NASHVILLE LIGHTS

JULIE CAPULET

Roxie

Nate Boone. My brother's best friend and the country boy I had a serious crush on all those years ago when we were both just kids. A lot has happened since then but a part of me never really moved on. Who am I kidding, *all* of me never moved on.

And now I'm heading back to Sugar Mountain to see my bestie—Nate's little sister—and to catch up with the extended Boone family, who have always felt like my own.

What I find is that Nate Boone is *alll* grown up, hotter than the Tennessee sun and not quite as forbidden as he used to be …

Nate

Roxie Tucker. No one knows about our history and our connection because I walked away and never looked back. I had to. She was a hundred percent off-limits.

I haven't seen her in years, until she shows up out of the blue, so beautiful it hurts. And I now know why I could never even think about getting real with anyone else. Because they're not her.

I shouldn't, of course. She's like family. And my life is complicated.

But she's too perfect and the pull is too strong. She's my dream and the one I could never let go of. I lost her once and I have no intention of losing her again. She's mine. She's heaven on earth and I'm a hundred percent addicted.

Now that I've had a taste of forever, this time, I'll risk whatever it takes to keep her …

Nashville Lights is a steamy standalone small town brother's best friend romance, starring a sweet & sassy band manager and the love of her life.

Music City Lovers

Nashville Lights

1

ROXIE

"HAVE FUN, Rox, and stay out of trouble." My oldest brother Kade's familiar drawl sounds as tired as I feel.

My phone is perched on its holder on the dashboard and I can see on the video call that Kade is back at his house downtown. He has a few houses in Nashville and he keeps a spare apartment for me at the one that's just off Broadway. I know he's got a gig tonight at the Lucky Seven. Not a solo gig, but he's agreed to be a guest for a couple of friends who are performing.

We've had a grueling few months of touring. My three brothers are the Tucker Brothers Band, and currently have songs at number one, two, four, seven, eight and ten on the Billboard charts. As manager of the band, I'm as exhausted as they are. We hit thirty-eight cities and did forty-eight sold-out shows over ninety-nine days. It was by far the biggest tour the band has done and it's taken their fame into overdrive.

"I will, KJ. You have fun too. And please get some rest." I can't help adding, "Finally." He knows I'm not referring to the tour with that last comment. I'm talking about the recent breakup with his hellish girlfriend Carmen. None of us could stand her, mainly because she made Kade's life miserable for the entire five months they were together. He told us he broke up with her but there was something cagey about the way he'd said it. I'm starting to wonder if he's actually done the deed yet. I'm pretty sure it's a sure thing, I just don't know if he's telling us what we want to hear until he cowboys up and lets her down gently. She was never going to go without a nightmarish meltdown. "I hope you're okay."

"Don't you worry about me, darlin'. You just make sure you're getting some good R & R at the Boones' place. Don't let them wrangle you into doing any farm work."

"Nope, I'm going to be sitting on that wraparound porch enjoying the view of Sugar Lake with my feet up and my phone on silent mode."

"Good girl."

"I'll talk to you in a few days."

"Say hi to the Boones for me."

"I will. Later, KJ."

I end the call and crank the radio up. Miles of open

highway stretch out before me as I cruise along in my faithful old pickup truck with the windows down. My brothers tried to insist I let one of their drivers take me or at least take one of the new cars they bought me that are sitting in the huge garage underneath the band's Nashville warehouse. But if I'm going back to the farm, there's no way I'm doing it with a chauffeur or in a fancy sports car. The Boones would laugh me straight back down the dusty dirt road.

AFTER MONTHS of being cooped up in crowded tour buses and arena green rooms, the warm summer breeze feels like heaven on my skin.

I drive past cornfields, barns, and the occasional rundown gas station. For once, my phone isn't buzzing with concert schedules, press releases, or my brothers' bickering in the family group chat. I finally have a moment to breathe.

Don't get me wrong, I love being the manager of my brothers' band. And I'm good at it, they keep telling me. With forty-eight sold out shows and six of the new album's tracks currently in the Billboard Top Ten, I'm hardly going to argue with them. The band is riding a high and we're making more money than we know what to do with. But I'm twenty-three years old and bone tired.

Three solid months of packed stadiums, screaming fans and non-stop life on the road takes its toll. I might not be the one singing or playing my heart out every night, but it's just as demanding keeping everything behind the scenes running smoothly. Corralling the rabid crowds, making sure security is air-tight, staying in touch with the label and organizing all the publicity is just the tip of the iceberg.

It's also a lot of work keeping Kade, Travis and most of all Vaughn steady and focused on what they need to focus on. Kade has been dealing with his awful relationship. Travis is head over heels with our new opening act, Ruby Hayes—who's insanely talented and who I'm also managing. And Vaughn is just…Vaughn. As wild as always, and even more so now that he also thinks he's in love. With Ruby's sister, no less. Which of course Travis isn't happy about at all.

I can always trust Vaughn to stir things up.

It's safe to say that for the first time in my life, I'm ready for a real break. Three blissful days in the country to clear my head and catch up with my best friend is just what the doctor ordered.

As if on cue, my phone rings.

Dakota flashes up on the screen and I hit the accept button. "Hey, Dee."

"How long until you get here?"

"I'm only around fifteen minutes away."

"I can't wait to see you, Rox! I have the biggest surprise."

"What surprise?"

"You'll have to wait and see." Dakota almost lost her mind when I called her a week or so ago and asked her if she wanted a visitor for the weekend. "It's been way too long since you came out to Sugar Mountain, Rox. I have a lot to fill you in on. Hurry up and get here already. I just made iced tea and put a bottle of white wine in the fridge. And of course Betty-Ann and Tobias are in the kitchen making your favorite fried chicken with cornbread and all the fixings."

"You have no idea how heavenly that sounds. I haven't had a home-cooked meal in I don't know how long. I'm in need of some serious R&R that involves having none of my brothers within a fifty mile radius."

"You get my brothers instead," she says. "But we can avoid them as much as possible."

"You and your brothers—and of course Betty-Ann, Louise and Earl—are the reason I'm staying in Tennessee and not spending a week on a sun lounger in Cabo. I can't wait to see all of you."

"Well, if I'd known Cabo was an option, I'd have packed my bags," Dakota laughs. "The farm won't be anywhere near as luxurious."

She thinks I'm exaggerating when I say there's nowhere I'd rather be, but it's true. Sugar Mountain Farm has always felt like my second home. It's not really a mountain. It's more of a series of sloping hills and picturesque farmland—and the closest thing to a real home that I've got.

The Nashville warehouse and the various apartments my brothers have bought for me don't really count. I have plenty of money to buy my own houses, but they keep buying buildings or compounds with lots of living spaces. Which they insist I live in. To keep an eye on me, they say.

My brothers are my home, in a sense, especially since we spend so much time together. And also because our parents died young and they've always felt responsible for me. But on the back end of a tour as intense as this one was, we all need some space.

I've spent every summer from the moment I was born, right up until I left to work with my brothers, visiting my Aunt Louise and Uncle Earl. Uncle Earl is my father's brother, even though it's safe to say the two men couldn't have more different personalities. Earl is a cheerful teddy bear of a man. My father was much more complicated, and those dark complications ended up cutting both his and my mother's lives short—something I don't want to revisit in my thoughts right now. I'm too happy.

So I let my memories drift back to Aunt Lou and Uncle Earl. They never had children of their own, but Aunt Lou's second cousin and lifelong best friend Betty-Ann, her husband Gus, and their five children live right next door. Sugar Mountain Farm is theirs. And it was their house that was literally bursting at the seams with love and laughter and all the best things about family and home.

The smells of apple pie and fresh-baked bread.

The sounds of laughter and good-hearted bickering.

Pots clanging with the promise of our next home-cooked meal.

They welcomed my brothers and me with open arms right into the middle of all that, from before my memories even begin. They became our family in the truest sense of the word.

The two houses sit side by side, with a joined driveway. Aunt Lou and Uncle Earl's farm and house are smaller, the house always neater because they didn't have five children running wild. Aunt Lou always made up beds for the four of us, but we hardly ever spent a night in them. We were having too much fun having sleepovers with the Boones, camping in tents, building blanket forts to sleep in and generally living our best lives.

So it's the Boones' house I remember most fondly. Half the memories of my life are in that house—and all the best ones.

I know every inch of this road. And with each landmark—the old red barn where I learned to dance, the Country Store where we used to go for triple-scoop ice cream cones that would drip over our fingers in the summer heat, and the familiar road signs that mean I'm getting closer—I feel another layer of the tour-hardened manager I've become peel back, and I'm ten again, bursting with the fizzy excitement of summer.

It's the one place I can guarantee will make me feel like myself again. The blinding stage lights are suddenly a million miles away, and I'm surrounded by nothing but cornfields and the warm Tennessee sun.

"What are your brothers up to this weekend?" Dakota asks. "Don't they all fall to pieces when you're not there?"

"Pretty much."

Most of the time, I'm cursing the fact that three grown men rely on me as much as they do, but I know I'd miss the buzz of excitement that surrounds them if I wasn't doing this job. Not to mention the fact I don't trust anyone else to have their best interests at heart, especially now that they've gone stratospheric.

I sort of stumbled into being their manager by default. They weren't getting along with their former manager and, since I've taken care of the three of them my whole life anyway, I stepped up and started organizing their schedules and making their phone calls. One thing led to another and when Vaughn fired their former manager out of the blue after an argument, it made sense for me to take on the role. I've been doing it ever since, learning on the job and mostly loving every minute of it.

All three of my brothers are insufferable at times but, even so, I couldn't love them more if I tried.

"You know I saw Kade when he came to see Nate, not

too long ago," Dakota says, "but I haven't seen Travis or Vaughn in ages. They haven't been back here since before they became superstars."

"Well, they're no longer the ragtag Tucker boys you grew up with, that's for sure." I'm not sure she'd be able to reconcile those ragamuffin kids she remembers with the rockstars who now have the world at their feet—and every possible temptation thrown at them on a daily basis.

"Anyway," I say, "I'm only going to be gone for a few days. Even the Tucker brothers can survive that. And besides, Travis and Vaughn are so loved-up with their new girlfriends, they won't even notice I'm gone. One thing about my brothers, once they fall, they fall *hard*."

"I think my brothers will be the same. I'm not sure why I say that since none of them are in steady relationships right now, but they're all secretly romantics at heart."

"Maybe it's something in the Sugar Mountain water," I laugh. "Anyway, all four of us need a break. You know how it is working with family."

"Oh, trust me, I get it." Dakota has four brothers and they all still live and—mostly, at least—work on Sugar Mountain. "Luke and Leo spend half their time bickering and fighting like they're still eight years old. They drive me crazy."

I picture the twins wrestling with each other non-stop when they were kids. Those nights when we all camped out under the stars or slept in a row on the big front porch, they were always rolling around like two little hell-raisers.

It feels strange to imagine my brothers back here now that their lives are so vastly different. Once upon a time we were sun-kissed kids running wild. We didn't care about our skinned knees or our thrift store clothes. We loved the simplicity and the contentedness of the country life, which felt so charmed to us. It was a welcome respite from the rougher edges of our "real" life in the city, where our parents' lives were slowly but surely imploding.

"So, when's the wedding?" Dakota asks. "I can't believe Travis is engaged."

It was big news when Travis proposed to Ruby on stage on the last night of the tour. The internet blew up with replays of the big event and Dakota called me immediately after it happened.

"They haven't set a date yet. But I don't think Travis will want to wait too long. He's absolutely besotted. So's Vaughn. And that's something I never saw coming: Vaughn in love. But I must say it makes both of them a lot easier to keep in line. All I have to do is threaten to tell their girlfriends how obnoxious they're being and immediately they're all contrite. Works like a charm."

I'm mostly joking, but there's an edge to it I hope Dakota doesn't hear. I'm thrilled that Vaughn has found love with a nice girl. Gigi is a country bumpkin and a sweetheart. I've gotten to know her a little and I'm really not sure if she's ever had a mean-spirited thought in her life. She has a purity of spirit that's almost saintly. For Vaughn to fall for someone like that is a wild relief. He's a changed man, and for the better. I no longer have to sweep groupies out of his dressing room every morning or stop strangers slipping pills into his pockets. For Gigi, Vaughn is willing to do literally *anything.* Even reform.

I just hope it lasts.

"What about Kade? Is he still with that girl none of you liked?"

"No, thank God. He just recently ditched her. We're all so relieved."

"Well, it's good he got rid of her, then. But it sounds like you like Travis and Vaughn's girlfriends? You approve?"

"Not that they consult me on these things," I laugh, "but yes. They're both beautiful, inside and out. Even if I have to yell at the boys for being late all the time because they spend so much time in bed, I have to admit they're writing the best songs of their careers. Gigi is really good for Vaughn. Then there's Ruby of course, my newest artist and now sister-in-law-to-be. She's a major talent."

Dakota's silent for a beat. "That must be so busy for you, Rox. Managing both the band *and* Ruby. How do you juggle it all?"

"It's busy," I admit. "It requires a lot of patience and even more caffeine. Plus I'm thinking of taking on two other new artists." I sigh, stretching my neck out and hearing it crack. "I swear I feel like I've aged ten years on this tour."

"Sounds like you definitely need a break. Do you ever get any time for yourself? I mean, when's the last time you went on a date?"

I have to think for a minute, it's been so long. "Um...maybe, like, over a year ago? I went out with that drummer from Austin once, but then we hit the road again. Oh, and there was that sound engineer who basically stalked me but he wasn't my type at all. Kade ended up firing him and threatening to kill him. Anyway, I don't really have time, Dee." It's true. I absolutely do not have time for dating. "There's also the small matter of spending 24/7 with my three extremely overprotective older brothers."

"I hear that." Dakota definitely gets it.

Even before I started managing the band, I'd always avoided getting serious with anyone. Not that I could ever tell Dakota the reason why.

"Well, I know you think of them as surrogate brothers," Dakota says, "but in fact my boys are not related to you at all, and three of them are eligible bachelors. None of them—aside from Tobias and he doesn't count in that way—are in a relationship right now. So you can take your pick."

"Stop." But my stomach flips. I do not want to talk about Dakota's single brothers. "Seriously, I love Luke and Leo, you know I do, but they are not going to settle down any time soon. They have new girls every time I talk to you."

"It's true." I can practically hear Dakota's frown. "They both seem allergic to commitment. Plus, whoever one of them dates is going to have to put up with the other one. The two of them are practically inseparable."

Luke and Leo are identical twins who used to speak their own secret language when they were tiny boys. "Yeah, maybe they could date two girls who are identical twins. That might be the only solution."

"Poor girls, is all I can say." Dakota exhales a pained laugh. "So, I guess that just leaves Nate."

Heat creeps up my neck and warms my cheeks. I've never been able to bring myself to tell her about my secret kiss with her oldest brother all those years ago. I figured it was just a teenage crush and the torch would burn itself out over time.

I guess I'm about to find out.

"Things are complicated for Nate right now," she says. "He's got a lot going on."

I know what she's talking about. Kade and Nate have always been close and they check in on each other regularly. When we were kids, they were best friends. They're the same age, almost exactly. Kade is three days older. Kade has filled me in on some of what's going on in Nate's life and, even though I don't know all the details, it sounds like a lot.

I don't push Dakota on the details now. I know I'll get

the entire lowdown over the weekend. "It must be nice having him back home again."

Kade and Dakota have both kept me up to date with Nate's house on the farm, which he built himself. It took him a long time to do it, but he moved in a while ago and now lives there full-time. "Oh my god, Rox, it's *such* a cool house. It was good timing, too, considering he's now got full custody of Daisy."

"I heard about what happened from Kade. He went to the funeral. It's so awful, Dee."

Around six months ago, Nate's best friends and business partners, whose names were Jed and Laney O'Leary, died in a head-on car crash on a rainy night. They were both killed instantly. The only thing that made the whole story a little less tragic is that their six-year-old daughter Daisy was at home that night with a babysitter. Kade told me Jed and Laney had been out to dinner on a date night, their first in almost a year.

They named Nate in their will as the legal guardian of Daisy. So Daisy's been living out on the farm with Nate and the whole Boone clan ever since the accident happened.

"Nate's so good with her," Dakota says. "Daisy adores him. They're really cute together. You'll see when you get here." My stomach does another one of those light flips. "And Ma of course loves having Daisy around. Your Aunt Lou, too. But it's still hard, as you can imagine. Nate's trying to process everything and make sure Daisy is okay, while also working on his business—without his business partners—*and* he's also overseeing a lot of the workings of the farm. I'm not sure how he's holding it all together, but you know how Nate is."

"Yeah." I *do* know how Nate is. Stoic, steady, always trying to do the right thing by everyone else. He's been a workaholic ever since his dad died of a heart attack when Nate was seventeen. As the oldest of five kids and the son of a devastated widow who needed him to step up and take control, Nate did exactly that.

It's why he left the farm for a while, to build his property development company. After his father's heart attack, it was up to Nate to make sure they didn't lose the house and the land. The farm was struggling back then. He had to somehow make enough money to ensure his mother could stay in her family home and that everyone got fed.

I see the sign for Sugar Mountain Farm Road and take the turn. I know from my memories that the dirt road is 1.2 miles long. "How's the farm going?"

"The farm's great. Nate's been pouring money into the place, which obviously helps. And with Nate's help, Luke and Leo have really been working some magic. They've both really stepped up and they're both really good farmers, as it turns out. The farm is more profitable than ever. They're diversifying the land and getting into some new areas. You'll see when you get here. And Tobias and I…well, we've been busy too. I can't wait for you to see it."

"See what?"

Dakota's words come out in an excited gush. "Okay, I can't keep the secret any longer. I've been *bursting* to tell you. But I wanted it to be a surprise."

"Tell me what, Dee?"

"Well, remember how Tobias wanted to start up his own restaurant?"

"Yeah."

"And you know how I've always kind of loved the idea of starting an event planning business?"

"Yeah."

"We know it's a long way to come all the way out here just for dinner, so we've set up a small boutique B&B. It's also a wedding and event venue. Think farm-luxe chic. We've been run off our feet with bookings and we're not even officially open yet. Can you believe it, Rox?"

"Dee! Why didn't you tell me any of this? That sounds amazing."

Dakota laughs. "I didn't tell you because you were on tour. I know I can reach you for emergencies, but you don't have much time to just jump on a video call and chat for an hour. And besides, Tobias and I kind of wanted to surprise you when you finally got out here. We knew you would eventually and we hoped it wouldn't be too long."

Guilt pangs in my stomach. I know I'm not the easiest person to have as a best friend when most of the time I'm too busy to reply to texts, let alone schedule chats or actual real-life meet-ups.

"I can't wait to see it." When we were kids, Dakota was always the one who was planning our little tea parties and decorating our picnic tables with wildflower bouquets. And even from a young age, Tobias was in the kitchen creating elaborate delicacies. He hand-squeezed our lemonade and not only frosted the cupcakes but created little sugar fondant decorations to sit on the tops of them. "We have so much to catch up on, Dee. I'm almost here. I can see the house."

"I can see your truck! We're all so excited, Rox. Okay, I'm hanging up so I can tell all the others you're here."

"See you in a minute."

As we disconnect the call, my heart feels like it might burst with happiness to be back here. I'm also attempting to tone down the butterflies erupting in my stomach now that I know there's a very good chance I'll run into Nate Boone during my stay. And I really don't know how to feel about that.

My Aunt Lou and Uncle Earl, Betty-Ann, Dakota and the boys were all such a staple of my summers, they feel ingrained in my bones. They're a part of who I am and I realize I've left it way too long to come back to them.

As for Nate, I remember so well his crooked grin, the way his eyes would shine when he laughed, and how I would catch sight of him walking across the lawn to the farmhouse in his low-slung jeans and his t-shirt slung over one suntanned, gracefully-muscular shoulder.

A lot has happened since I've been back, in both our lives.

As I pull up in front of the house, the welcoming farmhouse brings back a thousand golden memories.

I park my truck and take a deep breath. I'm not just coming back to a place. I'm returning to a family and a world I left behind, one that holds pieces of my heart I didn't even realize I'd kept locked away until right now.

2

ROXIE

"SHE'S HERE! SHE'S HERE!" My excitable best friend comes running out the front door, screen door slamming behind her, sprinting down the steps. I'm enveloped in a deep, joyful hug.

"Hey, Dee." I sigh. It's one of those restorative sighs that somehow goes a long way toward replenishing my supply of soul food.

"It's been way too long, bestie." She slings her arm around my shoulders and we walk up toward the house. "I see you haven't upgraded your ride even with all that money you've got now."

"I like Bertha." It was Dakota who named my truck when my brothers gave it to me for my sixteenth birthday. And it was Nate who tuned it up so it stopped making the clunking noise every time I tried to start it. Even though I don't drive it much these days, it's been reliable ever since.

Betty-Ann is waiting on the porch. I texted my Aunt Lou last week and she told me she and Earl had a charity dinner event held by her sewing circle tonight but would absolutely cancel it so they could spend time with me. I texted back and told her they should absolutely go to the dinner and I would see them in the morning and that we had the whole weekend to catch up. She finally relented. The Boones' farmhouse kitchen is where she spends most of her time anyway, chatting with Betty-Ann as they cook, sipping iced tea (and sometimes sherry) and gossiping about the local townspeople in nearby Sugar Falls, which has a population of somewhere around four thousand— more than enough to give them plenty to talk about.

"Hi, darlin'." Betty-Ann hugs me. "Welcome home."

"It's so good to be here."

Betty-Ann blots her eyes with the tissue she always keeps stuffed up her sleeve. "When are those brothers of yours coming for a visit?"

"They'd all love to. But their schedules have been pretty busy."

Stepping back into the Boones' huge kitchen feels like time-traveling. I'm suddenly fifteen again. The wooden floorboards creak in the same places they used to, the smell of fresh-baked cornbread and hot coffee fills the air, and there's that familiar, homey chaos of a family living out loud.

I lean against the counter, feeling the texture of the worn wood beneath my palm, and for the first time in months, I let myself finally relax. If I close my eyes, I could be back in the middle of one of those golden childhood summers with all nine of us Boone and Tucker kids tumbling in and out of the back door for lemonade and fresh-baked chocolate chip cookies, a whirlwind of knobby knees and skinned elbows.

We spent those summers running through the fields, leaving laughter tangled in the cornstalks, and conquering the creek like small, soggy overlords, crowning ourselves with wreathes of leaves and making pets out of frogs who didn't hop away quick enough. When the evenings came around, lazy and low, our skin tingling from the sun's kisses, we'd all pile onto the porch with its big table laid out with mountains of home-cooked food, finally sitting still long enough to eat some of Betty-Ann and Aunt Lou's fried chicken, potato salad and apple pie. Then we'd stay up late telling ghost stories until us Tuckers were occasionally ushered back to our beds next door—except for all the nights I'd stay in Dakota's room because we couldn't bear to be separated. Or the many, many nights we all camped out on the front lawn or swung hammocks from the rafters (depending on whether we were pirates or cowboys that day).

As I look around the kitchen, Luke and Leo are just coming in the back door, kicking off their work boots, looking wholesome and wide-shouldered, their shirts and windblown hair both dotted with errant pieces of hay.

"Well, if it isn't Roxie Tucker," Luke drawls, his

familiar grin lighting up his face. "Come over here and hug your second favorite Boone."

Leo nudges Luke out of the way and gets to me first. "That would be me," Leo laughs and I can't help laughing along with him. The two of them are tall, strapping, good-looking country boys and I have no doubt they have half of Sugar Falls county drooling over them both.

After the hugs have been attended to, the two of them pick right back up into the playful debate they were having over who's the better grill master. The twins share one of the cottages on the farm, which is within easy walking distance of the main house. Despite their debate about grilling, I have no doubt they reliably turn up to Betty-Ann's table every mealtime.

"Everyone knows my ribs are the talk of Sugar Falls," Luke boasts.

Leo shakes his head. "Keep dreaming, brother. Last time you tried to grill, the fire department had to get involved."

I see Tobias coming through the hallway door. "Hey, Rox." I get yet another heartfelt bearhug.

I hold his burly shoulders and look up at him. With his light brown hair and bright hazel eyes, he and Dakota could easily have passed for another set of twins. He used to be a skinny little freckle-faced kid, but Tobias has gotten tall and filled out a lot over the past few years. "Wow, look at you," I beam. "When did you get so *hot*?"

Tobias grins. "I've always been hot. And when did *you* get so seriously gorgeous? Holy fuck, girlfriend."

"Tobias Boone," Betty-Ann scolds him softly, but there's more love than heat in it.

Tobias is the second youngest Boone sibling, just a year older than Dakota and me.

Even when we were very young children, Tobias always preferred playing with us girls, rather than his older brothers. Dakota and I were tomboys but we still occasionally dressed up in tutus and pink costumes whenever the game of make-believe we were playing called for it. And Tobias was right there with us.

We all knew and accepted from the word go that Tobias was gay and it never felt like a thing that had to be worried about or questioned. It made me love the Boone family even more, that they fully embraced this part of Tobias with their characteristic whole-hearted love and good humor. Even in a small Tennessee community like Sugar Falls, especially all those years ago, the Boones celebrated Tobias, occasionally teasing him in the same, good-natured way they teased each other, and Tobias was encouraged to fully bloom into his true self.

Now, I keep in touch with Tobias almost as much as I do with Dakota. When I'm on the road or feeling overwhelmed by life, our group chats are often the one thing that keep me sane.

Betty-Ann was always thrilled by Tobias's flair in the kitchen. Slightly dismayed that none of her other children had any interest in cooking, baking or spending much time indoors at all except to eat and sometimes sleep, Tobias was always creating culinary masterpieces. But he would never follow the recipes. He always embellished and made them his own. So instead of homemade biscuits, we'd have "mixed berry cornmeal biscuit short-cakes with macerated fresh berries served with home-made vanilla and lemon zest whipped cream," or something equally over the top.

We always knew that one day he'd become a chef or start his own restaurant, so I'm excited to hear more about his and Dakota's plans for their "farm-luxe chic" restaurant and B&B.

I notice then there's a little girl sitting quietly at the table, coloring. She watches me with huge blue eyes as Tobias releases me from his hug.

"This must be Daisy," I say gently.

Tobias goes over and picks the little girl up. She wraps her arms around his neck. "Daisy," he says, "this is Roxie. She used to practically live with us every summer when we were all about the same age as you are now. Roxie, meet Daisy."

"It's very nice to meet you, Daisy."

Daisy leans closer to Tobias and whispers, "She's pretty."

Tobias grins. "Yes, she is. And she's nice too. Do you want to show Roxie what you're coloring?"

The little girl nods and I sit down next to her as Tobias places her carefully back in her chair.

"This is so beautiful, Daisy," I say. She's coloring a picture of a butterfly. "Is pink your favorite color?" It's a safe guess, since the entire butterfly is pink.

She looks up at me with those wide blue eyes and barely nods.

"Mine too," I tell her.

She notices the necklace I'm wearing. A gold butterfly, as it turns out.

"I like your necklace," she whispers.

The necklace was a gift from a Nashville jewelry designer who randomly sent it to me. I'm definitely not an influencer. When I have time to post on social media at all, it's usually something to do with the band, or my brothers, or being on tour. Occasionally I'll post things about my life on the road or a good restaurant recommendation or a brand of clothing I like. I don't have time to do more with my platform than that, but I do have a huge following. I'm sure most of the people who follow me are hoping to catch a glimpse of whichever brother they're most in love with. Last I checked, I had around seven million followers.

People and companies often send me gifts or products they're hoping I'll promote. My assistants go through all the stuff and, if they think it's something I'll like, they'll show it to me. They put the rest of it aside and at this point most of my spare room in Kade's building off Broadway is full of these gifts.

My assistant showed me this necklace a few months ago and I loved it. It was made by a woman who hand-crafts one-off pieces of jewelry. At the time, I put it on and posted about it. The woman later reached out to my assistant and told her to thank me. She'd sold out of every piece she's ever made and has enough commissions to buy herself a house.

I haven't worn the necklace for a while but saw it on my dresser as I was leaving this morning and, on a whim, put it on.

But now, I think there's someone who likes the necklace even more than I do. I reach for the clasp and take it off. "I think it would look prettier on you, Daisy. Would you like to wear it?"

Her blue eyes get even wider. She nods.

I put the necklace carefully around her neck and do up the clasp. "There. It's yours now."

Tobias and Dakota have both watched this exchange and Tobias winks at me. "What do you say to Rox, Daisy?"

"Thank you." Daisy holds my hand. "Do you want to help me color? I have two pink crayons."

"I'd love to."

She hands me one and we color as the lively conversation swirls around us.

Leo is still giving us a play-by-play of the inferno Luke caused with the barbecue.

It's like slipping into a warm embrace, this easy, familiar banter that feels like it's part of my soul.

Tobias, always the peacekeeper, chimes in from where he's gone back to his task of meticulously chopping vegetables and dumping them into a boiling pot. "Boys, there's only one way to settle this. A cook-off. We vote on it. The panel's decisions are final. Loser does dishes for a week."

"Deal," both brothers say in unison, and we all laugh again, knowing full well this "cook-off" will be another epic Boone family event—which will probably involve flames, charred ribs and possibly wrestling.

"We'll do it in your new kitchen, Tobe," Leo suggests.

"You absolutely will not go anywhere *near* my new kitchen," Tobias says. "That kitchen is my new sanctuary and I do *not* want it being burned to the ground before we've even welcomed our first guests."

Betty-Ann wields her wooden spoon like a conductor's baton. "You also won't be doing it in this kitchen," she adds. "You can have a 'barbecue-off' and you can do it outside. Now why don't the two of you channel all that energy you seem to have for bickering and use it to do something productive, like set the table."

Dakota rolls her eyes playfully. "Mom, you know they're allergic to anything that resembles housework."

"Oh, I certainly do know it." But the boys—or, more

accurately, *men*—are dutifully getting the knives, forks and plates.

Even though Betty-Ann scolds her children, she obviously adores having them around her. I remember her saying when we were kids that she'd rather have her children making mischief at home than doing it somewhere else. "How are your brothers, Roxie? You still keeping them in line? You always did, even as a little girl."

"They're harder work now than they ever were as kids," I laugh.

Leo leans against the counter next to me. "Seriously, Rox, the boys' latest album is all anyone can talk about around here. You're turning them into legends."

"I just manage schedules and egos. The music is all them."

"And you couldn't have done the same for us, huh?" Luke smirks, kissing Betty-Ann's cheek as he passes her, carrying a stack of plates. "You can manage my ego anytime."

I get up to help.

"You stay right there," Dakota orders me. "That butterfly needs more pink. Seriously though, Rox, you should listen to these three. They've got a local following now."

This gets my full attention. "Who does?"

"Nah," Leo elbows Dakota. "We're just amateurs compared to the Tucker boys."

"You guys play?" We all used to play instruments and

sing together when we were kids, putting on little concerts that we demanded the adults listen to. Dakota, Tobias and I were mostly banging on things just for fun, but the older boys, from both families, all had talent.

"You'll have to listen to them while you're here." Tobias wipes his hands on a dishcloth. "We want to hear more about your glamorous life on the road, Rox. It must be wild watching the band play to sold out stadiums every night."

Wild doesn't even come close to describing it. "Honestly, it's hard work. There are parts of it I wouldn't change for the world, but it's also…crowded and noisy and there are nights, especially on the tour bus, that do get tiring. Not that I'm complaining. It's amazing how much everything has taken off. We're enjoying it while it lasts."

Dakota puts a glass of milk in front of Daisy. "Roxie's three brothers are in a band," Dakota tells her. "They're really famous. You've probably heard Uncle Nate play their songs."

"He likes to sing them," Daisy says.

"Nate sings their songs?" For some reason, the thought charms me.

"Of course," Tobias says. "Everyone around here does."

"Everyone in the whole damn country, more like," Leo says, handing out beers. "Rox? Beer? Wine?"

"Sure. Wine would be great, thanks." I don't usually drink but what the hell, I'm on vacation for the weekend.

After a few more minutes of chatter flowing round the table and Daisy quietly observing as I open my bag to check a message that just vibrated on my phone, her small hand reaches for the tube of lipstick I just pulled from my purse, her fingers barely touching it.

"What color is that?" she asks, her voice full of fascination.

I smile down at her and pass her the tube to examine. "It's called Pink Kisses."

"Can I put some on?" she asks soulfully, her eyes like pools. How could anyone refuse this kid anything?

"How about just a tiny bit," I suggest, and she nods seriously as if we're sharing an important secret.

I dab a little on my finger and touch it to her lips. I'm a little shocked when she climbs onto my lap, where she whispers into my ear, "My Mommy used to wear pink lipstick."

Dakota and Tobias are both watching Daisy do this, like it's unusual.

She softly fingers one of the shell buttons on my cowgirl shirt, which is a delicate pink and white plaid.

"I got this at one of my favorite stores in Nashville. Same with the boots." Daisy glances at my boots, which are brown suede with pink-stitched flowers. Daisy gasps when she sees the bright colored stitching. These boots are without a doubt the best damn thing I own. Daisy clearly has taste.

"I'm going to ask Uncle Nate for some boots for my birthday," she says softly, her smile with its faintest dab of Pink Kisses. "Do they have pink ones?"

"I'm sure they do. You could get a matching hat too."

Daisy's eyes light up at the thought.

"You already asked Uncle Nate for a pony, didn't you?" Tobias laughs.

"I'll need boots to *ride* my pony."

"Of course. My mistake." Tobias grins at me. "It's good to have you back, Rox. Lou and Earl are beyond excited to see you."

"I'm surprised Lou didn't come barreling over here the minute she heard your truck on the driveway," Luke says.

"She and Earl are at her sewing circle's annual dinner event," Betty-Ann informs him. "She said she could hardly wait to see Roxie but she's on the social committee and it was too late to cancel."

"Now that is a level of restraint I didn't realize your aunt had," Dakota laughs. "She talks about the four of you coming home on practically a daily basis."

"I'm excited to see them both."

"You need to get the boys out here again soon, Rox," Leo says. "We need a proper Tucker-Boone reunion."

"Absolutely. Maybe we could do something for Thanksgiving. Although Kade has his solo tour and

Travis has been hard at work on some new songs. But I'll see if I can pin them down."

"It's been ages since we've seen Travis and Vaughn." Dakota puts a gorgeous, artistic arrangement of wildflowers in the middle the table.

"They're rockstars now, Dee," Luke points out. "You wouldn't catch me hanging out here with you country bumpkins if I had thousands of screaming fans throwing their panties at me every night."

"Luke William Boone," Betty-Ann warns, her eyes darting to Daisy.

Luke holds his hands up in apology. "I just mean, I get it. They've got bigger fish to fry now."

"Well, Roxie managed to make it back," Dakota says.

"That's because she's missed the undeniable charm of the Boone brothers, isn't that right?" Leo comes up behind me and plants a kiss on my cheek which makes everyone, including Daisy, laugh.

"Y'all know I'm only here for Betty-Ann's cooking."

Tobias clears his throat.

"And yours, of course, Tobe. That goes without saying."

"Honey, ignore my boys," Betty-Ann says. "We're all just glad you're home."

Outside, there's the sound of tires on gravel. Daisy hears it and lights up with excitement, climbing down off my lap and running toward the door to peer out the window.

"It's Uncle Nate!" She pushes the screen door open and disappears out the door.

My heart skips a beat at his name.

I knew there was a good chance I'd run into him, but…*now?*

Seeing the others was like a homecoming, talking to them in the kitchen like slipping back into the long-ago, comfortable version of myself that I'd almost forgotten existed.

But just the mention of Nate's name does something weird to my insides. Am I expected to sit here and eat dinner with him too, like nothing ever happened and he hasn't held onto a big chunk of my heart all these years?

My stomach is fluttering and my heartbeat is in my throat. I do my best to keep myself calm, to stop the heat from rising to my cheeks and the secrets from writing themselves all over my face.

3

NATE

Two hours earlier...

I PULL into the parking lot of a downtown office building, wishing I was anywhere but here. I almost yank off the damn tie I'm wearing. The suit might as well be a straitjacket.

Jed was the one who used to handle this side of our property development business. The meetings with stiffs were *his* area of expertise. My area was getting my hands dirty, dealing with the contractors and making sure the day-in-day-out operations ran smoothly. Overseeing the construction, managing the building sites, dealing with the surveyors and so on. And Laney handled the books.

Now that they're both gone, I've got way more on my plate than there are hours in the day to deal with it all.

I slam the door of my truck, not giving a damn that

it's covered in mud from my early morning drive through the farm to give Luke and Leo a hand getting started with the hay harvesting. They've got plenty of farmhands on deck, but it's a big job and I wanted to make sure they've got it under control.

My meeting today is with a guy I can't fucking stand. He's a developer from Seattle who's trying to cash in on the Nashville boom that continues to creep further out. The asshole had never even *been* to Tennessee until a month ago. He contacted me by video call last week and I could immediately tell he's half con-artist and half greed-driven douchebag.

Jed was good at dealing with people. I'm…not.

I don't have the patience for jackasses, especially if they're only interested in making a quick buck without giving any thought whatsoever to the land itself, the heritage, the surroundings, and especially the people who happen to be a part of the place he's intending to destroy. People who have lived here for generation upon generation. People who *care* about the place and how it's handled and preserved.

People like me.

All this guy cares about are the dollar signs.

Jed used to say it all the time and I can still hear him scolding me. *As much as I admire your scruples, man, at least part of the reason we're here has to be about making some money.*

And we have made money. A lot of it.

My biggest problem with this project is that the farm

this guy wants to turn into an overcrowded hell-hole of a development is right next door to Sugar Mountain.

At four hundred acres, ours is a big farm by Tennessee standards. Over the past ten years, I've worked my guts out, along with the rest of my family, to turn it into a seriously profitable piece of land. My dad died of a sudden major heart attack that killed him before he even hit the ground. I was seventeen. He'd been in poor health for a while, but it was still a shock to all of us, that he could suddenly just be gone like that. Especially for Ma. Our father was a hard worker, but he'd been stuck in his ways and refused to embrace any of the changes that would have helped him get out of some serious debt.

We've turned all that around. But it's taken a shitload of hard work.

I walk into the meeting room without knocking.

Four suits stand up.

One steps forward, looking nervous. "Mr. Boone, good to see you. Julian Fuller. Thanks for coming." He's even greasier in person than he was on screen. He holds his hand out and I shake it briefly. His hand is weirdly cold. And soft. Which doesn't help my mood and in fact makes me feel like punching him in the face.

Jed, damn it.

"Nate, these are my business associates, Wesley Crane, Everett Olsen and Darren Smith. Gentlemen, this is Nathan Boone."

I shake the other men's hands and each one has me

feeling more like walking out of this meeting than the last. I already know this is a waste of time. And I fucking *hate* wasting time. Especially when Daisy is waiting for me.

All four of them are pale corporate types who've probably never stepped foot on a farm in their lives. Hell, they look like they've never even seen the sun. I'm easily half a foot taller than all of them. A strong wind could probably blow them over. I'm tempted to suggest we go down to the local steakhouse and order them up some red meat.

"Julian tells us you have some reservations about taking this project on," the one named Everett begins. "But also that you're the best, most reliable developer in Tennessee. We'd like to try to change your mind about whatever your reservations might be."

"Please, Nathan, take a seat." Julian motions toward the chair at the head of the table. I pull it out and sit, glad for the small distance from their clusterfuck of paperwork, spread out in neat little piles.

They all take my lead, taking their seats. "We're very impressed by the developments you built in Taylorville and East Grove last year," one of them says. "We've heard nothing but good things about your company. We're interested in having you spearhead seven new high-density developments we're currently in the process of getting consent for, all within an hour of Nashville. The first one is local to your own property, Julian mentioned."

I look the guy in the eye. And I take my time. "Everett, is it?"

"Yes."

"Everett, did you know that there are more than seventy thousand farms in Tennessee?"

"Uh. No, I didn't realize it was that many."

"Did you know that the average farm is family-owned and somewhere between a hundred and two hundred acres, some of which have been in families for generations?"

"Uh…sure, but—"

"Did you know that almost forty percent of the land in Tennessee is farmland?"

"Um, no, I don't have all the statistics—"

"You should. And did you happen to know that the number of farms and farmers is decreasing at a rate that's alarming to a lot of Tennesseans?"

"No. No, I didn't know that. But—"

"Did you know that more than 360,000 people in Tennessee are employed in agriculture and forestry?" Of course they don't. They don't know jackshit about anything. They don't know what the Tennessee rain feels like on your work-dusty skin. Or the smell of fresh-cut hay on a hot August afternoon under the Tennessee sun.

Everett looks uncomfortable at this point.

I don't wait for his reply. "Did you know that the collective production values of those seventy thousand farms pumps more than five billion dollars a year into the economy of Tennessee?"

"No, but Mr.—"

"These numbers are important to Tennessean farmers, Everett." I pause to make sure I'm not about to lose my temper and throttle one of them. "Tennesseans, including me, are invested in preserving as many of the family farms as we can. We think about our kids and our grandkids and we want to make sure Tennessee isn't completely bulldozed into parking lots and strip malls before future generations have a chance to experience it like we have."

Julian exhales an uneasy chuckle, like this is some kind of fucking joke. "We definitely understand all that, Mr. Boone. But progress means change. We currently have seven hundred clients interested in buying small land parcels in Tennessee. *Seven hundred*," he repeats. "With more people—Californians, in particular—signing up every single day. These are people willing to pay top dollar for a partial acre of land."

"And be squeezed into the countryside like sardines," I point out gruffly.

"A 0.2 acre section is all many families require, Mr. Boone," says the one named Darren. "Townhouses are very desirable. Especially with country views."

"You're telling me you want to put *seven hundred houses* on a hundred and fifty acre property." I don't ask it. I state it as an unbelievably stupid idea.

"Yes. That's what we're proposing."

Fucking hell. "The infrastructure required for seven hundred houses would drastically change the landscape of the entire area. And I'm not just talking about the views. I'm talking about the traffic, the impact on the ecosystems and the wildlife, the businesses that would be required to feed, school and provide for all the needs of that kind of population growth. The carbon footprint of a project like that—"

"Mr. Boone," interrupts Wesley. Or Everett. Or Darren. Who the fuck cares. "You—and all of us—stand to make a *significant* amount of money out of this project. We're talking multi, *multi* millions. Let's keep our eye on the ball."

I've had just about enough of this. "How about this, Wesley: you keep your fucking eye on *your* fucking ball and I'll keep an eye on mine."

Damn it all to hell, Jed. I don't know how he smiled his way through meetings like this every day of the week. My tie feels more like a noose around my neck with every passing second.

Daisy will be waiting at the house and once again I'll be late because I so often get held up by assholes like these.

I look at these watery-eyed men and all I can feel is contempt. They're quiet now, in the wake of my rant.

Jed and I started this company when we were both twenty-two and our skillsets were well-matched. He was the people person with a good-natured knack for dealing with clients. He knew how to talk sense into people like this and appeal to their sense of integrity, no matter how deeply it might be buried under all those layers of greed.

I was good at dealing with the nuts and bolts of the ground-breaking and the building—and do it in a way that was in the best interests of the community, the history of the place while also doing my best to preserve the aesthetics of the countryside. Making all of the above line up can be a juggling act. And I can admit that, without Jed, I'm dropping a few fucking balls.

"Look," I say, mining deep for an inkling of patience. "I don't disagree with you guys. Progress *does* mean change. You're right. And I have no problem with change. But I can't—and I won't—agree to the kind of change that's going to destroy Tennessee."

Sure, I could take on a project like this, cash in and retire. And have all the time in the world for Daisy.

I'm already pretty close to being able to do that, come to think of it, or way past the point of being already there. But these projects should never be *only* about the money.

Either way, I'd rather be dirt poor than see seven hundred houses built on the doorstep of Sugar Mountain.

I'll fight them tooth and nail with everything I've got.

"Mr. Boone, I don't think you understand the amount of money we're talking about here," Everett pleads.

"And I don't think you understand how easy it would

be for me to kill this project with one five-minute phone call." Which is exactly what I plan on doing. I can't blame them for trying, but there's no fucking way. I can admit my people skills are severely lacking today. I've barely had five hours of sleep a night for months on end, with Daisy's nightmares and my own tossing and turning with worry about everyone I care about, who all seem to need my help.

Julian correctly reads the room. "I think we've gone as far as we're going to go with this today. But Mr. Boone—please—read through this business proposal here when you've had some time to go through the numbers. I'm sure you'll be impressed by just how lucrative this project could be for you." He slides a manila envelope over to me.

As much as I'd like to tell him to shove his manila envelope up his pasty white ass, I see this as my out.

I stand up from the table, taking the envelope. "I'll look it over."

Julian and the others stand. "Could we reconvene in, say, a week? Same time, same day?"

"I'm afraid the answer to that question is no. I'll call you if I change my mind or if hell freezes over, whichever comes first. Nice meeting y'all," I add, because manners are still ingrained in me even if patience isn't. With that, I walk out.

4

NATE

I MAKE my way out to my truck and throw the manila envelope into the back seat, where I don't have to look at it during my drive. I loosen my tie, and decide it's the last time I wear one.

The engine roars to life, a growl that matches my mood.

I think of home, relieved as fuck that I'm headed there now.

I think of Daisy's laugh, the one that bubbles up every now and then, a pure, perfect sound that makes all the bullshit fade out.

I can admit the sound of Daisy's laughter is all too rare these days.

Which is to be expected. Her parents just died. She's a grieving little girl with a world of emotions that she can't possibly begin to understand or process.

But there should be some lightness, right? She should forget, sometimes, when she's picking wildflowers, or when she's digging into one of Ma's apple pies, or when she's being served her favorite strawberry sundae at the diner in town.

Most days, I'm going out of my mind, stewing about whether I'm giving her the best life I can and wondering whether I'm good enough for her. I know I can never replace her parents, but I want to be the best possible second option.

Deep down, I'm not sure I'm hitting that mark. Particularly when the nightmares seem to be getting worse. Every time she cries out for her parents, I wipe her tears, read her stories, and do my best to ease her fears. When she sobs like her little heart is breaking, a piece of my own heart breaks right along with it.

I've barely made it out into the bumper-to-bumper traffic when my cell phone rings through the Bluetooth. I bought this brand new truck the week after I became Daisy's legal guardian. To be honest, I prefer my old blue Chevy pick-up truck, which was built before safety standards were a thing and is now parked up in the shed.

Amanda flashes up on the center console.

Fuck.

Just what I don't need right now.

I'm tempted to let it go to voicemail. But that's not how you handle family—because that's what she is now—even when they're aiming to take a piece of yours.

Amanda Sullivan-Smith is Laney's older sister. The same older sister who was shocked beyond belief at the reading of the will, when sole custodianship of her six-year-old niece wasn't given to her.

It was given to me.

Possibly because she's a card-carrying bitch: Laney's exact words. The two of them never saw eye to eye. Laney was five years younger than Amanda and was the free spirit of her family. Their father was a preacher, their mother a devout stay-at-home mom and home-maker, because any other option was considered ungodly to them. Jed, a boy from what they considered the wrong side of the tracks, with mischievous blue eyes and a lust for living life to the fullest, did not fall into the category of what they saw as an "acceptable" choice. Laney chose Jed when she was seventeen years old. Her relationship with the rest of her family deteriorated after that and the two of them spent more and more time with us.

Amanda never approved of Jed—who turned out to be far more successful and wealthier than any of the Sullivans.

Jed and Laney knew how to pack the most joy into each day they possibly could. Laney always said Amanda was allergic to joy, or any kind of happiness at all.

I knew well before Amanda did that she was the last person Laney and Jed would have chosen to raise their little girl.

Amanda, however, didn't get that particular memo. She's been bitter and twisted about it ever since.

I tap the speaker button with a sigh. "Hey, Amanda." I make a point of injecting a note of cautious civility into my tone. "I've just come out of a meeting, so if you want to speak to Daisy, you'll have to—"

"It's after six," she interrupts. "Working late again, I see." Another crime I've committed, obviously.

"On my way home now. Daisy was helping my mother and my aunt bake an apple pie when I talked to her an hour ago."

"Nathan," she says, and there's a pause, a deliberate softness there that catches me off guard. Amanda is never soft, or gentle. She's fierce, cold and very determined. "That's the whole point here. *Your* mother. And *your* aunt. Not Daisy's *own*. I know we both want what's best for her."

I can hear the restrained urgency in her voice, the unspoken plea of someone who isn't ready to back down but knows they've hit a wall. So she's trying a different tack.

She's hired a team of lawyers, which I'm sure is costing her an arm and a leg. More than she can afford. We both know she doesn't stand much of a chance. Laney and Jed's will couldn't have been clearer in its wording. They stated in no uncertain terms that they wanted me to become Daisy's legal permanent guardian if anything happened to them.

As much as I disagree with Amanda, I understand her concerns. She *does* want what's best for Daisy, like we both do, and Amanda is convinced I'm neglecting Daisy because I work so much.

I can't entirely blame her for that.

"Amanda, I get it. Laney was your sister. I'm sure I'd have some of the same concerns if the tables were turned. But we have to remember that this arrangement is what Laney and Jed wanted for Daisy. The court isn't going to side with you on this one. Not when the lawyers confirmed that their wishes were so clearly stated."

I hear her bristle through the phone. "You might be winning for now, Nathan, but Daisy is a Sullivan, whether you like it or not. She belongs with her *family*. The judge will see that soon enough."

Laney once told me that Amanda was always jealous that Laney had a daughter. Amanda had sons. According to Laney, they don't get along with their mother at all and have always preferred their father.

Maybe Amanda saw the death of her sister as her last chance to have a daughter of her own. I hope Amanda doesn't see it that way, but I can't help but wonder. Either way, it's not happening.

I rub a hand over my jaw. I'm still two years off thirty, but I feel a decade older tonight. "Laney and Jed obviously thought of the Boones as family too, Amanda. Daisy has spent half her life on the farm. She loves it there. It's a big part of her family legacy, we both know that. She knows it. She remembers her parents being there. We talk about her memories of them all the time."

"Be that as it may, blood is thicker than water. You *are* like an uncle to her, Nathan, no one's saying otherwise. But Daisy has a whole family eager to welcome her home."

There's a flicker of something like guilt that flares up inside me. It's true, after all. Daisy does have a family beyond the boundaries of Sugar Mountain.

But Laney and Jed *loved* the farm, and they thought of my family as their own. Jed and I met the first day of high school and from that day, he spent most of his time at our place. Jed was an only child and the farm was a hell of a lot more fun than his small rundown house in town.

When Laney and Jed got together in eleventh grade, she started coming along with him.

As soon as they could afford to, they bought a small property across the road from Sugar Mountain Farm. They spent Easters, Thanksgivings and Christmases with us. When Daisy was born, she was welcomed into our family like one of our own.

It was no surprise to me that they wanted Daisy to be raised on the farm. Not flown to Ohio, where Daisy has never even been, to live with an aunt she's only met a handful of times.

I happen to know Laney could barely stand to spend time with Amanda, and she thought Amanda's husband Derek was insufferably dull. She complained that their two teenage sons spent most of their time gaming, which Laney always thought was a colossal waste of time. Especially when you could be swimming in the lake, swinging on the rope swing or going on hayrides.

"I know you won't stop fighting this," I say, my voice steady. "And believe it or not, I respect that. But I won't stop fighting it either, Amanda. Daisy's where she needs to be. With me. With people Laney and Jed loved like their own." *More than their own,* I don't bother mentioning. "Now, I'm going home to have dinner with Daisy, my sister, my brothers, my mother, my aunt and my uncle, who all adore Daisy and who are pouring all the love they possibly can into every day with her. Just like I am."

"I'll also mention that I've communicated my concerns to my lawyers about your…lifestyle."

Here we go. "What lifestyle?"

"I took the liberty of googling you. As is my right in a situation like this. I don't know if you're aware, but a number of…*women* have posted about you. Online."

Shit. "What women."

"The ones you occasionally go out with and apparently spend the night with."

Damn it.

Laney was actually the one that saw it. She and Jed had a good laugh about it. It was probably a year and a half ago. A woman I met at a local fundraising event who happened to be some kind of "influencer" posted a photo of her and me on her social media. I give money to a bunch of different local groups and the town paper asked for a photo of me at their event. She insisted on standing next to me. I'm not proud of it—and it turned out to be a terrible mistake—but I went home with her that night. I can't even remember her name.

She later posted the photo, with a caption along the lines of: *Turns out the hot country boy is a well-h#ng superhero on steroids in the s@ck. If you see this, Nate Boone, freaking call me, you sexy beast.*

Or something like that. I never heard the end of it from Laney and Jed.

She wasn't the only one. There was the woman I went out to dinner with the night the accident happened. Who's been hounding me ever since and who might also have posted something. I have no idea.

But, hell, all that was *before* I became Daisy's legal guardian. I'm single and have been for a very long time for reasons I'm not going to analyze right now. But I never signed up to be a monk.

"That happened a long time ago, Amanda. A year or more before Daisy came to live with me. Which makes it none of your concern."

"Be that as it may, the lawyers did agree with me that it's concerning that there isn't…well, a traditional family unit. You're a single man who apparently…plays the field. And you work long hours. It's not exactly an ideal situa-tion for a child who recently lost her parents."

Her words sting, because they're not entirely untrue.

"I'm doing my best," I say, the defensive edge in my voice betraying my frustration. "I've cut back on my hours. Daisy's well-being is my top priority. She also has a close-knit family and community who will do anything for her. I'm doing everything I can to try to make sure she's happy."

"I'm sure you are, Nathan. But the fact is, it may not be enough. My lawyers are in touch with the social workers and I've been told they'll be making their decision within the month."

"I've been told that too. So we'll be in touch." I've had enough of this tonight. "I hope you have a great night, Amanda. I'm sure we'll talk again soon. Goodnight."

I end the call before she can fixate on more of my flaws.

I love Daisy with my whole damn heart, but whenever Amanda calls, her comments dig into me like sharp claws. She's a wife and mother with two kids of her own. She *could* give Daisy a conventional family unit. Cousins to grow up with. A mom *and* a dad. Not the setup I've got back at the farm, with my hodgepodge of siblings and my mother and aunt taking turns looking after Daisy, with me working six days a week. Doing our best to make it work.

That kid deserves the best, and there's an insistent part of me that wonders if that happens to be me.

I drive along for a while, grateful when the city lights are fading in my rearview mirror.

My phone rings again through the Bluetooth.

To my relief, it's not Amanda calling back. It's a number I don't recognize.

I press the answer button. "Nate Boone."

"Mr. Boone, good evening." Another uptight-sounding woman's voice. "My name is Ainsley Beal and I'm a social worker for the state."

"Social worker?" My people skills are at an all-time low right now but I make a point of toning down my gruffness. "What kind of social worker?"

"Children's welfare. Amanda Sullivan-Smith just called me. At her insistence—and it's not unusual in these types of cases—the court has ordered a home visit by the Child Protection Agency to your place of residence. To make sure Daisy's situation is as optimal as possible."

Optimal. "Okay."

"Mrs. Sullivan-Smith feels it's necessary, and we agree. If you're unwilling to comply, Mr. Boone, the judge will take that into consideration as he considers Daisy's case."

"I'm more than happy to comply. Visit whenever you want. When did you want to come by?"

"These are unannounced visits, Mr. Boone."

"Oh. Right. Well, Ms…"

"Beal."

"Ms. Beal, I invite you to come by any time you want. Ideally, you'll choose a time when Daisy and I are home."

"Yes, I've heard that your extremely full work schedule is an issue."

"Everyone has to work, Ms. Beal. Even you."

"Indeed. Except those fortunate stay-at-home mothers who can dedicate all their time to their children and their home, as Mrs. Sullivan-Smith continues to point out."

Jesus. "I'd prefer not to be this petty, but since Amanda is playing dirty, then I'll meet her halfway. Are you also going to be visiting Amanda's house? Because you might want to check in on the welfare of her own children, who game too much, are medicated, and are struggling in school because their brains have been taken over by their addiction to dopamine. Daisy wouldn't thrive in an environment like that. She deserves better."

"And you feel like you're able to give her…better?"

"I sure as—…yes. All I ask, Ms. Beal, is that you consider Daisy's happiness the most important thing. She doesn't know her aunt. Except for the funeral, Amanda hasn't been out here once to see how her niece is doing. She hasn't called her, or me, to check in on how Daisy is doing."

"Noted, Mr. Boone. This isn't personal, I might add. I know it's what Daisy's parents wanted, but that doesn't mean that your home is automatically the best place for her. We do have to consider the fact that you're a single man who lives alone. In cases that are contested like this one, judges do often side with the party who offers a more traditional family environment."

"My family is very close-knit, Ms. Beal, and Daisy has a lot of good people making sure she's safe and happy and well-cared for at all times."

"We'll take note of all that during our visit."

"As I said, you're more than welcome to come by any time."

"Good. Thank you for your cooperation, Mr. Boone."

"Of course."

"You can expect a visit in the coming weeks."

"I'll look forward to it."

Like a hole in the head.

5

———

NATE

PULLING into the dirt road of Sugar Mountain Farm, I do the same thing I always do. I take a deep breath. Every time, it feels like the weight of the world lifts a little when I re-enter paradise.

Of course it isn't paradise at all, just a sprawling four hundred acre farm with a scenic lake, rolling hills and a small river winding through it, miles from town. And it comes with all the problems that go along with the day-in-day-out hard work it takes to make a buck out of it.

The scent of the gritty road dust through my rolled-down window is as familiar to me as the rhythm of my own heartbeat.

It's not long before the farmhouse comes into view in the distance. We recently painted it and the place looks more inviting than ever, its windows glowing with the soft, warm light of home.

I have my own house now, which I built myself. It's further along the dirt road from the main house, perched on its own hill with trees surrounding it and a nice view out over the river. It's always been my favorite place on the farm.

Jed and I designed the house together. Once Daisy came along and Jed and Laney bought their own property, he got busy fixing up his own house and I worked away on mine, but we'd often help each other out. It took me almost three years from start to finish, but even I can admit it turned out better than I imagined it.

I was glad I'd worked so hard on it, every spare minute I had. The month after I put the finishing touches on the house, it became Daisy's as well as mine.

With Luke and Leo's help, I boxed up most of Jed and Laney's stuff, put it in one of our storage sheds, and rented out the house. When Daisy's older, she can decide what she wants to do with it.

I brought home all the stuff I thought she might want close to her. Her toys, all the photos we could find, and a few keepsakes of her parents' I thought might make her feel like their memories were still very much with us.

In the six months since then, we've made the front guest room Daisy's own. Ma and Dakota and Tobias helped decorate and they didn't hold back. They told me what to do and I built it, painted it and put it together.

Daisy's got pink walls, a pink four-poster bed, a hand-built two-story princess's castle, a tent full of pillows and blankets, along with stars and photos that hang from its pitched roof, two comfortable pink velvet reading chairs in a reading corner next to the window, a built-in pink bookshelf, a stocked closet full of (you guessed it, pink) princess and cowgirl outfits, and a window seat that catches the sun and looks out over the view.

For all that pink, it could be gaudy as fuck, but Dakota and Tobias know how to decorate. It's tastefully done, like something out of a decorating magazine.

When she's a little older and has had more time to process everything, I'll show her the details of our house that were her dad's ideas. And there were plenty of them.

If only it hadn't been raining that night. If only they hadn't been in such a rush to get home and see their little girl. If only I'd kept him busy just a little longer, and they'd canceled their date night, like they so often did because of all the work that always needed doing.

None of the regrets will bring them back.

The driveway of the farmhouse is, as usual, full of pick-up trucks.

I pull up alongside Luke's and kill the engine.

The sound of laughter and the clinking of dishes drifts out the screen door and the open windows and, for a moment, I allow myself the simple pleasure of being back where things make sense.

There's another truck parked next to Leo's that gets my attention.

It's Kade's old truck. Aqua and white. It still has that

old pair of horns he stuck on the grille back when we were lean, sun-bronzed kids.

The exact same truck he gave to his little sister the day she turned sixteen.

Before I can even think about this too hard, the door bursts open and Daisy bursts out, all strawberry blond curls and boundless energy, charging toward me like I'm the finish line of her favorite race. "Uncle Nate!"

I crouch down just as she leaps into my arms, her tiny body full of a warmth and trust I'm not sure I'll ever deserve.

"Hey, Daze," I murmur. She smells of sun and home and the apple pie she must have been tasting as she helped bake it. "Did you miss me?"

"Uh-huh," she nods. "Uncle Nate, *look*." She's unusually animated tonight. Daisy points to her lips, which are barely painted with a dab of pink lipstick. "It's called Pink Kisses. My new friend let me wear some. And she let me wear *this*." It's a tiny gold butterfly necklace.

"Your new friend, huh." Let me guess. Just thinking of her being here feels like a jolt directly to the heart. We haven't seen each other in years. I've seen her once since that day…almost eight years ago now.

"Did you have your meeting in the city?"

"Sure did," I reply, straightening up with her in my arms and walking us toward the house. "But the whole time, I was counting the minutes 'til I could get back to my favorite girl."

I carry Daisy up the wide front steps I helped my dad build when I was around Daisy's age and I pull open the screen door. With Daisy's arms wrapped around my neck, I take in the scene—Ma serving up fried chicken and homemade cornbread, Luke and Leo in from the hayfields arguing and drinking beer, Dakota and Tobias setting the food on the table.

And there she is.

Sitting at the far end, sipping a glass of white wine.

Roxie Tucker.

Our eyes meet, and there's that jolt again, but a thousand times stronger now that she's actually *here*. In the very same room. Breathing the same air and filling it with that special brand of electricity she always seemed to carry around with her.

How'd she get so fucking beautiful?

She's always been beautiful, but *Holy Mother*. She's bloomed into a full-blown goddess, sophisticated and citified but still with that country girl edge.

My little sister's best friend, and my childhood best friend's little sister, who hasn't been back since before her brothers' career went into overdrive. Or at least not when I was around.

Dakota never mentioned Roxie was coming for a visit. Kade never mentioned it either, even though I talked to him around a week ago. We talk once a month or so. He told me he had the time, now that their tour is over, to catch up for a beer sometime soon.

I place Daisy down on the chair next to Roxie's and make a point of not staring, even though it takes everything I have not to. Roxie Tucker is no longer the gangly teenager running wild that I remember. No, the woman in front of me is all grown up…and *holy hell*. My addled brain can hardly handle the extent of how fucking gorgeous she is, sitting here all almost-innocently like she isn't detonating a bomb in the middle of my chest right now.

Her dark hair still hangs as long as it always did, but it's thicker now, cut in a fancier style, falling in shiny waves that catch all the golden light of the antique pendant lights hanging over the kitchen island.

Those same vivid blue eyes that used to spark with mischief now hold a depth that's downright intoxicating. The years peel away and I'm nineteen again, battling with myself for not being able to resist kissing my best friends' little sister.

She was a kid then. She caught me off guard once and I allowed it. More than allowed it. I was fucking destroyed by it, in the best possible way. But it was a mistake. Of course it was. She was only fifteen.

She's not fifteen anymore.

My family is doing their usual thing of joking and chattering like it's going out of style, but I barely hear any of it.

"Roxie Tucker," I drawl, trying like hell not to be

transfixed by the shape of her mouth and the way she's filling out that cowgirl shirt.

Damn it. I force myself *not* to react to her the way my body wants to. There are children present. And younger brothers who would love nothing more than to turn an old, speculated-about spark into tonight's entertainment.

"Nate Boone," she says, almost sassily, maybe tuning in to the fact that my greeting isn't so much a greeting as it is a long-built system of defense. There's not a single day that's gone by that I haven't at least once lingered over that memory of our long-ago kiss.

Damn, that kiss was sweet. The sweetest I ever had.

Our eyes are locked as we both deal with the shock of seeing each other again. Her smile is slow, her eyes full of all those old memories of our childhoods together, and also the ones just the two of us share. I can practically feel the air crackle with her wildfire effect.

Keep it together, Boone.

Daisy tugs on my hand, a reminder that I'm not just Nate Boone, I'm Uncle Nate, and there's comfort and an anchor in that. The rest of my life might be a blur of problems to be solved, but I'm solid as a rock when I'm Uncle Nate.

"Uncle Nate, this is my new friend," Daisy informs me, as if I'm not already acutely aware of the woman who's suddenly filling the room with a whole different kind of light. "Her name is Miss Roxie and she's *so* beautiful."

She sure the hell is.

"Can I get some pink cowgirl boots, Uncle Nate? To wear when I'm riding my new pony?"

"Of course you can," I hear myself say.

"Look at Miss Roxie's. They have pink on them!"

I've spent ten years trampling all my emotions down into some deep reservoir inside myself, where they can't affect me too much. I've had too much work to do and too much tragedy to cope with and too many people to take care of to let any of it rise up enough to actually *feel.*

I do it again now. She's here for the weekend and only the weekend. Then she'll be back on the road, her life full of traveling the world.

I'm a father now, or close enough, with commitments that take all my time and focus.

I almost don't do it.

I don't know if I can control myself enough *not* to give away all those deep-rooted feelings I've had for Roxie Tucker my whole life, right here in front of my very observant family.

So I steel myself. I lean in and kiss her cheek, keeping my tone as light as I'm capable of. "Hey, Rox. Good to see you again."

The scent of her, of hothouse flowers, warm sunshine and all my best memories makes me almost dizzy.

"Good to see you too, Nate. You look…good. A little more buttoned up than the country boy I used to know, but I like it." More of the sass, but she's gentle about it, like she knows I'm only wearing these city clothes because I was forced to by circumstance.

I pull off my tie and take off my jacket. "I might as well be wearing a noose and a straitjacket. And those stiffs from Seattle weren't worth dressing up for."

Our gazes hold even though I'm trying not to drink in the sight of her like I've been wandering across a desert for the past eight years and suddenly come face to face with a lush, gorgeous oasis. *Fuck, she's pretty.*

"How'd the meeting with the developers go?" Luke asks, and I'm relieved by the distraction.

"About as well as I expected it would. It was a ridiculous plan which I'll be making sure never happens." Leo hands me a beer and I take a long sip. "Get all the hay in?"

"Around eighty percent of it," Leo says. "We'll get the rest of it in tomorrow morning. The weather report says it's not supposed to rain until sundown."

"You better hope they're right." If I'd helped them, we would have finished the job today. But I've learned by now I can't be in twelve places at once. We all had to learn how to Get Shit Done a long time ago and despite my twin brothers' happy-go-lucky attitude, most of the time they're reliable. "I'll give you a hand if we do it early. I've got to be at the Barrington project building site by one."

The twins are both hard workers and strong as fuck, but they're also a lot more laid back than I've ever been.

Luke is more of a natural farmer. He's genuinely passionate about learning new things and he reads up on all the latest farming technology and techniques.

Leo's more of a numbers guy and the more business-minded of the two. Which makes them a good team.

But neither of them has the relentless drive I have. What they'd rather be doing most of the time is jamming together and making music. I don't begrudge them this. Hell, *I'd* rather be sitting around making music too. But life isn't like that.

The farm and all the challenges that go along with it don't keep them up at night, and I'm glad. They haven't had to carry the brunt of the burden of the responsibilities of the mortgage, the bank, the insurances and so on, but whatever. That's my job.

Tobias places a huge platter of fried chicken on the table in front of the girls. "Ladies and gentlemen," he says, "this evening's menu includes extra crispy fresh buttermilk fried chicken with paprika seasoning, skillet-baked cornbread, apple slaw, and home-harvested green beans. Ladies first. Rox, Ma, Daisy, Dee, get in there before these boys have a chance to clean the plate. And save room for dessert. Daisy helped with the pies and they are masterpieces."

A small hand touches my arm. "I helped, Uncle Nate."

I look down at Daisy's angelic little face. "I can't wait to taste them, darlin'."

"Still warm and served with homemade vanilla ice cream and home-grown blackberries," Tobias adds.

"Wow," gasps Roxie, and I am beyond grateful that I'm now seated with the tablecloth providing coverage, because her breathless gasp does things to me that are not suitable for family occasions.

I've dated a lot of women over the years, but nothing ever really took. I remember one woman I briefly dated was there the last time I saw Roxie. It was around five years ago. I'd gone to play pool with Kade and the boys at some bar in Nashville and I was pissed off because the woman—whose name I can't actually remember—made a huge deal out of the fact that Roxie and I talked for a while. I broke up with her before we even left the bar and never saw her again.

I remember holding myself back from going after Roxie that night. I almost *couldn't* hold myself back. But with her being not quite eighteen at the time and with her brothers surrounding her like a brigade of hell-bent body-guards—and me among them—I hadn't. I'm practically *another* brother, or at least that's how we all saw it at the time. In those days, I had a lot to prove and a mountain of responsibility I didn't fully yet know how to handle.

But that was a long time ago. And the thought flares tonight like a neon sign in a bar window: I am not, in fact, Roxie's brother. Not even close.

There have been a string of mostly one-night-stands between then and now. Occasionally the loneliness and the animal urges become too much to bear and I'll go out with someone new. But none of these "relationships" last. None of them *mean* anything to me. I can barely remember their names, even *when* I'm with them. Which has led to more than one pissed-off meltdown.

I've been accused of being cold-hearted and unfeeling. Of not being capable of love. Of using people.

The problem is, it's all true. I chalked it up to the fact that I work so much and I don't have time to give them the kind of commitment they always want and cry about because I don't give it.

Deep down I think I've always known why, even if I haven't allowed myself to fully acknowledge it for what it is. And I realize now that all those women were wrong.

About all of it.

Here, with the raucous sound of my family's conversation and laughter surrounding me, I do my best to deal with the wrecking ball that's currently pummeling its way through my soul.

Maybe I always knew. Maybe I just never allowed it enough oxygen to fully sink in, because it was a thing that happened when we were kids and I always figured she'd moved on. Or that her brothers would never allow it. Or, more accurately, that *I* would never allow it because she was too young and too close to home.

But now, with her scent and the sound of her laughter branding itself onto my broken, unfeeling heart, all those shattered pieces feel like they're sealing hotly back together. The forging force of it kick-starts my pulse into a slow-burning high gear, as though it's just realized what it's pumping for.

The reason I couldn't love anyone else is suddenly crystal clear, like the clouds have cleared away and the sun is shining directly onto the little hell-raiser sitting at my kitchen table with her mischief-glinting blue eyes and her thick dark hair and that banging little body that I'd fucking kill for.

It's because none of them were her.

6

ROXIE

Nate Boone.

In a suit.

Not just any suit. Armani, if I'm not mistaken. I've organized enough fittings for my brothers leading up to events and awards ceremonies to recognize that by now.

It's not quite what I'm expecting. But I can't help but study the way the suit fits his big frame in *all* the right places, showing off the strong, athletic body that's so jacked it looks like it's about to burst through the freaking seams.

The first thing I notice about Nate Boone is that he's just as swoon-worthy as he's always been, but the swoon-worthiness has somehow gone into overdrive. His handsomeness has seasoned into full-blown masculine virility in the prime of its goddamn life. The suit porn only adds to his hotness, even though it's clearly uncomfortable for him, like it's clashing with the rest of his rugged, beefed-up he-manliness.

Wow.

Nate Boone has definitely changed. The boy I remember, all long limbs and easy smiles, has filled out, his presence almost too big for the room—and definitely more than big enough for that suit.

The other thing I notice is that Nate Boone looks… tired. It's a sort of bone-weariness that draws my attention. Combined with his over-the-top gorgeousness, this detail is basically the equivalent of waving a red flag at a girl whose full time job is looking after her three very demanding and very in-demand older brothers.

I didn't exactly *choose* to be my brothers' guardian angel, but the job chose me and I've grown to love it. Plus I happen to be pretty good at it.

I can't take credit for any of the music, but in the early years it was me who first encouraged them to start writing their own songs instead of doing covers of other people's. Travis and I sat down at the kitchen table and I told him to play me something original. We actually wrote the lyrics to that very first song together. It ended up being their first number one hit.

Vaughn probably would have spiraled out of control a long time ago if I wasn't there, day in and day out, keeping an eye on him. He'll usually toe the line for me, because he knows I worry about him, and he doesn't like me worrying. Of the four of us, Vaughn is the wildest.

He's also the one who's internalized a destructive, misguided and twisted guilt over losing our parents. This has manifested in a way that's made him punish himself by drinking too much and taking too many drugs. We've talked about it a lot. Along the way, every time he got close to an edge, we'd rally around him and pull him back from it. Especially me.

I'm relieved that he's come through the other side of all that and he has Gigi now—who, I'll admit, has a power over him I'll never have and would never want to have. For her, Vaughn will do *anything* to become the best version of himself. All I can say is thank God he's found a girl who has that kind of sway over him. Now all he has to do is keep her. Luckily, the two of them are obsessed with each other and they seem to me like soulmates.

As for Kade, he's so soulful he sometimes gets carried away with it. I don't think he's ever been clinically depressed or anything like that, but he *feels* stuff. Deeply. He sometimes needs to be reminded that the weight of the world isn't actually on his shoulders. And *I'm* the one who mostly does the reminding. I tell him to write a song about it, which always helps. Kade's pouring-your-heart-into-the-music songs are the ones that have won the most Grammys.

Kade also probably would have stuck with his nightmarish ex Carmen if I hadn't convinced him, once and for all, to break it off with her.

Kade and I had a long talk about how unhappy he's

been. He admitted he hadn't thought of it that way. He was grateful I reminded him that he used to laugh a lot more. He used to have fun. He used to *be* fun. So he finally bit the bullet and left her…or so we all hope. I need to follow up on that as soon as I get back to Nashville and check in on him.

So, because of my brothers, I'm attuned to sensing when things aren't going quite right in people's lives. Nate Boone has a world-weary edge to him. Like he hasn't put his needs before anyone else's in a long, long time.

I could help him see that.

Maybe…he needs me.

He's the adolescent crush I never really got over, that's now literally staring me in the face and forcing me to confront it.

Nate Boone is—even though, to be honest, I've never allowed myself to think of it this way until right now—The One Who Got Away. I was too young and too controlled at the time by my family to follow my heart. My parents were fighting a lot, my dad drinking too much, and then we had to deal with their sudden death, which was beyond devastating. All the way through, it was overwhelming. My brothers were the ones who were there for me. I needed them for my own stability. Collectively, they were my rock. And deep down I knew they'd never allow it.

All the girls were after Nate Boone in those days. He was young, hot, and a little bit wild. He was also considered family. None of it was a recipe for true love at the age of fifteen.

But now…*holy shit.* Seeing him again after all these years is giving me a crazy rush of realizations.

He's the one I saved myself for, all this time. Because no one I've met along the way has even remotely compared to Nate Boone. I loved him. I think I still do.

I force myself to slow down with all these over-the-top thoughts.

All that happened a long time ago. I'm sure he's moved on from any feelings we once had for each other. He probably has a girlfriend. Of course he does. I mean, freaking *look* at him. He probably has women falling at his feet all over the county.

Our eyes meet for a charged moment, but his family surrounds him, wanting his attention.

"We're honored by your presence, Mr. Corporate," Luke teases. "Just don't touch a farmer with those fancy clothes or you might get hayseeds on it."

"Trust me, I won't be wearing it again any time soon," Nate mutters, his gaze holds mine as he takes in the look of me. The change in me. And there have been a lot of those.

"Watch out, everyone," Leo grins. "He's always grumpy AF when he wears the suit."

"Leo Angus Boone," comes Betty-Ann's predictable scolding.

"I said *AF*, Ma."

"I know what it means," Daisy announces in her soft little angel's voice. "Uncle Luke says the F-word all the time. So does Uncle Tobias."

Both men give their mother guilty looks.

"Don't you listen to them, sweetheart." Nate ruffles her curls gently with his big, suntanned hand. "They're just rednecks who don't know any better."

"What's a redneck?" Daisy asks innocently.

All the brothers laugh.

Even Nate smiles, and I'm quietly, utterly dazzled.

Despite his gruffness, there's an underlying warmth in his interaction with his brothers. I've missed watching their bond play out over long, hot summer days. My brothers have their own messy bond, of course, but it's more of a life-on-the-road bond, not a this-is-home-and-we-like-it-that-way bond.

His attention is on me, careful but rapt, like it's just the two of us alone in the room. Our connection feels sparked and brimming. Those teenage summers fall back into clear focus and I can practically feel the brush of his lips against mine.

Once and once only.

Daisy tugs at Nate's hand. "Uncle Nate, do you like my butterfly? Miss Roxie is helping me color it."

He's looking at me when he says it. "It's beautiful."

He pulls off his tie and takes off his jacket.

Jesus, the man is cut.

I've followed his career from afar and from Kade's

updates. Nate is a successful property developer and businessman now. Despite the suit and the muscles, I can still see the lean farm boy he used to be. He always kept his hair on the longer side, long enough that it would fall over his eyes and make my stomach do somersaults. It's thicker now, and still long enough to almost clash with the suit—or it might if he didn't look so damn hot in it.

He pulls up the chair next to Daisy's and takes a seat, answering more questions about his day.

It's jarring to be sitting here at the same table with him after all this time of having him live rent free in my head for so many years. Day in, day out, like a little devil sitting on my shoulder in his suntanned, buff, long-limbed image, never really allowing me to get over him.

God, I was so in love with him.

With his golden eyes and that beguiling V above his low-slung jeans that you could see whenever his buttoned-up shirt was open or he took his t-shirt off—which was all the time because we were always swimming or having water fights or the boys were working in the hot sun.

The Boones were like siblings. Yet something set him apart from that. He felt like *mine*, in a way I could never quite explain.

We were just two kids in our extended tribe, going about our business of having the time of our lives. He was another one of my playmates and my protectors, and nothing more.

Still, as we grew older, I became more and more spellbound. I'd never seen a human being who was so physically *beautiful* before. I was endlessly fascinated by him.

I was fifteen the summer Nate Boone turned nineteen. It was too much of an age gap, of course. We were in different phases of life. He barely gave me a second glance, treating me exactly like he treated Dakota and Tobias. Like an annoying kid sister who was fun to tease every now and then but was mostly just an afterthought. My brothers were his *real* friends. The six of them were closer in age and played music together, drove into town to meet girls, smoked cigarettes sometimes and even drank whiskey.

I was barely even a fully-fledged woman yet. And I was sheltered because I had three older brothers who wouldn't think twice about beating any boy to a pulp who so much as looked at me. Not that they ever had to because we usually traveled in a pack and no one would dare. All three of my brothers were built even then and they all had a wild edge that people didn't mess around with.

But that summer, something bubbled up inside me, burning me with new, confusing feelings that dug into my body and soul. My fascination with Nate Boone deepened. I could hardly bear it. He drove me crazy with his graceful muscles and his lazy smile. It wasn't fair that he barely seemed to notice I was alive, aside from kidding with me, along with my brothers, like I was a child.

I didn't *plan* to do it. I can't even remember why I

went out to the barn at dusk one hot late-August night. I might have been looking for one of my brothers. Tobias and Dakota were in the house. Tobias was baking and Dakota had fallen asleep, I remember. We'd had a late night the night before and we were emotional that day because it was our last weekend at the Boones'. Our parents were coming to pick us up in a few days and none of us ever wanted to go back to the city after our long idyllic summers at Sugar Mountain.

I didn't expect to find him alone out there. He was asleep in a big pile of hay. I even remember what he was wearing. Faded blue jeans and an ancient light blue t-shirt that was tight across his shoulders and chest. He wore work boots. He was long, lean and deeply tanned. One of his muscular arms was bent, crooked behind his head.

A low, dust-flicked beam of late-day sunlight landed directly on him, painting him in soft golden light.

"Nate?" I'd whispered.

He still didn't wake. His dark brown hair almost touched his shoulders and was sun-bleached at the ends.

I lay next to him in the hay, carefully, on my side so I could gaze at his peaceful face. He looked younger than nineteen when he was asleep. A lot of the time he had a serious expression, like he was thinking about all the things he needed to do. I knew he had a lot of responsibility already. It was one of the reasons we still came out for the summers, so the boys could help out around the farm.

But the worry was gone in that moment and something about the absence of it broke my heart a little. I wished he didn't have to worry so much or work so hard.

Keeping still for a while, I listened to the evenness of his breathing, taking in the beauty of him and memorizing it, somehow knowing that I might not see him again for a long time. Or maybe ever. The boys were already starting to get serious with their music and I knew we might not be coming back next summer. I remember my eyes stinging at the thought, and the warm slide of a tear.

"Nate?" I whispered again.

He stirred lightly, turning on his side to face me, but his eyes didn't open.

Nate Boone looked so gently sunlit and gorgeous in that dusty old barn, I couldn't help myself. I leaned closer. I kissed him. Slowly at first, because it was my first kiss. Sweetly. I loved him so much. He played the starring role in all the best memories I'd ever had. He was a sun-golden dream and the only thing I ever wanted.

I think it was me that deepened the kiss but it might have been him because he sort of hummed a growl when he woke up. Or maybe he thought he was dreaming. Because he *kissed* me. He opened my mouth with his, which shocked me a little at the time, and pulled me against his warm, hard body. It was hard in places I wasn't *used* to it being hard. And *big*. Pressed up against my stomach as he rolled me back in the hay. I loved the heaviness of him. His tongue was in my mouth and his hands were in my hair and the fiery love and *need* in that one minute of sparked intimacy was like nothing I'd ever experienced.

I don't think I've ever been that happy before or since, if I'm being honest.

But then he must have *actually* woken up because he slowed himself down. To this day I've always been grateful he didn't jump away as soon as he realized. He took his time. He knew he wouldn't go any further, but he allowed himself—and me—one more kiss. Tasting me and kissing me with such tenderness and so much heat, it's no wonder I've never been able to get over him. It was a perfect, sweet, hungry, life-changing kiss.

I would have given him anything and everything that night.

"Roxie," he whispered, his voice deep and smoky and as smooth as music.

"Yeah?"

"You know I can't."

I knew. The timing wasn't right. I was fifteen and we were family. If my brothers had walked in on us right then, they might have hurt him, best friend or not. They *would* have hurt him. Maybe very badly. They were hot-headed, impulsive kids back then. "I wish you could."

"I wish I could too."

He smoothed my hair from my face. Then he shifted his weight like he was about to get up.

I held the front of his t-shirt with my fist, to keep him there. "Nate?"

"Yeah?"

"I love you," I whispered.

There have been times, of course, between then and now that I've remembered those whispered words and I've cringed. But mostly I'm glad I said them. Because they were true.

Nate grinned down at me softly. Then he carefully loosened my fist and lifted himself off of me. "See you around, Roxie Tucker."

It was a goodbye, we both knew that. He left and, after a while, I went back inside and silently cried myself to sleep that night. And quite a few nights after that too.

I was pretty sure he avoided me on purpose because I didn't see him again before we left for good.

"Rox?" Tobias is laughing. "Earth to Roxie Tucker."

I smile and shake my head a little, feeling the heat rise to my cheeks, both at spacing out like that and at the memory, which I haven't thought about in that much detail for a long time. I don't usually let myself because it digs up a special brand of something like pain or regret but not quite either that always feels raw.

"Sorry," I grin. "I must be a little worn out from all the touring. What did I miss?"

"Poor dear," Betty-Ann croons. "You must be exhausted, honey."

"I'm sure I'll sleep well tonight," I admit. "But it

won't be until *after* this amazing dinner. Thank you so much, Betty-Ann. Tobias. Dee. Daisy," I add. "It's so nice to be here."

"It's so nice to have you here." Tobias says. "And we were just saying that we'll take you over to the lodge after dessert. If you're not too tired."

"The lodge? Is that the B&B?"

"The full name is The Sugar Mountain Lodge," Dakota explains.

"I'm definitely up for the grand tour. I can't wait." I take a bite of the fried chicken. "Oh my god, this is incredible."

"We aim to please," grins Tobias.

"When's the grand opening?" I ask between bites, in awe of how good this food is.

"The weekend after next," Dakota says. "We're already fully booked for almost four months."

Luke helps himself to a generous portion of fried chicken. "I just hope you control your guests and we don't find them wandering all over the farm. I like to take a skinny dip in our pond every evening and I don't want to shock anyone with my—"

"Don't even think about continuing that sentence, little brother," Nate says.

"We've already got signs up, telling guests not to wander onto the working farm part of the land," Tobias tells us. "They've got their own area."

"You could put up a sign that says 'Beware of Skinny-

Dipping Rednecks'," suggests Leo. "That should scare them away."

Dakota slaps his arm lightly. "Don't encourage him."

"Might need to add a few adjectives to the sign," jokes Luke.

Leo laughs. "What, like 'moronic'? 'Idiotic'? 'Microscopic'?"

"I was thinking more along the lines of 'king-sized'," Luke grins.

"Would you two stop?" Dakota groans.

"You *are* pretty tall, Uncle Luke," Daisy says earnestly.

"Thank you, Daisy." Luke's green eyes glint. "That's exactly what I meant."

"We're going to have to kick you two out if you can't behave in polite company," Nate says, and the banter continues but the twins obey and barely rein it in. But their respect for their older brother is obvious.

I let the laughter and lively conversation settle around me and enjoy the best meal I've had in a very long time, occasionally stealing glances at Nate, who's cutting up Daisy's food for her into little pieces.

Tobias spreads some butter onto her biscuit.

I can't help but think that, even though losing her parents must be profoundly difficult, she's lucky to have such a loving group of people doting on her.

And it strikes me how much I've missed these small everyday interactions that come with being a family in a real place—not on a stage or a tour bus or in a studio or hotel.

Nate's phone rings in his pocket and he pulls it out, checking the number. "Sorry, everyone, I better take this." He mumbles something about being back in a few minutes, then heads out the door.

There's a general murmur of acknowledgement from the rest of the family. They're clearly used to Nate being interrupted and distracted by all the things he's dealing with.

I find myself caught off guard by the intensity of my curiosity.

Is he okay?

Is it one of his girlfriends?

He paces across the porch, his figure through the sash windows a blend of strength and weariness. Something tells me he's not talking to a girlfriend. Unless she's nagging him about something. He seems pissed off by whatever they're talking about.

I try to concentrate on the conversation around the table, but my mind is on Nate. It's clear that he's shouldering more than just the weight of business deals and a new kind of parenthood. There's a depth to him now, a complexity that wasn't there before. Layers of unrelenting stress are clearly a part of his life now.

After a while, he comes back in. His amber eyes are lightly bloodshot, from lack of sleep, maybe. It does nothing to detract from how insanely good-looking he is.

"I'm sorry, but I'm going to have to deal with this. There's an urgent payroll issue that the manager on call was supposed to have taken care of. But I can't get a hold of her. I'll have to go up to the house to use my desktop."

"You need a hand with anything?" Leo asks.

"No. I got it. Thanks."

Tobias gets up from the table. "At least take your food with you. And I'll get you some pie too."

"Thanks, Tobe. Daze? Come on, sweetheart."

Daisy's eyes fill with tears. "But what about the *ice cream*? It's the best part. It'll *melt*."

"We can bring her up to the house after dessert," Dakota offers. "It's still early. She could come over to the lodge with us and we'll drop her off after that. Is that okay?"

"*Please*, Uncle Nate." Daisy stares at him with pleading blue eyes. "I want to have ice cream with my pie and then go to the lodge with Miss Roxie."

Nate nods, like he wishes he could do that too. "Sure, honey. If that's what you want to do."

"It is."

"Are you okay with that?" Nate asks me, and the question and its delivery in his deep, husky voice does things to me I'm really not prepared for. *I'm not over him. I never was over him.* And my problem—which I didn't actually realize was a problem but it very definitely is—is that...*I still love him.*

I've always loved him and I still do.

"Of course." I smile at Daisy, because the intensity of him and my reaction to it is going to give me away. I softly wipe a tear on Daisy's cheek with my thumb. "We'll have fun."

"I'll see you after that, then. I'm sorry, everyone," he says again. Nate's gaze lands on me. "I'll, uh, I'll see you later."

Daisy and I watch him go as the others return to their food and their laughter.

I smooth a strawberry-blond curl back from Daisy's face and when she looks up at me I feel a deep connection to the concern in this little girl's eyes. She misses him already.

And so do I.

7

ROXIE

We drive along the winding dirt road in Tobias's white pick-up (mine was politely deemed too ancient to guarantee a six-year-old's safety). It's twilight now. The sky is lavender and the moon is rising.

"I'd forgotten what it's like to be out in the country like this," I muse. "Look at all those stars."

"Do you know what the Big Dipper is, Miss Roxie?" Daisy's in her car seat next to me in the back seat. She reaches for my hand and the light, heartfelt clutch of it is comforting to me in a way I can't name. The thing is, *I know how the enormity of this little girl's loss feels.* I was older than she was, but I also lost my parents in a gruesome, tragic car accident. I don't know if she can somehow detect this about me, but I feel an immediate bond with this lost child.

Then again, she's not *really* lost. She has Nate, the

rock of all rocks. And the beautiful, boisterous, close-knit Boone clan. Like me, she wasn't alone in her grief. But it doesn't mean you feel it any less.

I get a sudden wild and surprisingly raw craving to *also* have Nate, the rock of all rocks, as *my* rock too. And the close-knit Boone clan as *my* clan. Not just on an occasional visit, but to belong here. To be *his* and *theirs* and to become one with this magical place that's already so much a part of me. I've missed it and them—*and him*—so much more than I realized.

"I can show it to you if you want," she offers sincerely, her inky blue eyes solemn.

"It was your Uncle Nate who taught me about the stars, a long time ago."

"Uncle Nate shows them to me too," she tells me. "He always asks me to show him the Big Dipper and I find it every single time."

"I bet you do." I remember the night. I was maybe twelve and we were all camping out on the porch. We were all laughing and talking like we always did. Nate pointed out the North Star, the Big Dipper and the Little Dipper, but I was the only one paying attention. I remember him smiling in that lazy way he had. To this day, when it's a clear night I can always find the constellations he showed me and they always remind me of Nate. "He must be a good teacher because I can find them every single time too."

Daisy smiles, holding my hand a little tighter.

We turn around a bend and I can see the lodge coming into view. It sits on the edge of the largest pond on the farm. The water reflects the lights of the buildings and the moon and stars.

"There's the lodge!" Daisy whispers.

"The main entrance is off Southern Road," Dakota says. "No one will be driving through the farm to get to it. Luke and Leo were adamant about that detail. So we're trying to keep it as separate as possible."

"How long did it take you to set this all up?" The magnificence of the buildings comes into full view. "And why didn't you *tell* me about all this?" There are at least seven buildings, one large one and six or seven smaller ones. I'm guessing the large one is the restaurant and the smaller ones the accommodations.

"We've had the idea for so long." Tobias turns into the long entranceway and we drive under the Western-style gate, where *The Sugar Mountain Lodge* has been sculpted under the arch with chopped birch logs. "We've been talking about this since we were kids. But we couldn't afford to build it, at least not the way we wanted to. Nate came to us around a year ago when we were both at a loose end and said he had some money to invest. We sat down and came up with a business plan. Then he brought in one of his teams to help us design and build it."

"He basically threw a shitload of cash at the project," Dakota continues. "At first we weren't sure we should take it. It was such a huge amount of money and we didn't know if we could earn it all back. But Nate talked us into letting him do it. He said it was burning a hole in his pocket and he couldn't think of a better way to spend it. So he paid cash for the whole thing and now the three of us each own a third of it."

"Wow." I'm not surprised that Nate has money. All he's done since we were kids is work. But as we get closer and the grandeur of the lodge comes into full view, it's obvious no expense has been spared. This would have cost *a lot* of money.

"At least we have jobs now," Tobias says cheerfully.

Tobias and Dakota are both homebodies and they're both free spirits. They both went to the University of Tennessee, but they both got homesick and came back to the farm every chance they got. Tobias started his own small local catering company after he graduated, and once she graduated, Dakota took on a few clients as an interior designer. But their jobs have been sporadic and they've both been living at home—by choice, but I imagine it takes some of the stress out of life's inevitable daily expenses.

My besties are happiest when they're together and around their family. Something I happen to understand. "Who needs a job when you can create your own jobs. *Look* at this place. It's incredible." The buildings are made of black-painted wood, glass and black steel, a combination that's sophisticated and luxurious but still looks rustic and very Tennessee. There's a courtyard with arches overrun with rambling white roses, an outdoor seating area, an outdoor kitchen and even a pool.

"Nate got tired of us talking about one day building our dream business, which we've been doing since we were sixteen." Tobias parks the truck in a small parking lot next to the largest building. "So he insisted we make it happen."

"Nate's been *so* generous," Dakota adds, "that we have no choice but to make the place a roaring success."

"It sounds like it already is if you're booked out four months in advance."

"Social media helps." Dakota and Tobias both happen to have impressive Instagram followings, since they're both so artistic and know how to stage a photograph like it's what they were born to do. "The cabins are private so they can be booked by couples. But we're also doing bachelorette parties, weddings, engagement parties, anniversaries, baby showers and so on. These days so many people want Instagram-worthy settings, we put the whole business together with that in mind."

"It's such a great idea. You guys are going to be run off your feet."

Tobias turns off the truck and I unbuckle Daisy and help her climb out.

"You're going to *love* it, Miss Roxie. There are *so* many fairy lights." I offer my hand again and she takes it as we walk inside.

I gasp when I see the interior. The restaurant looks

like a very upmarket barn, with wooden beams criss-crossing across the vaulted ceilings. And Daisy was right: strung around them are hundreds and hundreds of fairy lights.

"Isn't it pretty?" Daisy tugs at my hand, dancing around me as we make our way inside.

"It's beautiful." It really is. Tables and booths are lit with stylish pendant lights. The place has a very luxe feel to it but at the same time it looks like, after hours, they might clear out all the tables and have a barn dance party. I notice that there's a stage at one end. "Are you planning to have live music?"

Tobias gives Dee a look. "We sure are." His reply is almost cagey, but I'm too overwhelmed by the lodge to dig deeper. "Come on, Rox. I want to show you the kitchen. You're going to freak out when you see this."

We walk past an expansive glass office to the kitchen—which is like something out of a Michelin-rated restaurant. "Tobias. It's your *dream* kitchen." I can't believe Nate paid for all this. We haven't even gotten to the outbuildings yet. This whole set-up must have cost millions. "You can finally put all those years of cooking practice to good use."

"The only reason I've come down to the house at all is to see you. But I basically live here now. We've got a little back room in the office with couches and a bed." His grin is adorably elated. It's possibly the happiest I've ever seen Tobias.

I give him a hug because I can't help it. "I'm so happy for you, Tobe. This place is going to explode with business."

"Thanks, honey. That's what we're hoping."

"Tobias has planned the whole menu—with some help from me, of course. He's obsessed." Dakota reaches like she's about to ruffle Tobias's hair and he ducks just in time.

"Do *not* touch the hair," he protests dramatically.

Dakota laughs. "I should know that by now, right, bro?"

"There's nothing you can do to dampen my mood, Dakota Boone, so you can politely—" he eyes Daisy, reigning in whatever colorful reply he was about to give— "leave me to it."

"Gladly. Daze, should we show Roxie the guest cottages?"

Daisy jumps up and down, clapping. "Can we look at the pink one first?"

"You have a pink cottage?"

"It's got a pink door," Dakota confirms. "It's the honeymoon suite."

We say goodnight to Tobias and leave him to his late night macaroon baking session.

"We're going to take your truck, Tobe. Do you want us to pick you up after we drop off Daisy?"

"No, I'll sleep here. There's still so much to do before

the grand opening." He's already opened his laptop and has also turned on several of the ovens.

It's nice to see the both of them so passionate about their new business. Both Tobias and Dakota have, at times, been a little bit aimless. But now the two of them are bright-eyed and excited.

What a gift Nate's given them. A life that revolves around the one thing they've always wanted to do. And now they can.

Dakota, Daisy and I walk along a manicured gravel trail through a grove of trees, shrubs and more rambling roses. I get the grand tour of all six bungalows, which are as luxurious as the main building and all have their own unique charm. "I'm wildly impressed, Dee. Can I move in?" I joke.

"You can live with me and Uncle Nate!" Daisy exclaims. "We have three guest rooms."

"Well, thank you, Daisy." For some reason, the thought of Nate Boone's guest rooms makes my stomach do a funny little flip.

"We should probably head back there soon, Daze," Dakota suggests. "It's getting late."

"I don't like going to bed," Daisy tells us, her blue eyes earnest. "I have bad dreams. Sometimes Uncle Nate has to read me stories in the middle of the night because I can't go back to sleep."

Dakota and I exchange a brief glance.

Daisy's matter-of-fact sadness makes my eyes unexpectedly sting. For what she's had to go through, and from my own tragic memories of the worst night of my life. And now Daisy's got one of those too. "Uncle Nate got me three nightlights and I get to keep all of them on if I want to. They're Elsa, Tinker Bell and Ariel. Uncle Nate tells them to use their magic to me help get back to sleep. So that's what they do."

No wonder he looks so worn out.

I squeeze her hand. I can relate to the nightmares and the many sleepless nights that go along with loss of that magnitude.

Dee picks Daisy up. "You've got your princesses and you've got all of us, right, Daze? You never have to feel alone or scared of anything, okay? And now you've got Roxie too."

"You sure do, sweetie." And even though I'll only be here for the weekend and shouldn't be making promises like that, I find myself wanting it—*really* wanting it—to be true.

"Come on, Rox," Dee starts carrying Daisy toward the truck. "Uncle Nate will be wondering where *this* little princess is."

We climb into Tobias's truck and head back up the road toward the farmhouse, driving past it and further down toward the river. Dakota turns into a driveway that winds through the trees along the ridge. I don't remember this road being here.

And then we're pulling up in front of the most to-die-for house I've ever seen in my life.

It's made of rough-hewn natural-looking wood, the same black steel as the lodge, and glass. Huge windows take full advantage of the stunning river view. It's ultra-modern but with a traditional farmhouse twist. You can tell immediately that it was designed by a major talent, taking full advantage of the nature around it, blending into its surroundings seamlessly. And it's *big*. Three stories are stacked into levels that angle in places in different directions. Along the entire front of it is a two-level covered deck with seating areas, an outdoor kitchen and a hot tub. All of it looks over the ribbon of glittery water and the rolling hills of Tennessee.

"This is Nate's *house*?" I don't know why my question comes out as breathless. I always knew Nate Boone would be a success story, I just never imagined he'd create his own wonderland.

I see him then, sitting in a chair at the far end of the deck, talking on his phone with a laptop open on the table in front of him. He hears our truck and ends his call, getting up to walk over to us.

"Uncle Nate!" Daisy runs across the deck and jumps into his arms.

"There's my girl." He's talking to Daisy, of course.

But he's looking at me.

Wow.

Nate's dressed in faded jeans and an old, soft-looking flannel shirt that strains against his muscles.

Here's the Nate Boone I remember, except that now he's all grown up, all *beefed* up and holding an adorable child in his burly arms. The combination is enough to make every feminine urge I own suddenly wake up, like someone just plugged me in to an invisible charging station that's now pumping cravings into me like a very potent drug.

I've honestly never in my life thought about my *ovaries* before. But right now they're humming. Electricity pulses through my veins with a slow, warm awareness. Of myself. Of how I've never, ever had a love life besides the memory of him. *Because* of the memory of him.

All my cravings were always for him.

And now those cravings are on overdrive because here he is in all his low-slung-jeans-that-fit-like-they-should-be-illegal glory.

I don't know if Dakota is picking up on the sparks I can feel but she takes Daisy from Nate's arms. "It's been weeks since I got to read Daisy her bedtime story. Are we doing a bath first?"

"You sure, Dee?" Nate asks her.

"Of course I'm sure. Besides, you and Roxie haven't had a chance to catch up properly. She and I have all weekend together. Come on, Daze."

With that, Daisy says goodnight to Nate and Dee carries her inside. "Goodnight, Miss Roxie!"

"Goodnight, Daisy."

The door closes behind them.

Nate's hands are in his pockets now and he watches me with light amusement as I stand here sort of speechless. He nods toward the covered seating area. "You want to sit outside? I've got bug candles and a diffuser thing Luke gave me that does a good job of keeping the bugs away. And I think there might be a bottle of wine in my fridge."

"Okay."

I follow him across the wide boards of the deck in awe, not only of the view but of the grandeur and just plain awesomeness of this house. "It's amazing, Nate. You *built* this?"

"I had a lot of help. I've got teams of architects and builders attached to my contracting business. Daisy's dad Jed helped with the design. A lot of the ideas were his."

We go up the stairs to the upper deck, where the state-of-the-art covered outdoor kitchen—complete with a fridge and a flat-screen TV—take full advantage of the stunning view and the clear night sky.

He opens the fridge. "I've got beer, white wine and sparkling water."

"Wine sounds great." I sit in one of the comfortable Adirondack chairs and try not to stare at how good his ass looks in those old Levis, or how they fit him in that uber-masculine way that's making me feel warm and…tingly… in a *very* intimate place.

I've been alone with Nate Boone exactly two times in my life. The night in the barn when I kissed him and he kissed me back, and right now.

He pours me a glass and opens a beer for himself. Then he sits in the chair next to mine and half-grins in that slow, familiar way that used to beguile me. It has an even more profound effect on me now.

I might have been thirteen or fourteen when I first fell in love with Nate Boone. It was the kind of love that ruined me for anyone else. It's still ruining me.

I didn't even allow myself to admit that, until now. My psyche blocked it because I wasn't allowed to have him, but it was always there.

But now, it's as subtle as a freight train rolling through the middle of my world.

He was always the one.

Now all I have to do is to figure out what to do about it.

8

NATE

Roxie Tucker. Here. At my house.

For the first time in a very long time, I feel like I can *breathe* again. Like some unknowable weight has been lifted.

The weight of letting her go, and always knowing she was out there, alone and unprotected. The weight of knowing she could never be mine.

It's only now, with her standing in front of me, that I can see it all clearly.

The past six months have been hard in a lot of ways, but hard is what I'm used to. I had to keep my head down and become the man my family needed me to be. And now I'm doing the same for Daisy.

I haven't looked up for ten fucking years.

And it's come at a cost. I'm not sure I know who I am or what I offer outside of my commitments to this family.

Work and responsibility have consumed me for so long that it's easy to forget what it feels like to simply enjoy someone else's company.

Roxie Tucker isn't just *someone*, of course.

She's the addiction I've fought my whole life.

She was the one who was able to draw me out of my shell, even as kids. She was a rough-and-tumble little tomboy who could give as good as she could take. She was smart and sassy and she lit up every room.

They're the same age, but Roxie has always seemed older than Dakota. And even Tobias. More savvy and more focused. While Tobias and Dakota were figuring out what directions to take with their lives, Roxie jumped into the role of managing her brothers' band when she was barely out of high school—and did a damn good job of it. She is and always has been a firecracker.

There was nothing I could have done about our undeniable connection back then. She was still a kid.

After that night in the barn, which lit a fire in me I've never, ever been able to put out, I built a brick wall between us and made sure it stayed there. I did my best to put her out of my mind, for good.

It never worked.

Since then, the brick wall has remained up. Not just between me and Roxie but between me and most of the people I meet.

It's been staunchly in the way of me getting close to any and every woman I've ever been with. It's why they always accuse me of being cold and unfeeling. Because I am.

What's crazy is that here she is with her Pink Kisses lips and her sledgehammer. The brick wall in the middle of my soul suddenly feels like it's got a big fucking hole in it.

It's hard to explain how good that feels.

Sitting here with Roxie, I don't feel cold or uncaring or distant. My whole body is running hot and I want to pull her onto my lap, kiss her like I did that day in the barn, and watch the sun go down with her in my arms.

That's only the beginning of what I want to do to her.

Roxie clinks her glass against my beer bottle, her eyes twinkling. "Do you remember that time we waited until your parents and Aunt Lou and Uncle Earl were asleep and then snuck out to go night swimming in the pond?"

I smile at the memory. "Yeah. I threw stones at your window to give you guys the signal to sneak out and cracked it."

She laughs. "We got in so much trouble for that later. Kade climbed out the window and down the drainpipe and ended up falling into Aunt Lou's prize roses."

"Ma was waiting for us on the porch when we got back with the wooden spoon she used to threaten us with."

"I remember that spoon. But it was always an empty threat." She laughs. "Aunt Lou said she was going to ground us for the rest of the summer, but in the end she was more worried about Kade's scratches than the flattened roses. The next morning she cooked us pancakes and we were out the door before she could finish scolding us."

Her smile makes my pulse feel hot. I have to look away before she notices me staring at her lips, remembering how fucking sweet they tasted.

"And then there was that camping trip where we saw that shooting star," Roxie muses. "I must've been, what, twelve or thirteen?"

"Something like that." I watch her, struck by how the starlight still glimmers in her sapphire-blue eyes all these years later, just like it used to. "You made us all promise to make a wish before it disappeared."

Roxie nods, looking wistful. "I wonder if any of those wishes came true."

"Maybe some of them did." *Not all of them.* Then again, she's here. Our gazes hold for a second before she looks away. "At least one of your brothers must have wished for fame."

"Yeah. All three of them probably did."

When was the last time I sat with someone other than my family and just talked? I used to with Jed and Laney, of course, but we'd known each other so long, they practically felt like a few extra siblings thrown into the mix.

Roxie touches my arm as she recalls another memory that brings the laughter to her eyes, and I'm damn near consumed by the urge to pull her onto my lap and kiss her, to feast on the sweetness of her that hooked me all those years ago and never let go.

I want to, more than I've wanted anything in a really long fucking time.

But I'm not the carefree boy she remembers. There are new burdens now. Where would Roxie even fit into the precariously-balanced life I'm on the brink of losing control of every second of every day? There are a lot of balls in the air and I'm constantly worried about dropping them. She has her own busy schedule of sold out tours and life on the road.

But damn. *She's so fucking beautiful.*

Her hair was always pretty, but now it's thick and glossy, hanging in waves almost to her waist. She's still slim but she's filled out, from that skinny little tomboy into a full-blown woman with curves for miles, which I'm trying very hard not to stare at like a lovestruck fool. Her cowgirl style is more sophisticated now, with the fancy Nashville boots and the designer jeans—which I can't help noticing fit her like a fucking dream.

It's been a long time since I've felt the feverish pull of white-hot lust—and it's never felt *this* raw.

Lust isn't something I've had a lot of time for lately. I single-handedly run a three-person business and I'm the legal guardian of an orphaned six-year-old.

But the sudden appearance of Roxie Tucker is reminding me that I'm also a big, rough, red-blooded animal with needs that have been put on the back burner for far too long.

Take it down a notch, cowboy. It's Roxie Tucker we're talking about here. She's a hundred percent off-limits.

Or at least she used to be.

She catches me staring. Heat rises to her face, at my expression, maybe, and she bites her lip.

"Rox?"

"Yeah?"

I don't know what I'm about to say. Something, though. Something real.

The screen door slams open and Dakota walks out. "Mission accomplished. The princess is clean, snuggled into bed, all three nightlights are on and her two favorite stories have been dutifully read. But she wants to say goodnight to Uncle Nate. You ready, Rox?"

Roxie's gaze is still fixed on me and she does her best to hide her curiosity. And her disappointment. At the unspoken words. "Oh. Yeah." She adjusts her expression, smiling at Dakota. "Sure."

But that's the story of us, after all. All the things we've never said.

Or at least it was. Until now. Because I've made a decision that has already forged itself into my hot-beating heart.

"Bye, Nate." There's a long-buried sadness behind her smile I understand only too well. "Thanks for the wine."

"See you around, Roxie Tucker." I didn't mean to say

it like that—the exact same words I said to her that night in the barn.

Roxie's eyes are blue as all hell in the moonlight as she glances back at me.

She's the most stunning creature I've ever seen.

And that old ember of regret has suddenly lit itself into a bonfire, like a fucking phoenix rising from the ashes, transforming itself into resolve, lust and the kind of true love that only happens once.

Fuck regret. The memory of the girl I've always loved ghosted around me for years. And now the goddess who just turned up on my doorstep is quite literally the woman of my dreams, one and the same.

I want her. I want everything.

She's real.

She's perfect.

And she's here. For the entire weekend.

It's complicated. She's insanely busy and I'm a workaholic with a six-year-old in tow.

Then simplify it. Figure it out. If there are barriers—and there are—fight your way through them like a fucking Viking until she's knocked up with your baby and so happy all she wants to do is let you love her.

9

———

ROXIE

WAKING up in Dakota's room feels like I've time-traveled back to our tween sleepover days, minus the questionable fashion choices and boy band posters. I stretch out, half expecting those teenage relics to still be on the walls, but instead, I'm greeted by some genuinely cool art and the morning sun streaming cheerfully through the window.

I glance at the clock.

10:34.

Shit.

I must have been *really* tired. I never sleep in.

It probably didn't help that Dee and I stayed up until almost two just talking.

Dakota's side of the bed is empty, and I can hear the clangs and conversation of a house that's already awake and halfway through their busy day drifting under the chunky wooden door.

Sliding out of bed, I throw on some clothes from my suitcase—denim shorts and a tank top—twisting my long dark hair into a braid that hangs halfway down my back. My style has always been farm girl chic, but sometimes I have to wear more "corporate" style clothes when we're trying to put record deals together or when I'm organizing publicity. Just another reason why being back here at Sugar Mountain makes my soul feel so light. I can be the real Roxie Tucker who lives in cowboy boots and barely wears a scrap of makeup, instead of always having to be the one with all her shit together.

Padding down the stairs, the familiar sounds of the Boone household surround me like a comforting hug. There's the clink of dishes, the laughter of morning chatter, and the unmistakable scents of fresh-brewed coffee and home-cooked food.

The kitchen is a welcoming bustle of the Boone family morning routine.

"Roxanne Savannah!" Aunt Lou pulls me into a buxom hug the moment I step into the kitchen. It's been a while since anyone used my full name. My middle name is my mother's name, and it always kicks up bittersweet nostalgia when I hear it. "Child, it's about *time* you came back. What took you so long? We've all missed you and your brothers so much." Aunt Lou finally releases me and holds my shoulders, drinking in the sight of me. "Look at you, baby girl. You have no right to be this beautiful. Especially when you're being run ragged by all those troublesome brothers of yours. How's Vaughn?"

She strokes my hair, touching my face. All the little gestures that I remember from the warmth of the summers I spent at her house. "Vaughn's fine. He sends his love."

"Where is he this weekend?"

"He's…" He's shacked up with his new strawberry-blond obsession, but I don't mention that to Aunt Lou. She'll have a conniption—mainly from excitement because she wants to be a great aunt as soon as possible and no doubt Vaughn's babies will be her favorites. "He's in Nashville, taking some much-needed R&R after the tour."

"Sit down and tell me all about it, sugar pie."

Aunt Lou guides me to the table. There's no sign of Nate or Daisy or the boys, but the table is already in the process of being piled high with mountains of food.

"Mornin', Sunshine," Betty-Ann sets a mug of steaming coffee on the table in front of me. "Best get in quick before the locusts descend. The boys are out in the fields, but they'll be in before long."

"Thank you, Betty-Ann. I can't believe I slept so late." I hold the mug between my hands, blowing on it. "Usually I'm up with the birds."

"I kept you up far too late last night." Dakota pulls a tray of fresh-baked biscuits out of the oven. "Besides, you've been so busy, I figured you needed the rest."

Dee and I talked for hours, about the tour, about her and Tobias's business, about our currently-dismal love lives, and about life in general.

We talked about everything except the one thing I've still never confessed to anyone, and hardly even to myself.

But I dreamt of him last night, my subconscious digging up some particularly sweet forgotten memories. And new ones too. *Of the way he looked in the moonlight, allll grown up and hotter than any One Who Got Away has any right to be.*

I've seen him twice in the past eight years, but the half hour we spent together last night has hit me hard. *Will I see him today?*

"I haven't slept that deeply in a *long* time," I confess.

"You definitely needed it," Aunt Lou insists. "You also look like you need plenty of home cooking, Roxanne Savannah Tucker. Are they not feeding you on that tour bus?" Lou tucks a stray strand of hair behind my ear and plants a kiss on my cheek. "Skinny or not, it's so wonderful to have you home, honey."

Home. It sure does feel that way. "It's good to be here, Aunt Lou. How have you been? And how's Uncle Earl?"

"Oh, you know. We're fine. Your Uncle Earl is a little more hard of hearing these days and his memory isn't quite what it used to be, but other than that we're doing just fine."

With my back to the door and Dakota and Betty-Ann bustling around to get even more food on the table, I almost miss Uncle Earl shuffling in. He's older than Aunt Lou, and he's definitely aged quite a bit since I was last here.

"Morning, everyone," he holds a hand up in greeting as he slides into a seat at the head of the table. At first he doesn't notice me amongst all the activity of the chefs.

"Earl Tucker," Lou scolds him, "look who's here."

His eyes light up when he sees me. "Roxie. What a surprise." He struggles a little to get up, so I jump up to give him a hug. "When did you get here, honey? Just now?"

Lou pats his arm affectionately. "Earl, Roxie's been here since yesterday. You remember, we talked about it last night."

Earl chuckles, rubbing the back of his neck. In that moment, he reminds me so much of my father it takes my breath away. The similarity pulls at something painful and buried inside me. "Ah, yes, of course."

"It's great to see you Uncle Earl. You're as handsome as ever."

It's true. He might look older, but when they were young, he and my dad were stunning looking men. Vaughn looks a lot like both of them once did. Except he's taller and more built. Not to mention he acts like a maniac most days. Even so, everyone has a soft spot for Vaughn.

A gigantic plate of food is placed at my place setting.

"Hope you're hungry, darlin'," Betty-Ann grins.

Dakota laughs. "No one's *that* hungry, Ma."

"She's skin and bones!" Betty-Ann exclaims.

"It's true," Aunt Lou seconds. "Roxie, eat."

"Yes, ma'am." Obeying, I sit in my chair and pick up my knife and fork. "I don't even know where to start."

Scrambled eggs, two oven-warm biscuits with gravy, cheesy grits, fresh fruit, bacon, sausage, and skillet-baked cornbread dripping with homemade butter.

"Okay, this is next level, guys. You'll have to roll me down Sugar Mountain."

"Men like women with some meat on their bones," Lou informs me. "How's your love life, darlin'? Have those meddling brothers of yours let you spread your wings a little?"

Aunt Lou knows my brothers well. "Not exactly. Tumbleweeds are currently rolling through my love life."

"Maybe we could help, Betty-Ann." Aunt Lou perks up. "Plenty of handsome red-blooded country boys around Sugar Falls we could introduce you to."

Dakota laughs. "Like who?"

"A bunch of 'em are living right here on this farm," Lou replies.

"Lou, you're losing your marbles worse than me," Uncle Earl scolds her. "The Boone boys are practically Roxie's *cousins*."

"More like brothers," Dakota adds.

Nothing like family to spear straight to the heart of the very topic that gave me such sweet dreams last night

—and has always felt a hundred percent forbidden for the exact reasons they're happily bantering about.

"You all know they're not actually her brothers," Betty-Ann points out. "And neither are they her cousins. Any one of my boys would be lucky as sin to win a woman as beautiful and successful and sweet as Roxie Tucker. But my guess is she's looking for someone more mature than my twins. God knows I love 'em to pieces, but they still act like a pair of naughty schoolboys half the time. Plus they're still busy sowing their wild oats, God love 'em. I just hope they're being careful. Boys will be boys, after all."

"Amen to that," Earl chimes in, digging in to his own breakfast.

Betty-Ann tops up my coffee. "Then there's Nate of course but he's so surly these days and hardly ever home."

"Plus all the responsibility of a child to raise on his own, which hasn't been easy," Lou chimes in.

"Lord knows that's the truth," Betty-Ann continues. "Then again if he had a gorgeous wife to come home to, he'd think twice about his workaholic tendencies. Maybe it's exactly what he needs."

My stomach does another one of those swoops.

"Didn't he go out on a date with one of those girls down at the coffee shop a while ago?" Lou asks. "Every time I go in there, they're always asking about him. Then again, they ask me about him at the bakery too. And the library."

"Oh, you know Nate. Nothing ever lasts with him. I worry about that boy. I can't think of a single time he's dated a girl more than once."

I don't dare look up from my plate in case I somehow give myself away. And I'm not sure how to feel about or what to make of the information they're discussing.

"Anyhow, since tomorrow night's the hoedown, we can introduce Roxie to some of the local boys," Lou says excitedly. "Just think about it, darlin', if you married a local we could see you all the time!"

"Hoedown?"

"It's just a little last-minute thing we're putting together," Dakota explains. "A few bands will be playing and we're serving up a casual buffet dinner, that's all. At the lodge."

"Oh. That sounds like fun."

Betty-Ann and Lou aren't cagey about any information whatsoever, like Dakota and Tobias were earlier. "Luke and Leo are going to play a few songs," Lou says. "And maybe even Nate."

"Nate?" They all sang with the family band when we were kids—and they were all good, even then—but that's as far as it ever went, or so I thought.

"Nate's the one with all the talent, if you ask me," declares Lou. "Of course the twins are also talented," she quickly adds. "And they could charm the pants off a nun, just saying."

"Louise Mary Jensen Tucker," Betty-Ann chides her. "Those are my angelic sons you're talking about."

"Well, it's true and you know it."

Dakota pulls up a chair and sits next to me. "We didn't want you to feel like we'd invited you here just to listen to them play or anything like that, Rox. We know you're a high-powered manager now but there are zero ulterior motives to the hoedown."

"Got it," I assure her. "But I invited myself, if I remember correctly."

"True," Dakota smiles, helping herself to a piece of my bacon. "But the hoedown is a new development."

"Dakota Beatrice Boone, let the child eat."

"I need her help." I put my fork down because I'm already getting full even though I've hardly made a dent in my breakfast. "There's seriously no way I can eat all this."

"Her stomach has shrunk, Lou, because of her life-style." Betty-Ann sounds concerned. "Roxie, how long are you staying?"

"Just the weekend. I have to go back to the city on Monday."

"That's not enough time for us to feed you properly," Lou protests. "Child, you're wasting away. Can't you stay a little longer?"

All four of them are watching me hopefully.

"Well, the tour's over, so technically I'm supposed to have a few days off. But I—"

"It's decided then," Lou declares. "Two days isn't nearly long enough."

I'm wondering how long they think it'll take to both fatten me up *and* find me a local to marry. "I guess I could stay an extra day, but I definitely need to be back in the city on Tuesday afternoon. I've got a meeting with one of my new clients."

"Do it by Zoom or whatever they use these days," Betty-Ann suggests. "Nate does it all the time."

I take a bite of bacon and it's literally the best bacon I've ever tasted. "I wish I could, but she's flying to Nashville from Austin just to meet with me."

"How was your sewing circle last night, Lou?" Dakota, bless her, might be deliberately steering Lou away from the topic of both my overly-busy work schedule and my non-existent love life.

"Oh." She holds her palms up, as though she thought we'd never ask. "*Well*, Mildred Johnson is all up in arms about the new business venture of Mitch's. You remember the old Johnson barn on the edge of town, Rox?" I nod, remembering it as a place that sometimes held farmers' markets in the late summer. "Well, turns out Mitch decided it would be the perfect place for his new brewery. He's calling it 'Johnson's Jolly Juice' and now the whole town's in a tizzy over it. And apparently it packs quite the punch. Maureen O'Neill—you know her, Dakota, she chairs the town's historical society—well, her husband's taken a real liking to it. Maureen's telling everyone at Town Hall that the barn's a historical landmark and should be preserved, not turned into a glorified speakeasy."

"Only in Sugar Falls would a batch of home brew cause such a scandal," Dakota laughs.

Aunt Lou loves nothing more than a good scandal. "Mayor Simons had to get involved on account of all the biddies knocking on his door 24/7. He told them it's good for the town's economy. And he asked Mitch to bring some samples to the town meeting to make his case. But then half the council ended up tipsy. Even Maureen was dancing on the tables. She broke one of 'em and rolled halfway across the gymnasium."

The kitchen erupts into laughter.

The laughter, the lighthearted melodrama, the sense of belonging—it all feels like a breath of fresh air.

"I've missed you all so much."

Aunt Lou reaches over, giving my hand a gentle squeeze. "And we've missed you, dear. Don't leave it so long next time."

Earl nods, looking at me with misty eyes.

"At least consider staying a little longer." Aunt Lou blots her eyes with a tissue.

"I'll stay until Tuesday, then."

But if I'm being honest, three more days on Sugar Mountain doesn't feel like nearly enough.

10

ROXIE

Betty-Ann sets a final platter of food onto the table, a giant bowl of potato salad. "There. That's everything."

"Ma, sit and eat something, will you," Dakota says as Betty-Ann goes back to the sink and starts washing dishes.

"I'll eat up whatever the boys don't want. Anyway, I'm on that special diet the doctor gave me. No butter and not too much meat on account of my cholesterol. Takes all the fun out of it, if you ask me."

"I'll make a plate for you. You said yourself they're locusts, Ma. It'll all be gone."

Betty-Ann shrugs. "Well, they're working hard, they need the fuel. And I want to encourage them. They're doing a good job out there. Dakota, I made a batch of lemonade that's chilling in the fridge. Would you take it out to them and tell them lunch is ready?"

"Sure, Ma. You want to come, Rox? Or do you want to stay for more grilling and matchmaking suggestions?"

"I love you all," I tell them, getting up and taking my plate to the counter. "And thank you for that wonderful meal. But if I eat another bite I will literally burst."

"Don't you dare do any dishes, Roxanne Savannah," Betty-Ann scolds me. "You're on vacation."

"I can put one plate in the dishwasher." But she's already taking it from my hands.

"Do as your aunt tells you."

"I thought you said you weren't her aunt," Earl says.

"Oh, be quiet, you old geezer," Betty-Ann says, with love.

I grab some glasses to put on the tray Dakota is setting up with the large pitcher of fresh-squeezed lemonade and some of the still-warm buttered biscuits.

"See y'all soon."

I open the screen door for Dee and we walk out onto the porch, making our way toward the barn. Beyond it, the harvester is bringing in the baled hay, load by load. I can see Luke, Leo and Nate at the far side of the barn. The barn doors are open wide and the brothers are stacking the bales in the barn.

Shirtless.

We get closer and the sun is beating down in golden, dusty beams, directly onto the three of them, like God wants to showcase his masterpieces in perfect, luminous light.

Whoa.

The gangly boys I once knew are now big, muscular, sweaty men. I'm pretty sure every girl in Tennessee would pay good money to watch the Boone brothers throwing hay bales around in the hot sun.

The twins are gorgeous and they know it. They're young, cocky show-offs.

But it's not the twins I'm looking at.

Nate Boone's lean, boyish frame has filled out into a god-like specimen of full-blown freaking manhood. He's got the physique of a hard-working farmhand who must also work out. His muscles are taut and defined, glistening with sweat, rippling as he lifts the hay bales and tosses them to Luke to stack onto the mountainous pile.

You've got to be kidding me.

I used to gaze at him when I was a girl, knowing for a fact I had never seen a more beautiful human being. He was perfectly made even then.

But now, he's more than just beautiful.

He's hot as fuck.

And this is more than fascination. It's a deeply-buried craving that opens a flood gate inside me, surging through my bloodstream.

I want him.

He's the one I waited for.

I stand there, transfixed by the way his abs flex and quilt as he picks up a hay bale, the sculpted strength of his muscled, suntanned arms, the way the bright sunlight reflects off his too-long dark hair, tinting it shiny shades of red and gold.

Holy Dream Come True, Batman. He's perfect.

He looks up.

And then he smiles. That old crooked smile I remember so well. Like he can't help himself. Almost like he's…happy to see me.

His eyes are on my face, as darkly spellbound as I feel. Then his gaze moves over my body, taking in the fit of my tank top, my short jean shorts, my long bare legs, my cowgirl boots, before making their way back up to my face.

Nate's eyes paint warmth onto my skin, and deeper. I can feel his effect *inside* me, where it's somehow turned me into a ripe fruit that wants nothing more than to…*be eaten.*

I don't even know what's happening.

It's a slow motion awakening, and whatever beast is coming to life, she is *hungry*. I'm aware of a transformation taking place and I vaguely try to stop it, but I can't. I might as well try to stop myself from breathing.

I fall in love with him.

Just like that.

Right then and there.

Sure, I already loved him, from afar. A benign sort of worship that was more of a crush or a wish you don't really expect to come true.

This is different.

I fall *in love* with him. Like, *hard*. With a lusty ferocity that grips my heart like a hot squeezing fist that *needs* what it wants.

"Hey, Rox," he drawls, swiping some burly arm porn over his forehead to wipe away his sweat.

I want to lick his dirt-smeared chest like I've never wanted anything in my life.

His eyes are light, the color of whiskey on ice, and that usual frown of concentration and Getting Shit Done are suddenly gone. He's so handsome I forget to breathe.

Luke and Leo both stop what they're doing to watch their older brother, as though his relaxed, charmed, lazy grin is wildly out of character. Then they glance at me. Then back at Nate. Leo elbows Luke and they're both grinning like Cheshire Cats.

"Well, well, well," is all Luke says, but it's enough to break whatever trance Nate and I are locked in.

A light nudge pokes into my rib. "Rox?"

"Oh. Yeah?"

"I was just saying, can you take the tools off that hay bale so I can set this tray down?"

"Oh. Sure."

"'Bout time, Dakota," Luke laughs. "I was about to die of dehydration."

"Then carry a water bottle with you like a normal person would."

"I'm trying to save the planet." Luke downs the entire glass of lemonade Dakota just handed him.

"Get yourself a Stanley like a good little metrosexual. The planet will be fine."

"Who you callin' a metrosexual?" Luke looks offended.

"What even *is* a metrosexual?" Leo stuffs a whole biscuit into his mouth.

"Someone with more manners and dress sense than you, who wouldn't stuff an entire biscuit into their mouth like a Neanderthal."

"Mm phumpgry," Leo protests.

"Nate must qualify, in his Armani and deluxe, high-tech mansion." Luke elbows Nate.

"Nate is the last person I would describe as a metrosexual," Dakota laughs. "Nate's more like a he-man with brains. And one extremely expensive suit."

"So there." Nate elbows Luke back, but it's stronger than Luke's shove was and Luke pretends to almost fall over, which makes Nate smile. He's in a good mood today, reminding me of the carefree kid he used to be, running through the fields with my brothers and playing guitars all night long.

And now I'm curious. "High-tech?"

"Didn't you get the grand tour?" Luke asks. "Our boy here has *all* the bells and whistles, down to the ambient lighting and the stereo with sensors that recognize the sound of your voice. His house will actually play your favorite song when you walk into a room."

"Is that right?" I'm impressed. And it's true, I didn't

even go inside his house last night. We didn't get that far. We were too busy radiating with the buzz of seeing each other again to even get past the porch.

The same thing must be occurring to Nate. "Come by later and I'll show you around, if you want to see it."

Luke grins at Leo, raising an eyebrow.

Nate ignores them. "I've got a meeting until around five. Daisy's with Tobias. Baking a cake. He's taking her to a birthday party later this afternoon. Her first sleepover."

"Wow," Dee says. "That's a big deal, Nate. You think she'll be okay?"

We all know about the nightmares. "I told Harper's mother Kristie to give me a call any time of the night if Daisy wakes up in the night. It's just down the road so I can go get her if she needs me to. She's really excited about it so hopefully she'll be okay."

"You should check out the house, Rox." Luke's not about to let it go.

"Sure. I'd love to see it."

Nate's eyes hold mine and the heat in them burns me all the way down to my soul.

I glance over at Dakota and a light smirk brings out her dimples. "I'd come with you but Tobias and I have some stuff to do before the hoedown tomorrow night. And no, we don't need help."

Well.

I don't overthink it. But if Dakota, Luke and Leo are all entertained by the idea of Nate showing me his house

—alone, just the two of us—then it's almost like…this long-buried thing between us isn't quite as forbidden as it used to be. I mean, Betty-Ann basically gave us her blessing, in a roundabout way.

Not that there's anything to give her blessing *about*, of course. It's just…a whole different vibe than it used to be.

I don't know if my brothers will be as understanding, but I'm hardly going to worry about them. Most likely I'll have a civil glass of wine with an old friend and then be on my way. Besides, God knows all three of my brothers allow themselves to dive into their romances with gusto, whenever and wherever the mood strikes.

I'm not fifteen anymore so as far as I'm concerned, it's none of their business anyway.

Nate says to Luke and Leo, "I better hit the shower and head over to the Barrington site. You two can take it from here." Then he puts his hat on his head and tips it at me. "See you later, Roxie Tucker."

At least he didn't say *see you around*.

I guess it's a date.

11

———

ROXIE

DAKOTA and I spend the afternoon by the pool. The day is as perfect as it possibly can be.

Yellow loungers and matching umbrellas give the resort-feel of the place a festive atmosphere. Humidity buffers the rolling hills of rural Tennessee in a gauzy, romantic haziness.

After all the city lights, the greens of the trees and the blue of the clear sky are like a balm for my jaded soul. I feel myself relaxing like I haven't in a long time.

We're both wearing bikinis, straw hats and sunglasses.

"So, have you changed your mind about any of the locals?" Dakota grins. "Just think about it, Rox, we could be *actual* sisters."

"Let's not get ahead of ourselves, girlfriend. I've been invited to see if a high-tech stereo system can guess what my favorite song is and nothing more." But I'm relieved she's okay with…whatever happens. *If* anything happens. What I'm finding is that times have changed since I was fifteen, which shouldn't surprise me as much as it does. And I somehow get the feeling tonight is going to change my life. "Until then, don't bother me, I'm mainlining Vitamin D."

"You're so lucky you tan so easily. I have to burn before I tan. It's not fair."

"You shouldn't be tanning at all, Miss Dakota. Your skin is flawless." It really is. She's still very much a tomboy and rarely wears make-up. She doesn't need it. She's got a perfect complexion. She's filled out since our teenage years, of course, and she's still slim but curvier now, filling out her bikini like nobody's business. Her long brown hair is glossy with natural reddish highlights, matching her hazel eyes and the jaunty sprinkling of golden freckles across the bridge of her nose. "You're stunning and you know it. And I don't believe it for a minute that there's not a single 'local' that appeals to you. Come on, spill. If I'm going to be meeting some of them tomorrow night, I need a lowdown of the one—or ones—my bestie has her eye on."

The quirk at the corner of he mouth is full of mischief.

"Dakota Beatrice Boone. Tell me right now. There *is* someone."

She barely shrugs. "I wouldn't call it a *someone*. More of a we've-had-two-conversations-and-he's-hot, that's all.

And he's not a local. He's just visiting. He's a bull rider, believe it or not. He's from Montana."

"Wow. A rodeo hero? Sounds promising. What's his name?"

"Wyatt. His family are ranchers."

I elbow her. "Sounds even more promising."

She laughs. "We'll see. He's also the new shiny toy in town, and just passing through. Every girl is after him. Apparently he just broke up with a long-time girl from back home and he's still partly heartbroken, so of course everyone wants to be the one to fix his broken heart."

"But he's got his eye on you."

"Hardly. As I said, we've had two conversations. Anyway, all eyes will be on you. This whole town is obsessed with the Tuckers."

"The Tucker *Brothers*, maybe. Not their behind-the-scenes manager."

"That's until they get one look at you. You look amazing, Rox. Your exciting life obviously agrees with you."

"Thanks." I take a long sip of the iced tea Dakota brought for us. Since it's Dakota, she packed a whole cooler complete with ice and lemon wedges. "Aside from the bags under my eyes, you mean."

"They're not so bad," she smiles. "Nothing a few good nights' sleep won't fix."

Tobias's truck pulls up in the parking lot next to the pool. He lets himself into the pool area, looking cool with his sunglasses and flamboyant outfit. "*Damn*, girls." Tobias lets out a low whistle. "When did my sisters turn into Sports Illustrated cover models?"

"We're not calling her our sister anymore, Tobes," Dee tells him. "For…reasons."

"What reasons?"

"No reasons," I cut Dakota off before she can continue, then I deftly change the subject. "How'd the birthday party drop-off go?"

"Without a hitch," Tobias confirms. "They loved the cake. Twelve princesses were very impressed by the pink icing. It's Harper Mason's party and apparently Daisy goes there for playdates all the time. She was excited about the sleepover. And Harper's mother has been briefed on the plan if she wakes up in the night."

"Poor Daze," Dee murmurs. "Hopefully it'll go smoothly."

"Dakota Boone, get your sweet ass up out of that lounger and help me with the hoedown prep. And no you may not help us, Rox, so don't ask or insist. It won't be tolerated. You can remain poolside, relaxing."

"What time is it?" My i-Watch, a birthday present from Travis, is in my bag, up at the house.

"Almost five-thirty."

"Is it?" It's later than I thought.

"Roxie's going over to Nate's to get a tour of his house," Dakota tells him.

"Nice." Finally, a normal reaction. Tobias doesn't read anything into the innocent piece of information.

Dee leans over and kisses my cheek. "Enjoy. See you when we see you, honey."

"I'll see you both later on."

Once they're gone, I lower myself into the water to cool off. My heartbeat feels warmer than usual, radiating a slow glow of…anticipation, maybe.

It's a tour of his house, that's all.

I dry myself off, pull a pink sundress on over my bikini and head to Nate's.

12

NATE

My meeting ran overtime and I drive like a bat out of hell. By the time I get back to the house it's almost six.

Fuck. Did I miss her? Then I'll storm over to the house or the lodge or the pool or wherever she is and fucking find her.

Just as I'm pulling into my driveway, her old pick-up follows me. Behind the wheel is the prettiest girl I've ever seen.

No one's ever had the power to take my breath away like Roxie Tucker.

She steps out of her truck, wearing a practically-see-through pink dress over a pink bikini that's obviously still slightly wet, her long, glossy hair hanging in waves over her shoulders.

I'm fucking spellbound. And in serious trouble. I want this girl like I've never wanted anything in my life. My body and soul want to wrap themselves around her and make the girl who's always been my dream *mine*.

After all the years of missing her, of forcing myself to try to forget her, it's hard to adjust to seeing her again. And not just seeing her but being more dazzled than I know what to do with.

She's here and we're alone. For the third time in our lives.

"I'm going to have to talk to your brothers about upgrading your ride."

She glances as Bertha and smiles. "I've got plenty of rides, all parked in the garage under our Nashville warehouse, that I never use. She's still my favorite."

"I can see why." She might be old, but she's a beaut.

"I hardly ever get to drive her. Coming back here seemed like the perfect chance to take her for a spin."

"She running okay?"

"Like a dream. Ever since you fixed her."

I can't help smiling at that and it reminds me that I hardly ever smile anymore. Not until sunshine in human form came back to me. "You ready for your tour, Tuck?" It's a nickname I gave her when she was maybe ten or eleven.

"I'm more than ready for my tour, Boone." There's a twinkle in my girl's blue eyes. She's always been sassy, and now that I'm allowing myself to fully bask in her blazing glow, the burn of her blue eyes lights the long-simmering fire in my blood. "Are *you* ready for my tour?"

"I've been ready for your tour for a long time, darlin'."

Light flags of pink warm her cheeks and I hold her gaze, making them turn even pinker. Still half grinning, I lead her into the house, attempting to hide the fact that my cock is thickening hotly. *Fuck.*

I've had a serious dry spell lately. Part of the reason is because I'm busy. Part of it's possibly due to the six-year-old who's both infused my life with a new purpose but also taken it over almost completely. Most of all, though, because I have a hard time finding women that…appeal to me.

Because they're not her.

Now I know.

Deep down I've always known, but now the realization might as well be emblazoned across the sky in neon lights. *She's the one. She's always been the one.*

I hold the door open for her and she steps into the kitchen. A light gasp escapes her, causing my cock to thicken even more painfully.

"Nate. This is, like, my *dream* kitchen."

I know. Because I remember her describing it once, to Tobias, when we were kids. *It'll have windows across the entire side of it, looking out over Tennessee. It'll have a big table next to the windows where all my friends and family can eat together, and a window seat where you can sit in the sun and read your book and talk to whoever's cooking. It'll have a big island and those hanging lights. And a huge double fridge. It'll be modern but also country. When you step into it, it'll feel like you're home.*

She runs her fingers over the marble countertops, taking everything in. "It's amazing. You must…like to cook."

"I've hardly used it. I cook most of our meals out on the barbecue. And Ma and Lou drop off so many casseroles, I have around twenty of 'em in the freezer at all times."

She smiles, but she's distracted.

The kitchen opens out into a rustic but modern open-plan living area with a 72-inch flat screen mounted on one wall and a stone fireplace that takes up most of another. The other wall is made entirely of sliding glass doors that fully open onto the deck. There's a wooden staircase leading to the second floor.

"Nate," she whispers, her eyes bright. "This *house*."

"You like it?"

"It's a dream house."

It's *her* dream house. Because I always listened.

Now all I need to do is convince her to live in it.

13

NATE

"Can I look upstairs?"

"Of course." I step back. "After you." And if my life wasn't already painful, following the sweet, sassy little goddess who's haunted my dreams for eight years up the stairs makes it exponentially more unbearable. Or somehow perfect. Because she's *here*. And if I get my way, we're not coming back down these stairs until morning.

"Daisy's room is the first one on the left."

She wanders into it. "Nate," she gasps. "I can't believe this." She actually twirls around, exactly like Daisy did. "This was my absolute dream room when I was a little girl. You're a romantic at heart, Boone. No wonder Daisy loves you so much." She puts her hand on her heart and grins at me.

She's so damn sexy it hurts. The fading daylight

paints her in golden light, making her eyes shine like sapphires.

"I just do as I'm told. As soon as Daisy moved in, I told her she could have anything she wanted. So the first thing we did was paint it pink."

"It's definitely pink."

"It's the pinkest pink we could find."

We both laugh. The sound of her laughter washes over me, stirring up memories of summer nights under the stars.

I adjust myself in what I hope is a subtle move as Roxie checks out the tent, with all the glitter-covered stars Daisy and I made.

"This is so cool." She emerges from the tent, a dusting of glitter on her cheek, like she's made of magic. "Six-year-old slumber parties are the best. Too much candy, very little sleep, and lots of giggles. I'm sure she'll have fun. And she'll come back tomorrow totally wired. But it's all worth it to make her happy, right?"

"Always. I just hope I'm doing enough of that."

Roxie's eyes meet mine. "She seems happy, Nate."

"I hope she is. I'm not nurturing like Ma or Lou, or fun like Dakota, and I don't have limitless patience like Tobias. I can be her rock, though."

"She obviously adores you. You're her knight in shining armor and I'm not surprised. You always felt like that to me too."

It wasn't what I was expecting her to say. "Yeah?"

"Yeah."

"I didn't know that."

"You always made sure I was okay. You got the band-aids when I skinned my knees. You made us a bridge to cross the creek. You fixed my truck." Her smile is almost shy. *Fuck, I'm in trouble.* "You're doing an amazing job."

"Thanks. Her mom's sister is contesting custody. They don't think a 'bachelor' like me can provide a good enough home. They think Daisy should be with family."

Roxie is quiet for a moment. "One look at you two together and it's obvious she's where she's meant to be. And besides, you are giving her a family. Your mom and brothers and Dakota and Lou and Earl? It's pretty ideal, if you ask me. I don't see how anything could top that."

Roxie's faith, her instant defense of my bond with Daisy, hits me. "I appreciate you saying that," I manage roughly.

"It's the truth. Daisy's so lucky to have you, Nate."

We share a small, meaningful smile, and something shifts. No one else's opinion has ever really mattered much to me, but knowing Roxie sees me as worthy of raising Daisy suddenly means more than I can articulate.

"So, how's the 'bachelor' lifestyle treating you these days?" She even uses air quotes around the word. Digging for clues about my life, maybe.

"Well, Tuck, it's pretty quiet if you really want to know." I think back to the summer I turned nineteen and she was fifteen. I was overwhelmed by her. She was on the cusp of blossoming into the smart, brave, beautiful young woman she was always destined to be. I couldn't resist her even though I had to.

I'd never felt anything like what being around her stirred in me. Until I left and locked it away because she was too young and her family was my family. Now that she's here and she's blown the blockade off that room in my heart where I always kept her hidden away, I don't know if I can control the intensity of this surge of feelings.

My lust—which has been as locked up as the rest of me, because my life isn't only my own and no one I'm with is ever her—is suddenly a beast of fucking need that wants to be *fed*.

She's not just the woman of my dreams but also now a consenting adult who's capable of making her own decisions.

And this isn't just physical attraction. It goes soul-deep. She's always been able to *see* me in a way that no one else could. Not as the dutiful son or the responsible older brother.

As myself.

It almost shocks me how much I need her. How much I want her in my life again.

Roxie catches me staring and her cheeks get pink. "So…can I see more of the house?"

I've never stopped being in love with her. And I'm

done denying what feels like it's always been written in the stars.

Fuck everything. She's mine.

I slowly reach to weave my fingers through hers. Her lips part softly at the contact. "You want to see my room?"

14

—

ROXIE

Nate holds my hand, our fingers locked together, guiding me down a hall lined with photographs of the farm. Some are black and white. There are a few of his parents. There are baby pictures. Landscapes. Family portraits and polaroids.

There's one of him and a guy who could only be Jed—Daisy looks just like a tiny little girl version of him—with their arms slung around each other's shoulders, maybe in their early twenties. There's one of Nate holding Daisy, as a baby, with Jed and Laney in the background.

There are dozens of photos of our families together. One with Nate and Kade sitting on motorcycles, smiling for the camera. Another one of the two of them, shirtless in jeans, leaning against a fence they'd been fixing.

There's one of Nate with all three of my brothers, somewhere in town when they used to travel as a pack.

One of Nate's whole family, before their dad's heart attack.

One with all nine of us as sun-kissed kids, proudly showing off a fort we'd built.

One of me and Dakota, dressed in our usual country cowgirl outfits. We might have been fourteen or fifteen.

It's our shared history.

"It's us."

"Yeah, it's us."

I'm sort of stricken by the beauty of the house and also by its familiarity. I could *belong* here so easily.

I don't know how he did it, but it's like he read my mind. All the little details. The big, inviting kitchen with its farmhouse table that's the perfect place to raise a family. The view of Tennessee that we always used to talk about. The dreamy pink princess's room. The photos of our past already in place. It can't be true, but it's almost like he designed all of it…for *me*.

Still holding my hand in his warm, rough grasp, he leads me into his bedroom. "This is it."

Nate's room is enormous, rustic and masculine but at the same time luxurious because it has so obviously been designed and built by people who are exceptionally good at what they do.

His bed must be one of those Californian kings. The wall of sliding glass doors opens out onto a balcony with its own hot tub and more stunning views. Off to one side of the bedroom is a massive walk-in closet and a spacious master bathroom. I get a glimpse of sandstone and a huge free-standing bath.

"It feels like you." *It also feels like me.* "Thanks for showing me."

Nate's fingers tighten on mine and he pulls me closer. For a long moment we just stand there, hands clasped. The air is electric. Just like it was all those years ago in the barn.

But this time there's no one outside waiting to tell us all the reasons we shouldn't.

Slowly, he reaches to tuck a strand of my hair behind one ear, calloused fingertips ghosting over my cheek. I don't mean to sigh softly.

"Rox…" he whispers, my name a fervent prayer on his lips. His eyes are a deep amber, full of all the dark beauty and summertime memories I've dreamed about my entire life. His warm palm slides around the nape of my neck, gripping lightly, raising all the tiny hairs on my body. "I don't care about anyone outside this room or what they think. I only care about what you want."

"I want you," I whisper back, remembering the day I said it to him that late summer afternoon. *I love you.* I always wondered if he felt the same way. From the way he's looking at me right now, I can see that he did. And he does.

I don't say it again now but I feel like he can read it in

the wild beat of my heart. *I've always loved you and always will. And if you don't take me to bed right now I'm going to get down on my knees and beg.*

His eyes barely crinkle at the edges and he's just so freaking sexy it's weirdly painful. "I'm going to kiss you now unless you tell me not to, Tuck. Even then I still might."

"It's about time, Boone."

His slow smile does nothing to hide the lust in his whiskey-dark eyes. "We sure have taken our sweet time. We've got some lost years to make up for."

Nate Boone finally—*finally*—lowers his mouth to mine. The kiss starts soft. Careful. Like he's almost over-whelmed with relief, maybe, and at the same time giving me the chance to pull away. But my lips part and his tongue slides inside, tasting me.

With a low growl, Nate tugs my hair back and claims my mouth hungrily. All the built up longing practically hums as our lips and tongues tangle.

I melt against him, my knees going weak. The taste and heat of him overwhelms my senses.

He catches me, holding me. He presses his strong thigh between mine and kisses me senseless.

It appears the cool, aloof Nate Boone suddenly has zero chill. And the idea that, after all these years, he might be as crazy for me as I am for him is making me melt with need. I can feel that my bikini is...*very wet.*

Nate pulls back, his thumb sliding along my jaw. "Roxie Tucker…"

"Don't you dare say, 'see you around' or I'll throttle you."

He smiles, but there's regret in it. "You know I had to leave back then. But tonight, darlin', wild horses couldn't drag me away. I'm just going to tell it like it is, because I have no interest in wasting any more time. What I'm going to do right now is to pick up where we left off a long time ago. I'm going to peel off that little bikini and taste every inch of that soft, perfect skin. I'm going to feast on you all night long until you're crying my name and have forgotten yours. So stop me now if you feel like I'm rushing you."

"Like hell you're rushing me, Boone. I waited for you. And I'm done waiting."

He blinks dark lashes. "What do you mean you waited for me?"

"I've…" It's almost embarrassing to admit. "I've never been with anyone else. Since that day."

His head tilts and his brows barely furrow. It's a second before he continues, like his brain can't quite fathom what I've just told him. "Ever?"

"I still live with all three of those overlords, remember. It's a recipe for a whole lot of nothing, as far as romance goes."

Nate's chuckle of disbelief is low…and wildly relieved. "You mean to tell me that the most beautiful girl in the world hasn't been kissed by *anyone* besides me?"

If it wasn't for the *most beautiful girl in the world* comment, his amusement might almost rile me. "It's not my fault, it's theirs. And yes. So hurry up already."

He smiles, blinking at me and dazzling me with mischievous joy at what I've just confessed. It's his playfulness that kills me the most. Stoic Mr. Weight of The World On His Shoulders looks…*happy*.

And it's all the invitation he needs.

His hand is still weaved through my hair, holding me in place with dominant possessiveness. "All right then, darlin'. You're really ready?"

I nod, watching his eyes. Of course I'm ready.

Still, I'm a little nervous.

This is it.

And he's *big*.

His smile lingers as his mouth eases over mine, and there's an edge to him. A hot, dirty volatility that's new. His tongue slides over mine in a silky, intimate plunge. A wave of soft, sexy warmth floods my entire body.

Nate kisses me like he's already inside me. It's intimate and it's so hungry I want to cry with need.

Each thrust of his tongue pushes a rising wave of lust into me and I suck lightly as he does this, tasting the drugging flavor of him. His groan is low and my inner muscles flutter at the sound. I've never been so freaking *turned on* in my life.

Nate lifts me easily, like I weigh nothing, sending a thrill through me. *He's so big. So fucking strong. He could do anything to me.*

I want all of it.

He pulls me close and I wrap my arms and legs around him.

"Fuck, Roxie," he breathes against my neck. Kissing. Biting. Licking. "You have no idea how much I've wanted this."

"Show me," I whisper. "I need to know I'm not dreaming."

He lays me onto his bed, holding his weight with his brawny arms.

Fascinated by the strength of his body, I let my palms run across his flexed biceps.

I get to touch Nate Boone.

After all those years of pining without even fully realizing it, because I'd long ago accepted that he was off-limits to me and that he'd moved on, it's suddenly like Christmas and a fairy tale all rolled into one.

Nate lowers his body, pressing the full weight of himself onto me. All I'm wearing is a thin beach cover dress—which has ridden up to my waist—and my bikini. I can feel the roughness of the denim of his worn jeans… *and the colossal ridge of his giant erection pressing against me… there*, demanding that my body cradle him intimately.

"*Oh*," I gasp.

He holds himself still, kissing me more tenderly this

time. "*Oh*, give me more, Boone? Or *oh*, you're going way too fast for an innocent little wildcat who's never been kissed except once. Rox, do you want me to slow down?"

"*No.*"

I can feel his smile as he takes my mouth in a lewd, brain-demolishing kiss. "Good. Are you ready for me, baby girl?"

"*Yes.*" *I'm so ready I'll die if you don't give me what I need.*

It's then that Nate Boone transforms from the guy everyone knows and loves as the provider and the steady, reliable workhorse, into a beast.

I watch it happen, like he's blooming into a version of himself that's only only only for me. Here, like this. Alone in his room. His eyes get darker and his grip becomes rougher and more possessive.

Nate's fingers draw circles around my nipples over the thin layers of my clothing. "Did you know, Tuck, that I've thought of you every single day? I held myself back from chasing after you, because I knew you had your own life now and I had mine and I just assumed that you'd left me behind long ago."

"I didn't leave you behind. I never left you. You left me." It pisses me off, come to think of it. "How could you do that?"

He pinches my nipples and I moan because the light pressure sends jolts of hot heat straight to my pussy, where his *huge* hardness is still pressed against me like a loaded, insanely beautiful promise. "You were fifteen."

"So? I *loved* you. I *told* you I loved you."

"You know all three of your brothers would have killed me with their bare hands."

"And what about the next time? You were with someone else. That girl who shot daggers out of her eyes at me all night."

"That's because as soon as you walked in I completely lost interest in her."

"You did?"

"I never saw her again."

"Why didn't you tell me that, Nate?"

"Because the band was just taking off and you were leaving the next day to go on a two-month tour, remember? The first big one."

"Yeah." I remember. "We were all completely caught up in it." It was a roller coaster of crowds and the non-stop frenetic energy that went along with sudden, crazy fame.

"You were. Understandably. The four of you were so tight and they expected so much from you. What was I supposed to do, ask you to come back to the farm with me, just as everything was going stratospheric for you? Admit it, Tuck, you didn't have time for me even if I *had* told you how I felt. And I was coping with all the shit going on here anyway. Not that any of that is an excuse. You're right. I should have told you then how I felt. I wish I had. Fuck, I wish I had."

"Rumors were that you had…girlfriends." My

brothers always talked about Nate Boone like he had a whole harem on the go.

"I never had girlfriends. I'm not going to lie to you, Roxie, I wasn't a choirboy back then. But none of them stuck because none of them were you. If you really want to know, I never actually even *liked* a single one of them. *You* were always the one I wanted. And you were always the one I couldn't have."

"I didn't *know*."

"Well, now you do, baby girl."

Nate pulls up my dress, taking it off. He pulls at the tie of my bikini top, letting it fall away, releasing the bouncy fullness of my breasts.

"*Fuck*," he growls. "*Look* at you. How can anyone be so fucking perfect?"

He takes my breasts in his work-roughened hands and squeezes them, rubbing his thumbs over the painfully-sensitive peaks. "Tell me," I whisper.

"Tell you what?"

"Tell me how you feel."

"You want to know how I feel?"

"Yeah," I barely breathe.

"Well, Tuck, I *feel* like nothing ever compared to you. Ever. Not even close. Not since that day in the barn. Since *before* that day, if we're getting real here. Everyone else just seemed so fucking *dull* in comparison. No one has your hair, with its little curls at the end."

He moves one of his hands from my nipples—and

I'm so warm and wet by now I can feel that my bikini is soaked through and is starting to wet his jeans—to finger an end lock of my hair, where there's a ringlet, as though fascinated by the softness of it.

"None of them have your cute little face. Your *face*, Tuck. I fucking love your face. Like a sultry little angel with a sprinkling of freckles and a sassy attitude that always felt like it was just for me. Mine. It's haunted me, because no one else has that. No one looks like you."

Nate runs his thumb along my cheekbone, like he's simply appreciating me.

"Or your blue eyes, Tuck. Do you know how *blue* your eyes are? I've never seen eyes so blue."

Nate leans over me and takes one of my nipples into his mouth.

I have never in my life felt anything remotely as good as what he's doing to me right now. Soft, strong suction and warm fire. His tongue flicks and his *teeth* gently bite.

I moan.

"I won't even get started on your *body*, Roxie Tucker. Because you were always off-limits and I was never supposed to look at how insanely gorgeous you are. But fucking hell, darlin'. Do you have any idea how hot and sweet and *beautiful* you are?"

I can't answer him or even think because he's sucking on my other nipple and I think I might be a puddle on the floor at this point. A warm pulse is taking hold inside me that feels like a lava melt of sensation getting ready to overflow.

"*Nate.*"

"Right here, baby girl, taking what's mine."

He's moving lower now, kissing a slow line down my stomach, making me squirm.

"And it's more than that. It's much more than how perfect you *look*. It goes bone deep. It's your smile and it's the sound of your voice. Your laugh. I love making you laugh." His tongue dips into my belly button and I gasp a squeal. "It gets me hard, Tuck, that's what it does. Really. Fucking. Hard."

And lower.

"It makes me fall in love with you."

Oh, sweet baby Jesus. He's pulling the string tie at the side of my bikini.

It's gone.

"And you're *kind,* Rox. You're fun and you're good and you're *real.*"

I'm squirming here, dying with need, totally naked, while Nate Boone nuzzles and kisses his way *closer,* murmuring against the low skin of my stomach.

"Do you know how *rare* that is? To find a person that's gorgeous, sweet, fun, sassy and just basically *ideal* in every possible way?"

He's pushing my legs apart.

"It *isn't* possible, Rox. It doesn't *happen.* Except for you. You're like a fucking *miracle* of beauty. You're the only one

I've ever loved. You're the one. You've *always* been the one. *That's* what I would've told you."

Nate licks his tongue over my clit and it's the craziest thing. I never, ever knew anything could feel this good.

A blooming pleasure rises inside me that's so powerful I don't know what to do with it. It's going to overflow. It's going to push me over an impossible edge I don't know how to handle except to hold onto him for dear life and just ride it.

But then he slows, licking with lazy intent. "You said it to me but I never said it back. And there's not a day that goes by that I don't regret that."

What?

There isn't?

His fingers stroke barely into me, finding a slow, wild trigger that forces the pleasure to an insane peak.

Oh my god, I'm almost there.

"I know we haven't seen each other in a while, but that's exactly how I'm so sure. I knew it then but I was too young and too green to fight everyone who tried to stand in my way. I can promise you I'll never make the same mistake again."

His mouth latches onto my clit, feeding greedily as his fingers glide.

Holy hell, it's happening.

It overflows, tipping me into a tidal wave of nearly unendurable pleasure, wracking through me in hot, lush waves. I writhe and moan his name as my body clenches hard, over and over.

My hands are weaved through his hair and I'm breathing hard, floating on the bliss of him.

Once the ripples begin to calm, I lightly pull. *"Nate. Nate. Come here."*

He climbs up my body, laying half on top of me and half next to me. I take his face in my hands and just savor his alpha gorgeousness. I don't know why I say *alpha*, but he is. He's so fucking big and built. Handsome and delicious and so outrageously *male*. I love this about him.

He kisses me. I can taste *myself* on his lips and it's the most connective, intimate thing. *"Holy hell*, Boone." I'm breathless and dazed. "I've never…"

"You've never what?"

"Had that happen before."

"Had what happen before?

"That."

His eyebrows lift. "Wait. You've never had an orgasm before?"

"No."

He laughs. "You're a band manager, darlin', not a nun."

"I'll remind you again that I live with my three brothers."

"That's no excuse. I can assure you all three of them are getting off non-stop and around the clock."

"Yeah. I used to feel like I was the harem manager as

well as the band manager. At least before Travis and Vaughn found true love."

"You haven't been looking after yourself, sweetheart. You've put them before you."

"Sounds like we both have the same problem."

"We're going to change that. Right now."

That's when I happen to glance down his body. His shirt is open and his jeans are unzipped and—*Lord above*. It doesn't surprise me that Nate Boone is huge *everywhere*, but…

Holy Alpha Male, Batman.

Nate Boone is freaking…*packing*.

15

———

ROXIE

I REMEMBER the feel of him under me, in the barn the day I kissed him all those years ago. He'd pulled me onto him and the hard ridge of him electrified me.

I never forgot how good he felt.

How big he felt.

His sculpted, suntanned chest is dusted with hair now, and the six-pack of his abs are defined. The arrow line of dark hair and the muscular V framing his hips are quite literally mouth-watering.

But it's his gigantic…*manhood* that holds all my attention.

It's *enormous.*

Hard as ridged stone and hot-looking.

My heart is beating fast.

How the hell will it fit?

"Don't be scared of me. We can take it slow. If you've had enough—"

"*No*." I'll never have enough of Nate Boone.

He bites back a smile, leaning back onto a muscular arm to give me time to adjust to how freaking colossal and turned on he is. A bead of moisture seeps from the broad tip of him and it's…crazily alluring.

I did that.

"Can I…touch you?"

"You can do any damn thing you want to me, darlin'. I'm all yours."

He's mine. I'm wondering how I got so lucky. And I'm trying not to be intimidated by the sheer freaking *size* of him.

"Take these off." I pull his shirt over his shoulders and he kicks off his jeans.

Wow.

Nate's body is long and sculpted and lean. The proportions of him are somehow ideal. Except for one giant detail that's maybe even larger than ideal for a newbie like me. Now I just need to figure out how to handle it.

I let my fingers brush against his insane pecs. When did he get so damn *jacked*? "D-do you work out?"

His grin is entertained. "Yeah, Tuck, I do. I have a home gym we haven't quite gotten to yet on the tour. And I work like a dog day and night, both on the building sites and here on the farm. I'm used to doing a lot of physical work."

"You're in…really good shape."

Another lazy smile. "Thanks. So are you. Best shape I've ever fucking seen."

My fingers rove lower, to his quilted abs. He really is…*very hard*. Everywhere.

His enormous cock is so outrageously…*engorged* it's making me feel bold and reckless. That bead of wetness is so tantalizing. *I want to taste him.* I already told him I'm inexperienced. I'm also female. My reaction to Nate Boone has always felt primal, and never more insatiable than it is right now.

Nate's breathing is heavier now.

I ease my fists around his hard length, fascinated by the hot silkiness and the rigid bulk of him.

I'm almost surprised by how *greedy* I feel. I lean in to kiss him, licking him lightly.

The taste of him is addictive, igniting a hunger in me that's new and voracious. I ease my mouth over the broad crown, suckling and licking.

His head drops back and he groans like he's in pain.

Then he eases me back, taking full control, lifting me and laying me down. He crouches over me, kissing me so hungrily, I'm drowning in him. The huge, heavy weight of his cock presses against my slippery pleasure, which is still rippling. He holds himself there. The waves are starting again, just at the light contact of his huge, hot length.

"I'm not coming 'til you're coming', darlin'," he drawls, his accent stronger with lust.

I arch up to him and the head of his cock slides against me, barely *into* me, rubbing my clit. Another orgasm—this one even higher—is waiting there and I need it more than I've ever needed anything. *"Please, Boone."*

I love him.

"You sure about this, baby girl?"

Sure about what? Sure about having pure, raw, unprotected sex because we've always wanted to? Because he's the one I've dreamed of for eight years and I feel like I might die if I can't get him inside me right now?

"I don't want to *just* have hot, dirty sex with you, Tuck. I want to build a life with you. I want to keep you forever. And if I fuck you with no barriers, I'm coming inside you. You don't pull out of nirvana. Just so we're straight."

And when nirvana's about to fill up your body and soul, you want all of it.

Sure, we probably shouldn't throw all caution to the wind. There could be some very real consequences. Somewhere behind my mind I know that. I also know that neither one of us cares about caution. We've spent years toeing every line, resisting what felt like it was meant to be, hoping and praying this night would some day happen. There's no way in hell we're holding back now.

We're in love and we have been for a long time. We've denied ourselves each other.

But not tonight.

I kiss him, gripping him, trying to pull him closer, almost panting with need.

He slips his hand around my neck and his thumb rests low on my throat. It settles me. He's in control and he'll take care of me. "I might not last long because you're so fucking sexy, but we've got all night. I've never done it bareback before."

"You haven't?"

"Of course I haven't. I was waiting for you." His smile is hot and so beautiful it hurts more than the stretching burn of his outrageous thickness barely entering me. "I love you, Rox. I always have."

The words, delivered just as his thick cock thrusts deeper, using the wetness of my reviving orgasm, brings tears to my eyes.

He's way too big. But he feels so fucking good.

"You ready to take all of this big cock, baby girl?" *God.* Nate Boone dirty-talking to me gets me even hotter. "You'll have to get used to me." He's kissing me like he's addicted, dipping his tongue into my mouth as he drives deeper, rolling his hips in a rough rhythm that's painfully splitting me wide open even as it rubs against some perfect sweet spot. "You ready to come again, darlin'?"

I moan. I *am* coming. The aggressive, ridged friction rubs the pleasure-pain to its breaking point, spilling over in a tumbling swell of lush ecstasy, bursting into bright stars of clenching rapture.

We're gazing into each other's eyes as my body milks him lusciously. He uses each squeeze to thrust deeper—and deeper—until he's fully inside my tight, wet, squirming body. I'm coming hard, stuffed so full, all I am is my lovestruck heart and his huge hardness lovingly gripped by the rippling, spiraling pleasure-glow.

"I'm inside my Roxie." Like he's in awe. "*Fuck, baby,* you feel too good."

I'm crying because my dream is happening in real time. I'm so insanely full of him, I can feel when his cock starts to throb, flooding me in warm jerking gushes. We're grinding and gripping to get as close as it's possible to do.

It lasts for a long time, this wet, pulsing, feral dance. The overload spills and wets my thighs.

After a while, the aftershocks start to calm. My fingers play in his hair as he kisses my lips lazily. I love his thick-silk hair.

"Move in with me."

"Okay." I'm not even sure if I can, all things considered. All I know is I never want to leave Nate Boone's bed.

"You're beautiful, Tuck. The most beautiful thing in the world."

I cup his face and he notices my tears, wiping them with his thumbs.

"Did I hurt you, darlin'?"

"In the best kind of way."

Turns out Nate is just getting started. His head dips and searches for my nipple, finding it. His tongue slowly traces the outer edge before he languidly latches on. Keeping the tender bud inside his mouth, he licks me. Feeding on me like he's drinking spiritual sustenance from my body. "I want to do this all night, every night, Roxie Tucker. I'm addicted and there's no getting rid of me now."

Deep inside me, where Nate's bulky cock has softened but not completely, my soreness dissolves into a fresh wave of desire.

He moves to my other breast, sucking and stroking with his tongue. His fingers slide down my body. He teases my clit in light, rhythmic glides until another orgasm washes through me, tugging voluptuously on the hot flesh that's wedged so deeply inside me, until he's fully hard again.

Nate's watching me with a beguiled expression, smoothing my hair. "I'll never get enough of you."

It seems to be true. Through the night, I lose count of the number of times he comes inside me. After all this time of wishing, we finally get to feast on each other and fulfill every craving. Neither one of us holds back, until

I'm crying his name again, grabbing fistfuls of his thick hair.

When the purple sky takes on the faintest shades of lavender, I drift into sated sleep, wrapped possessively in the strong arms of my dream lover.

ROXIE

I WAKE up in a cocoon of warmth. I'm curled inside a big, secure bearhug, being spooned from behind.

And fucked from behind.

It all comes rushing back to me. *I'm in Nate Boone's bed. He very thoroughly obliterated my virginity, many times over. And he's still inside me.*

The tiniest bit of common sense creeps in with the morning sun.

Are you actually trying *to get knocked up right now? Because it kind of seems like you might be.*

I mean…not exactly. I'm late in my cycle right now and I think it's safe. Then again, you never know.

But when you've missed someone *this* much, and yearned *this* hard for *this* long, and when you know for a fact that if you ever did want to get knocked up, he'd be the one and only one you'd want to do it, you tend to go with it. And when it's *this* special and *this* wanted and it feels *this* fucking good, you don't want to *waste* it by not letting things happen the way they will.

I don't know. I feel too good to analyze it right now.

I'm safe, wildly comfortable, very sore in the best kind of way, and happier than I can ever remember being.

Nate trails slow kisses across my shoulders, nuzzling and licking my neck. He gently bites my earlobe and kisses my face, his beard rough against my skin. His massive rock-hard cock is slowly thrusting, in, barely out, and deeper in.

"Mornin', gorgeous," he murmurs and I can hear his slow smile. "Takes a bit to wake you, Tuck. Then again, I did keep you up all night."

I bite my lip. "Hey, Boone," I gasp, arching back to take more of him. From this angle, he sinks even deeper. I'm tender but so hot for him I don't care. There's definitely pain but I'm so wet from the last time he came inside me that it's bearable. Who am I kidding, it's more than bearable. It's sweet pain and hot fire and I'm already getting close to tipping over another crazy peak.

Nate eases me onto my stomach, lifting and gripping my hips. He spreads my knees roughly with one of his, driving even deeper into me.

I moan into the pillow.

One of his muscular arms loops around me. The

other hand finds my slippery clit, making a little cage with his fingers, squeezing in a light rhythm, rubbing and playing as he fucks me hard and deep. I slide into another rich, ridiculously intense orgasm that tugs strongly around his throbbing thickness, pulling his own release from him in lusty pulls, like my body *craves* his seed and won't relent until it gets all of it. Another flood of liquid warmth pumps into me in hot pulses, overflowing down my thighs.

"*Roxie.*" He growls my name like a prayer as he comes. "*You make me come so fucking hard.*"

I'm pretty sure there's nothing on Earth that can compare to this. Turns out, getting thoroughly made love to by a big, lusty, well-hung country-boy-who's-all-grown-up is the best thing that's ever happened to me.

I think we just want to make up for all the time we've lost, all the years that have passed, when we could have spent them doing *this*.

I'm not sure I could ever get used to how good he feels.

Still inside me, he holds me in his arms. "I missed you, Tuck."

"I missed you too." I turn to look at his face and he kisses me slowly.

"I thought about contacting you a thousand times."

"You did?"

"Yeah. I did."

"You should have." It occurs to me then that I could

so easily have missed him. Something else could have come up this weekend and I could have stayed in Nashville and I never would have run into him like this. We never would have realized that we both felt like the other was the One That Got Away or the One That Never Quite Was. It feels like a huge misunderstanding. And it makes me never want to make the same mistake again. "I would have been so happy to hear from you, Nate."

"Well, you're going to be hearing from me a whole lot now, darlin'. I'm going to go make you breakfast in bed. Then we're taking a shower. Then I have to go pick up Daisy. Then it's up to you whether you want to hard launch at the hoedown. Since we just spent the night raw-dogging nonstop and you're moving in with me, I figure we might as well go hard and let the relatives deal with the fallout however they want."

I blink up at him. "I'm moving in." It's not quite a question and it's not quite a declaration. I was kind of distracted when I agreed to that.

"You said so."

"I mean, of course I want to. I'm just wondering how that will work. I probably can't just take off and not show up for my job. They rely on me for a lot."

"Maybe you could find some help and start delegating some of the work."

"Yeah. I'll have to talk it over with my brothers."

"You let them control you too much."

I can't help biting back a light smile at his sudden surliness. I trace my fingers between his eyebrows, smoothing the light furrow. "Probably. But I can't just leave them in the lurch either. Besides, you might need to do some delegating of your own," I say gently. "There's no point to me moving in if you're never here."

His expression is hard to read, but the lightly pissed-off scowl is, more than anything else, adorable. He's mad because he wants me here. "We'll figure it out." He traces my cheekbone with the back of his fingers. "I built you an office."

"An office?"

"Yes. An office."

"For me?"

"We never got that far on the tour because you jumped my bones before we could, but there's a lot more I want to show you."

"Like what?"

He tortures me by taking his time, a mysteriously smug smile on his face. "Well, there's your private office, then there's the sauna—"

"You have a sauna?" I remember the exact conversation once. We were all camping down by the creek one night and we were listing off things we'd put in our dream house if we ever got rich. Travis wanted a pool. Vaughn wanted a mechanical bull in his living room. Kade wanted a five-car garage with a Harley Davidson and a bunch of other cars I can't remember off the top of my head.

They all ended up getting everything they wanted—although Vaughn's mechanical bull happens to be in Kade's apartment. He somehow convinced Kade that was a good idea.

I said I wanted a sauna. "I can't believe you remember that."

"I remember everything, Tuck. There's also a recording studio in the lower floor. Fully soundproof."

He has a recording studio? "For…the band?"

"They can record here if they want." He's being cagey about something.

"What aren't you telling me?"

He just grins and blinks noncommittally.

"*Nate.* Tell me."

"Maybe later." He starts getting up and I already miss his warmth. "Anyway, like I said, we've already wasted enough time and I'm going to be real with you, like I said I would. I built this house for you. So, any time you want to move in, just do it."

"You built it…for me?"

"That's what I just said, isn't it?" Nate pulls his jeans on. I watch him do this and the view distracts me. *Wow.* He's all lean, hard masculine muscularity and giant already-semi-hard-again manhood. It makes me want to pull him back to bed so I can lick his sun-bronzed skin and…*suck on him until he comes.*

He catches me checking him out. "You're insatiable, darlin'. You trying to kill me or something?"

I laugh. "You're just ridiculously hot, that's all. And… reviving."

He gives me *that* smile. The one that kills me and gets me wet. "Breakfast first. Then more orgasms. Don't go anywhere."

"I couldn't move if I tried. I think it's going to be a while before I can walk again."

"Coffee, food and a shower will help." Nate reaches to check his phone, which is on the bedside table. He slides it into his pocket.

"All's well at the sleepover?"

"She braved it out. I knew she would. We talked about it."

"That's good, Nate. It's a big step. Come to think of it, I wonder where my phone is. I've got some explaining to do to your sister."

"I texted her last night and told her you were crashing here for the night."

"You did?"

"Yeah. When you pulled up. I told her we were going to share a bottle of wine and you didn't want to drive back until the morning."

I narrow my eyes. "How could you be so sure I'd end up in your bed, Boone?"

"I could practically see the sparks flying off you, darlin'." Nate smooths my hair and kisses my head.

"You're beautiful, perfect, and hot as fuck, gorgeous girl. Relax. I'll be back with coffee and sustenance."

Wow.

He leaves me and I actually pinch myself to make sure I'm not dreaming. I doze a little, too sated to move. I block the thoughts that are trying to force their way in.

How will my brothers react to our "hard-launch"? And Dakota? How will we even make this work? Nate and I are both extremely busy people with a lot on our plates who live hours apart. We also had unprotected sex—a lot. Why did I even do that? How should we handle it? Should I do something about it…today?

I sigh, but it comes out sounding more contented than stressed about all of the above.

Right now, I want to savor the moment. All I want to think about is how good he felt. *And how hard we came.* My obsession with him wasn't unrequited after all. It's real, it's shifted up several hundred gears and it's now on supersonic overdrive.

What if he was just getting you out of his system? Are you really ready for a relationship, a six-year-old—and possibly a baby? What are you doing, Roxie?

I'm getting laid, thank you very much, I defiantly tell my subconscious. *Finally. By the hottest man in Tennessee. So there.*

Nate returns with a large tray full of fruit, toast with homemade jam (I'd know Betty-Ann's homemade strawberry jam anywhere), blueberry muffins (also signature Betty-Ann), glasses of orange juice and steaming mugs of coffee.

See? He's perfect.

He hands me my phone. "You left it on the kitchen counter." Welcome back to reality. "I didn't look," he smirks. "But it's lighting up."

Just then, another text comes through. From Dakota.

> Are we sisters yet???

I sigh and show Nate. "I guess she's okay with it then."

Nate sets the tray down on a table and brings me a mug of coffee. "We don't care what anyone else thinks. We're fully-functioning adults. What we do is up to us."

"I know. We just happen to have extremely over-interested, meddling families." I scroll through all my messages. "Aaand, it looks like the Boone-Tucker grapevine has already spread the news far and wide. I've got missed calls from both Travis and Vaughn and a whole bunch of messages from both of them telling me to call them ASAP."

Another text comes through from Vaughn.

> ANSWER YOUR PHONE OR WE'RE
> COMING OUT THERE, SUNSHINE

I don't bother showing Nate that one, but I send a quick reply—in shouty all-caps, like he did, to emphasize my point—even though I'm sure it's an empty threat.

I'M FINE. GO WRITE ANOTHER ALBUM

Nate goes into the bathroom and turns on the shower. "They're going to have to get used to waiting until after I've given my girl another round of orgasms. We're making up for lost time. Come with me, Roxie Tucker. Time for another one."

17

NATE

I TAKE her empty mug and set it on the table. Then I lift her and carry her into the shower, which I designed for this exact purpose. It's huge, with four detachable shower heads and a cedar bench that runs the length of it. I've put two towels along it so it's comfortable for her.

The shower's full of steam now, like a tropical mist, to make sure she's warm and relaxed. I set her down on the bench and lay her back on it, resting her head on my lap. Taking some shampoo, I carefully wash her hair as she watches me.

"I thought of you every day, you know," she whispers.

"I thought of you every day too, darlin'."

I detach one of the shower heads and rinse her hair. The perfection of her face makes my chest ache. Her blue eyes, with long lashes spiked from the water, are blinking at me. Roxie's eyes are like rare sapphires in the sun, always catching shards of light. Her lips are pink and plump. Her long, thick, shiny hair is wavy and lush, lightly coiled at the ends.

I'm so fucking in love with her I feel almost insane with it. I wasn't prepared for this. I missed her, I knew that much. I knew I loved her from afar but I guess a part of me had come to terms with the fact that it wasn't meant to be. But the second I saw her again, she hit me like a fucking wrecking ball. I wasn't prepared for the intensity of it. My body is on fire for her. My soul feels bloody and hot with obsession.

And rage. She was out there this whole time and I didn't fucking chase after her.

Usually, I'm the peacekeeper. The guy who keeps everyone steady and everything afloat.

But I've just found my limit.

Let them try to keep us apart.

She's mine. I'll fucking kill to keep her. I'll fight for her with everything I've got.

I can take any one of the Tucker boys. Maybe not all three at the same time, but then again, I've got eight years of regrets fueling me. Anything's possible at this point.

I get their doubts about me. We all ran wild together when we were young. We were sowing our wild oats and discovering how easy it was to get women to fall in love with us—or at least in serious lust. It's something Luke and Leo are still doing and, as far as I know, so were Travis and Vaughn until not too long ago.

I'm not proud of any of it. I used women to slake my rage—which I was too hot-headed to realize was all about the fact that I couldn't have the one girl I truly wanted.

That's the version of me the Tucker boys know best and it's the reason they wouldn't want me going near their little sister. Not like it's a thought that's probably ever entered their head—that I might want to. They considered me a brother.

They still can. But times have changed. I'm not the punk I used to be. And Roxie isn't fifteen anymore.

They're just going to have to get used to the idea. Because I'm done worrying about them.

I run my hands over her body. Rivulets cascade from her breasts like she's some kind of otherworldly nymph who, on Friday night, just happened to step out of my wildest fantasies. "You and me are going to make the absolute most of each day from now on. The past doesn't matter. What matters is that we're together now. We're going to figure out how to make things happen exactly the way we want them to."

"Okay, Nate," she gasps as I tease her nipples. "So far today's the best day of my life, just saying. And yesterday."

"Mine too, Tuck."

I slowly make my way down her luscious body. Her thighs are streaked with my cum and I swirl it over her glistening pussy. She's heaven on earth is what she is.

Using my fingers, I push some of the dripping moisture gently back inside her.

"At some point we're going to need to talk about what we're going to do," she breathes.

"About what?" I tease her, letting my fingers slide slowly in and out.

"About that."

Once I'm satisfied that none of my cum is being wasted, I hold the shower head close to her pussy, centering on her clit. "I think we already know what we're going to do about it."

"We do?"

"I have a fully paid-for house that's yours. I have more money at this point than I know how to spend. I'll take care of you." And I can't resist. I lick her, sucking her clit.

This has gone beyond passion into something else altogether. Lust doesn't even scratch the surface. Obsession, deep love and blazing addiction make one hell of a cocktail.

I'm already hard but her little moans get me agonizingly harder.

I eat into her until she's moaning my name. The sweetest sound I've ever heard. I curl my fingers inside her, carefully, because I know she's sore. I've been rough and demanding. I use the cascading water and my tongue to soothe her. And feast on her. She's as sweet as honey. I milk her clit and she comes for me, crying out. I slide my tongue inside the rippling spasms, drinking her pleasure like a drug.

I wait for the waves to slowly calm. Then I use the shower head to bring her to another dreamy rise as I soap up her breasts and slowly wash her body.

"*Nate.*"

"Right here, baby girl."

"How can anything feel so good?"

"You just needed me, Tuck. To show you."

Roxie sits up, reaching up to kiss me. Her color is high and her eyes are a bright, vivid blue. "My turn," she smiles sweetly.

She takes the shampoo and pours some into my hair.

I kiss her as she washes my hair. "You're distracting me, Boone. Let me rinse you. Lay back."

I obey her, letting her do whatever she wants to me. Her hands are soft, slippery miracles.

She washes my chest. My stomach.

Then she soaps up my cock, sliding her fists up and down the length of me. I'm so fucking engorged it's painful. "Rox...*fuck*. Unless you want to get dirty all over again..."

"I'm not going to get dirty." She rinses me. Then she takes my hot, heavy hard-on in her hands.

Her mouth eases over the head of my cock, licking lightly. Taking more. Sucking on me sort of awkwardly, like she's not entirely sure what to do, as her fingers explore.

"*Roxie*. I can't hold on to this, baby."

"I don't want you to hold on to it, Boone. I want you to come in my mouth so I can drink you."

I groan as a freight train of pleasure erupts and I'm spurting hot cum into her mouth in bursting, milky jolts. I come *hard*. I close my eyes and grit my teeth just to handle the overload.

She swallows as much as she can, but it's dripping down her chin. She drinks more, licking my cock to clean me.

She's like nothing in this world.

I sit up and take her in my arms, gazing into her eyes, kissing her plush mouth. "I love you, Tuck. Move in with me. Don't you dare leave me, darlin', or I'll hunt you down and make sweet love to you until you agree to come home."

18

———

ROXIE

HOME.

Two days ago, I was trapped in the zone of wondering if something was wrong with me, if maybe there was a glitch in my ability to connect with anyone romantically. The few dates I did manage to go on always crashed and burned almost immediately. I was starting to think I might end up alone, because no one has ever compared to my long-ago first crush.

Right now I'm reeling.

I'm in love. Hard deep and for real.

And I'm already talking about moving in with him because I've always suspected and now I *know* he's the love of my freaking life. *Oh, and we're also playing with fire because we had unprotected sex all night long.*

It's a lot.

Nate gets my bag out of my truck for me and I put on a white cotton sundress and my cowboy boots.

"We can leave your truck here," he says.

"You want me to come with you to pick up Daisy?"

Nate's putting the dishes from breakfast into the dishwasher, wearing only jeans with a dishtowel thrown over his sculpted, suntanned shoulder—just when I thought he couldn't get any hotter—but my question makes him stop what he's doing and come over to me.

He's quiet for a few seconds, gazing down at me thoughtfully. He smooths a lock of my hair and I notice again how big he is. He's a good six or seven inches taller than me and probably outweighs me by two to one. He's rough when he wants to be but right now he's so gentle with me, it almost brings tears to my eyes.

"Roxie, I want you to come with me wherever I go. But you don't have to come with me to pick up Daisy. You can go to the lodge and we'll meet you there if you want. Everyone will be there, getting ready for the hoedown."

"What time is it?"

"Now? It's almost two. The hoedown starts at three. Listen, I get that this is a two-for-one deal. Which isn't what you signed up for."

"Where's the paperwork? I'll sign up now."

There's something heart-breaking about his smile.

"Seriously, Nate, I understand what I'm getting into. Daisy's your family now. Which means she's my family too." I didn't know two days ago that I was about to fall head-first into a ready-made family, and I don't exactly know how to feel about all of it, but I'm willing to take this as it comes. "I've fallen in love with Daisy too. She's my tiny little kindred spirit."

He stares at me for a long moment. "Thank you," he whispers, kissing me softly. For a big, rough alpha male, he can be so careful. "Besides, I would hate to send you into the hoedown lion's den alone. I think it's better if we go together and I can be your buffer."

"So…we're doing the hard launch?" I cringe. My night of hot sex with Nate Boone is about to be Sugar Falls' favorite topic.

His amber eyes are bright. "I say bring it on. We'll definitely be the hot gossip of the day. But by tomorrow it'll be old news and they'll be back to discussing who got tipsy at the sewing circle."

I can't help but smile. "Okay. Let's do this."

It's a beautiful day. Our drive along the country roads couldn't be more scenic. But my stomach is full of butter-flies at the thought of facing everyone.

Nate takes my hand. "Hey. Don't worry about a thing, Tuck. You've got me now. I'll handle everything."

You've got me now. It's pretty crazy when your dream actually comes true.

We pull up in front of a house with pink balloons decorating the mailbox, the porch and the front door.

The table on the front porch has eight or nine little girls dressed in pink sitting around it. A woman is pouring pink lemonade into pink plastic cups. The woman waves. Even the woman is dressed in pink.

"Daisy is among her people," I laugh.

As soon as we pull up, Daisy jumps up from the table and runs down the steps, a little pink and blond blur. "Uncle Nate!" She leaps into his arms.

Then she sees me get out of the truck.

There's a split second when I wonder if maybe this was mistake. Nate has become her whole world. Maybe it's too soon to add me to the mix.

But then her little face lights up. "*Miss Roxie*." Filled with awe. "You *came*." Like she wanted me to. Like showing up for her means something.

My heart melts for this sweet child who's missing something profound in her life that maybe *I* could help provide. I understand it, and a feverish pull in me wants with my whole heart to give it.

She squirms out of Nate's arms, running over to me. She takes my hand, and Nate's, and leads us up the porch steps. "Did you and Uncle Nate have a sleepover, Miss Roxie?"

We're within earshot, and all the little girls—and the mother—are waiting for my answer. "Um…well, we had a glass of wine and I decided not to drive back." It's Nate's white lie, after all.

The little girls gather around me, wide-eyed. Some

are bold enough to reach out to touch the fabric of my dress. "Isn't she *beautiful?*" Daisy whispers to her friends. "Look at her *boots*. They have *pink* on them. And look at her *lips*. That's the lipstick I told you about. The one called Pink Kisses."

The woman comes over and Nate introduces us. "Kristie Anderson, meet Roxie Tucker. Roxie, Harper's mom Kristie. Kristie and her husband Shane are old friends of mine and of Jed and Laney's. Daisy and Harper have grown up together."

"So nice to meet you, Roxie."

"You too, Kristie."

"You wouldn't be Roxie Tucker of the Tucker Brothers' fame, by any chance? Nate's mentioned that he grew up with the four of you."

"I'm just the manager. The boys do all the work."

"I know that's not true," Kristie laughs. "I used to be in the music industry myself, before having Harper."

"Were you?"

"I was the assistant manager for the Down Home Boys, before they got big and before I found out Harper was on the way. Shane and I got married and we moved out here, so I've been out of the scene for a while, but I really do miss it."

"My brothers have played with the Down Home Boys at a couple of festivals. They're nice guys."

"Yeah. Superstars now." She smiles as though remembering good times. "But I knew them back when they were lean, hungry kids." To Harper, she says, "Honey, why don't you help Daisy get her bag and her party favors together."

"Okay!" Harper holds Daisy's hand and all the little girls scramble inside to help.

After the commotion settles, Kristie pours Nate and I some lemonade. "That must be a huge job, Roxie, managing such a successful band. Every song on their newest album is in the top twenty."

"Yeah, it's going well. And it's definitely busy."

"I've often thought about going back to it," she says. "I'd love to. But I have no idea how I'd even go about doing that. It's probably been too long."

Nate nudges me lightly. "Roxie was just saying she might be looking for some help. Maybe the two of you could get together and talk it over sometime."

Kristie's eyes cautiously light up. "I would *love* that. If you're interested. I mean, I'm probably not qualified to do much."

"Anyone who played a part in launching the Down Home Boys is more qualified than most, I'd say." When Nate talked about delegating some of my work, I was quietly thinking it would be hard to find someone who could fill that role. My brothers are too used to me being at their beck and call. But now that Kristie's offering, and is clearly excited about the possibility, and has worked with one of the biggest bands in country music, the idea doesn't sound quite so crazy after all.

"Think about it anyway." Kristie says. "Nate can give you my number. Just reach out whenever."

"Thanks, Kristie. I will. Actually, if you want to give it to me now, I can put it in my phone."

She gives me her number and Nate asks her, "Shane's working today?"

"Yeah," she confirms. "Every Saturday, at least for now." To me, she explains, "My husband is a builder and a contractor with his own small business, but he's also been working to complete a business degree at night school. He's just about finished and I can't *wait* until he's done with it. This working full-time while studying for his degree has been a lot."

"Sounds like it."

Kristie glances at the door, which is still closed. "Nate, Daisy did wake up last night. She was crying and I was about to call you. But Harper and some of the other girls knew why she was crying. We all kind of gathered around her and talked about it and she calmed down. I stayed with her and they all eventually fell back to sleep. I would have called if she hadn't stopped crying, but she seemed okay. I asked her if she wanted to stay and she did. I just wanted you to know what happened."

Nate nods, and that weight-of-the-world heaviness is back. "Thanks, Kristie. I appreciate it."

"We may see you at the hoedown later, depending on what time Shane gets home, and how tired Harper is. I imagine all the girls will need an early night tonight. Once the sugar high wears off."

Daisy's ready and we say goodbye to Kristie and the other girls before loading Daisy and all her stuff into the back seat of Nate's truck.

And we're on our way to the hoedown.

19

———

ROXIE

"You ready for this?" Nate asks me. "Here we go with the hard launch."

"Ready as I'll ever be."

By the time we get to the lodge, the party is already pumping. It's a family affair, with children running around and people of all ages enjoying each other's company. Guys wearing their baseball hats backward are drinking beer, older ladies are sipping (possibly fortified) iced tea, groups are playing corn hole and other lawn games, laughing as they catch up with old friends. The scene is like a living snapshot of all the best things about country life.

We get a lot of glances, a few waves. One or two whistles. But with Nate's arm securely around me, my nerves are gone. I get that unexpected feeling again, of being *home.*

The front doors of the barn have been rolled all the way open. A band is playing on the stage up at the front corner of the barn—and they're good.

Tables are decorated with gorgeous flower arrangements and are full of people. A bar that's been set up along one side is bustling, and a buffet is being loaded up with food. I see Tobias at the far end of it, surrounded and distracted by catering staff.

Dakota's carrying another flower arrangement, which she sets on a table near the bar. She sees us and runs over.

Nate's arm is still around me, his other arm holding Daisy.

"Bout time y'all showed up." Dakota beams at us.

"Hey, darlin'." Even when he's talking to his sister, that low Tennessee drawl gets me…hot.

Would you stop?

It's a major…adjustment, to *be* with him now, after all those years of dreaming about it. "You and Tobias have done an amazing job, kid," Nate tells Dakota. "This place looks incredible."

"You know we couldn't have done it without you, Nate. And I need to talk to you about stealing my bestie." She takes my hand. "But not until after I talk to *you*." She gently kisses Daisy's cheek. "How'd the party go?"

"Fun."

"You stayed the whole night?"

Daisy nods, biting a finger.

"Proud of you, pumpkin." Dakota touches the back of her hand to Daisy's cheek with affection.

But nothing can distract Dee from pulling me toward her office. "I need to borrow her for a few minutes," she calls back over her shoulder. "We'll be back in five. Actually, probably more like ten."

Nate watches us walk away. He looks almost like…he misses me already. Almost as much as I miss him already. *Damn, that man is gorgeous.* He always could make my knees go weak.

As we walk away, though, I can't help noticing several other women are also staring at him.

It's not surprising that Nate Boone, especially holding his adorable little Daisy, attracts attention.

But it riles me. *He's mine.*

He doesn't seem to notice how many eyes are on him.

Are they past lovers? Local girls he's partied with before?

I believe everything Nate said to me. It all felt so natural when we were alone together. So real and so true and so easy. But this small separation reminds me that we still have the entire outside world to navigate.

Dakota pulls me into her office and shuts the door, leaning her back up against it. "Tell me everything."

"I'm definitely not telling you everything. He's your brother."

"Just tell me…general stuff. Not specifics." She's practically bursting. "So…*did* you?"

"Did I what?" I bite my lip, feeling a light heat rise to my face.

"Oh my god, I knew it!" Dee squeals, squeezing my hands. "We're going to be sisters for *real*."

I'm still acclimatizing to my new status as…Nate Boone's *lover*. I don't even know how to categorize it yet.

It's a little daunting to have it scrutinized and fawned over by an entire small town, starting with my best friend. All I can do is cowgirl up and face it head-on. So I just it tell it like it is. "Dee, I love him. I've always loved him."

Dakota's eyes fill with tears. "Rox, I mean, it doesn't shock me. I was *there*, remember? I saw the way you used to stare at him."

"I tried not to. We were all too close back then. And too young. At least I was, I guess. I never told you this, but I kissed him once."

"You did?"

"And then he left."

She's quiet for a few seconds. "Rox, it would never have worked out back then. For a lot of reasons."

"I know."

"But it can work out now."

I nod. "Yeah," I whisper, not wanting to somehow jinx it. "I hope it can."

"I've never, ever seen my brother look at anyone the way he looked at you on Friday night, Rox. The feeling is obviously mutual."

"I haven't seen him for so long. But when I got here, I

think we both just *knew*. And we didn't want to waste any more time."

We're both crying now. "I'm so happy for you, Rox. And obviously for him. And mostly for me."

I laugh through my tears. "I don't know why we're crying."

"I just hope it was...no, I'm not even going to ask that. You're right, there are some things a sister should not hear about."

"True. All I can say is I'm glad I waited for him."

More tears pool in her eyes.

There's a loud pounding on the door, making both of us jump. "Dakota!"

"Oh, shit. It's Luke. Or Leo. They're ready to play."

"Play?"

More pounding. Dakota opens the door to both the twins, standing there, guitars slung over their broad chests and actual pieces of wheat sticking out of their mouths, like someone drafted up two stereotypical "hot, wholesome country boys" and with their magic wand somehow brought them to red-blooded life. "Dee, we're ready. The other band is on their last song. Hey, Rox!"

Leo's greeting is so enthusiastic it's obvious they've heard the news. It's confirmed when I'm embraced by one twin, then the other, with all the energy of young bulls on stampede. My hot and heavy night with their brother is clearly a cause for celebration. "Nothing like the country air to re-kindle old flames, eh? We attribute his vastly improved mood entirely to you, gorgeous."

"Um, thanks, I guess," I manage, from inside their testosterone sandwich.

"Would you two stop?" Dee scolds them, pulling them off me.

Washed up, shaved and in their best flannel shirts, there's no denying the middle brothers are handsome men. The guitars only add to the effect. But all I can feel is how much I miss their older brother. "You guys are going to play some songs?"

"We've been working on something special," Luke says, all green eyes and cocky grin. "A couple brand new songs."

"Not at all entirely for your benefit, Roxie," Dakota clarifies. "Just a casual late-afternoon session."

"A casual late-afternoon session of breaking every heart in town, especially for listeners of the female persuasion." Leo winks at me.

Dee rolls her eyes. "As long as they don't swoon to the point where they need medical attention again."

"That did not happen." Now I'm curious.

"Unfortunately, it did," Dee confirms.

"We can't help being irresistible to womankind, Rox," Luke smirks. "It's baked into our DNA."

"Out, you two." Dee guides them out of the office. "Get up there and play your hearts out. Make sure you play that song about the Sugar Falls sweetheart. Everyone loves that one. And don't play any Tucker Brothers' covers. Roxie's heard all those."

"As if we would," Leo calls over his shoulder as they make their way toward the stage.

Dee and I find the Boone table and I'm grateful that at least some of their attention is diverted from me to Luke and Leo, who get a big cheer as they climb onto the stage.

Aunt Lou and Betty-Ann make a space for me and pat the seat between them, which I squeeze into, both of them kissing my cheeks and fawning over me. It could be awkward—since they're basically congratulating me on getting laid by their own son and close-enough-to-a-son. But I'm too riveted by the sight of Nate in the near distance, talking to a woman.

A very beautiful one. Wearing a green dress that shows off her abundant curves.

Daisy, Harper and some other kids are holding popsicles and running around.

The woman touches Nate's shirt as she says something to him, her eyes full of...something. Longing. Pissed-off disappointment. Hope.

Nate's fists are shoved into his pockets and he kicks the ground with his boot. He says something to her.

Whatever it is, it gets a reaction. She glares at him, half with rage and half like she's about to burst into tears. She spits out a reply then walks away.

What the hell was that about?

I can guess and I don't like it one bit.

Were they together?

Recently?

How recently?

Was he just breaking up with her then?

Nate wanders back in this direction.

He sees me and his gaze holds mine. There's a dark challenge there, to go ahead and get mad about whatever it was just happened there. Because something clearly did. But there's also that slow, hot almost-smile that does what it always does. It kills me. It grips my heart because he's so beautiful and there's not a damn thing in this world I can do to stop from loving him.

Right now, I hate that. That his hold on me is so easy and so resolute.

He comes over to me, just as Luke and Leo start playing. The music's loud. Everyone starts cheering. A few girls scream their names.

Nate curls his warm, rough hand around my neck, letting it rest there. *Just like he did when he was deep inside me. To calm me. To reassure me. To anchor all the wild, tumbling feelings that make me lose all control.*

The light squeeze communicates a bond I want so badly to believe.

He has some explaining to do. But it'll have to wait.

Nate's hand slides to gently tug at my hair…*exactly like he did when he held me down and filled me so completely, pumping me full of his hot cum.*

God, he felt so good.

Stop it.

Daisy runs up to him asking for a quarter for the gum ball machine and I start to fully register that the music the boys are playing is…*really* good.

Luke's on the lead guitar and Leo's on the bass. They're much more polished than I might have expected. The two of them have clearly been playing together so much they can practically read each other's minds. They're amazingly in sync. They've got a natural rhythm and it's easy to see that they've put in their ten thousand hours, which takes their talent to a whole different level, as obsessive practice tends to do.

Luke starts singing, his voice smooth and melodic, and when Leo joins in, my jaw drops. Solo, they've got decent voices, but together they sound incredible. And this is original music.

I'm already thinking about record labels and how I might pitch them. A younger, hotter Florida Georgia Line. Sexy, suntanned twin Morgan Wallens.

A whole cluster of girls is now up at the front, some dancing and singing along, some just staring with love-struck awe.

This music would sell. The whole package of the good looks, the easy country boy charm, the way they play off each other with self-assurance, good humor and musical finesse…would *sell*.

"They're incredible," I say to Betty-Ann and Aunt

Lou, who both beam at me like they're so proud they could burst.

We all watch them play another song. And another. More people are dancing now and the whole party is having fun, like people can't help but do when music is this catchy and this good.

Dakota and Tobias both come over and stand next to Nate. Tobias sees me and grins at me devilishly. He mouths *I love you sister. You okay?*

Love you more, I mouth back. And I barely nod.

It's the *you okay?* that gets me.

I love them all so much. I want to stay here and live my life here. So much I feel like bursting into tears.

Get a grip, girl.

I'm feeling weirdly emotional.

There's no reason to cry, or want to.

Unless Nate Boone turns out to still be the player he once was.

Can I trust him? Did that woman in the green dress trust him?

Maybe I should have thought this whole thing through a little more carefully before I saw him for five minutes then jumped into bed with him and threw all caution to the wind.

Yes, you should have.

My anguish at the thought of him with someone else feels disproportionate, already. It feels like more than a human heart would be able to withstand.

I'm so in love with him.

I can weather some storms but what kind of hurricane are we talking about here?

I guess he'll just have to convince me (again) tonight beyond a shadow of a doubt. Or I'll be on my way, broken-hearted. With a baby.

Jesus, Roxie, calm down and listen to the music. Stop getting so worked up just because your heart is on overdrive.

The twins hit their final note and the crowd cheers.

"We love you, Sugar Falls," Luke drawls into the microphone. "Tell all your friends about the Sugar Mountain Lodge. It's going to be *the* destination in Tennessee."

"Goodnight, y'all," Leo follows. "And don't go anywhere. We've got a special guest playing tonight. Some of you might know him. He's shy so make sure you give him a Sugar Falls welcome."

With that they take their bows to their screaming fans and leave the stage.

"Who's the special guest?" I ask Dakota.

And where's Nate?

That's when I see him.

With a guitar.

Walking onto the stage.

20

———

ROXIE

NATE'S FINGERS ease over the strings and lightly pluck as he tunes his guitar.

God. That guitar. It's the same one.

It's the guitar I painted, a long time ago. I might have been nine or ten. Pink with white flowers.

I don't know why I did that. Some creative urge and it was there. My brothers were mad about it, that I would desecrate a guitar like that—with pink, no less.

It was a good guitar, Vaughn had lectured me. *It's got a pure tone. And now we can't use it.*

But Nate would still play it. He said the tone got even better after that.

He kept it. Because it reminded him of me.

Nate strums again. And he looks out over the crowd. Finding me.

His stage presence is insane. Before he even plays a

196

single note, the entire crowd goes silent, just watching him. He's got that brooding, sexy depth to him that, on stage, is somehow amplified. Your gaze just wants to drink him in. You're waiting with breathless anticipation for him to do something.

He plays a few chords, his fingers deft and skillful. I go instantly wet—*oh my god*. Because I know how good it feels to be played by those strong, rough, skilled hands.

And then he starts to sing.

Holy This Can't Be Happening Right Now, Batman.

He was already perfect.

His voice is as smooth as whiskey, somehow matching his soulful golden eyes with their rims of dark lashes. He's got a deep, smoky, musical, rasped tone that's perfectly in tune.

Wow.

Nate Boone can fucking *sing*.

He's got a crazy star power I don't know if I've ever seen before in an undiscovered artist.

My brothers are showy on stage. The wildness of them—and all three of them combined—appeals to their fans on every level, with their good looks, their heartfelt lyrics and their country soul.

Nate's got something deep and slow-burning. Just serious pure, raw talent that gains momentum as you watch him and takes on layers that awe.

Why why why has he been hiding this?

When we were kids, all the boys were gifted musicians, with the exception of Tobias who would rather be screeching Britney tracks along with Dakota and me than learning the guitar.

But it was always my brothers who burned for it, who had the gall and the energy to make a career out of it or die trying.

Nate was already burdened with mountains of responsibility. I guess back then it was easy to mistake that for someone who didn't *want* it badly enough.

This is a talent he's kept under wraps, beneath his ever-reliable persona, the one his family needed from him —and still does. It breaks my heart that he's never had the chance to indulge his talent when he should have been showing it off all along.

With each note he sings, I can see more of the real, unfiltered Nate Boone break through. Because this is who he is. It couldn't be more obvious that this is what he was born to do.

It's the same Nate I saw when we were alone together, tangled in sheets, hot and sweaty. The thread of vulnerability. The heartfelt sincerity. The fiery passion. All entwined.

Nate Boone is a musician in the true sense of the word.

And *I* can do something about making sure he realizes how freaking good he is.

When he sings the final note of the song, the crowd erupts into a standing ovation so loud Daisy and her friends, who are sitting around hay bales near the front, clap their hands over their ears.

Nate performs three more songs. Each one of them digs itself more deeply into my soul.

I didn't think it was possible to fall even more in love with him. But he just figured out a way to get me to do exactly that. I'm slayed. I'm scared but at the same time I feel braver than I ever have.

I might be pregnant with his baby.

And right now, there's nothing on this entire Earth that I've wanted more than for that to be true.

21

ROXIE

NATE and I say goodnight to Dakota—who scolds me for hardly spending any time with *her*, the Boone I came to visit.

"What does he have that *I* don't have?" she jokes, then quickly realizes her gaffe. "Wait. Do *not* answer that question."

I give her a hug. "Thank you, Dee. For making this happen tonight. For showing me."

"What did you think of our boys?" Her question is lightly cautious, as Nate goes to find Daisy's bag.

"I think your boys are all going to be superstars, that's what I think."

Her green eyes are bright. "Really?"

"Absolutely really. I can't believe I didn't *know* about this, Dakota."

"I mean, would you ever consider taking them on?"

"Of course I would. Before someone else discovers them and beats me to it."

Her hands hold her face. "I can't believe it."

"Well, believe it, girl. All three of them have the kind of X factor that sells records like nobody's business. Tomorrow we can all sit down and talk it through. I'll go through my offer and the steps we need to take, then we'll start making a plan."

"Oh my god. Thank you, Rox."

"Thank *you*. I only wish you'd called me out here sooner." I see Nate coming back, Daisy nearly asleep on his shoulder and a pink bag in his hand. "We'll talk tomorrow, okay?"

Another long, genuine hug. One thing about the Boone family is they know to freaking *hug*.

It's then that I notice a man standing back from us, sipping on his beer and watching the band. He keeps glancing over at Dakota, like he's waiting for her.

"Who's that?" He's tall and good-looking with dark hair flicking out from under a cowboy hat. "Is that *him*? The rodeo hero from Montana?"

"I don't know if he's a rodeo *hero*. And nothing's happened. We've just been talking, that's all."

"He's *hot*, Dee."

"*Shh*. Nate's coming back."

"Okay, I better go, sweetie. Have *fun* tonight. Good luck with Mr. Montana."

She laughs. "Thanks. Goodnight, Rox. Love you."

"Love you too."

Nate and I make a quiet exit from the hoedown, which is starting to rev up a few gears as the second half of the evening gets underway.

Daisy's eyes barely open as she's buckled into her car seat. Before we've even pulled out of the lodge's parking lot, she's fast asleep.

"I have a whole lot of things I need to talk to you about, Boone." But first things first. I ask the question gently. "Who is she?"

A sideways glance and a low not-quite-laugh. It's a few seconds before he answers. *Is there anything sexier than Nate Boone's suntanned, muscular, hair-dusted forearms as he grips the steering wheel? I don't think so.* "No one you need to worry about, darlin'."

"Please be honest with me. I want to know who she is."

He sighs. "She's someone who wanted a whole lot more than I was ever willing to give."

"What's her name?"

"I can't remember."

I give him a look. "Don't bullshit me, Boone."

"The thing is, Tuck, it doesn't matter what her name is."

"When's the last time you saw her?"

"I saw her tonight."

His dark eyes are glittering in the darkness. He loves my jealousy. "Before tonight."

For a second I think he's pretending to mull it over. But then he says, "Six and a half months ago to the day. We had dinner."

I'm a little surprised by how precise he is about it. "You had dinner?"

"Yes."

"Then what?"

Another sigh, and this time it's heavier. "Rox, do you have any idea where *you* were that night, six and a half months ago to the day?"

"What does that have to do with it?"

"Do you know where you were?" he asks again. Almost patiently but not quite.

"No. On tour. I can't remember where exactly."

"You were in Denver."

"How…do you know that?"

"Because I followed your tour schedules."

"Why?"

"So I knew where you were."

"The band?"

"Nope. You."

His cryptic answers are confusing me. "I don't understand what you're saying."

Silence.

"Nate?"

"There were a lot of nights I thought about showing up. Just knocking on your hotel door in whatever random city you were in and seeing your face when you opened it." He's quiet for a few seconds. "A lot of nights. But never more than the night she and I had dinner. It was *that* night I decided I'd track you down and tell you how I felt. Because I was so fed up with feeling so empty when I was supposed to feel…something. *Anything.* And I just didn't. I just never fucking did."

"You…didn't?"

"No."

"Why didn't you come find me?"

"Your next three shows were going to be at Red Rocks. I was going to come to Red Rocks."

"Nate. Why didn't you?"

"That's what I was doing when I got the call. I was booking the ticket."

"What call?"

"That was the night the accident happened."

The accident.

Jed and Laney's accident.

At the realization, my hand flutters to cover my mouth.

"Things got real complicated after that. I don't think I've come up for air since. Not until you walked into the kitchen the other night. Then there was suddenly more air than I knew how to breathe."

"I'm sorry."

He pulls the truck up to the house and turns off the engine. His eyes are dark in the moonlight. "Don't be sorry, darlin'. Just don't go accusing me of loving anyone else. Because it's just never going to be true."

I feel almost stricken with love for him. Here I was, walking along my whole life, minding my own business and secretly pining for a lost boy I once loved, only to be swept away by a tidal wave of everything I never thought to even wish for.

"We good, then?"

"I think we're more than good, Boone."

A slow grin flashes. "Come on. Let's get the exhausted little princess into bed. Then I've got some plans for you."

Nate carefully lifts Daisy out of the truck. I follow him up to her room with her bag. We take off her shoes and her little glittery pink jacket and tuck her into bed. Nate kisses her head and makes sure all three of her nightlights are on.

Then he takes me by the hand and leads me back to his room.

He locks the door and switches on the baby monitor that's next to the bed. "So I can hear her if she wakes up."

He comes over to me in the low light. We're quiet and it's a relief, after all the raucous activity of the day. His room is a luxurious haven.

Nate slides his warm hand around the nape of my neck. His dark head bends and he eases his mouth over mine. His mouth shifts, catching at my top lip, then the lower one, opening me. His tenderness, with the dark, heavy lust simmering just behind it, makes me go shame-lessly wet.

"You had quite an ace up your sleeve tonight, Boone." I look up into his whiskey-fire eyes and see everything I've ever wanted. "Why didn't you tell me?"

"Tell you what? That I sing every now and then?"

"'Sing every now and then'? Nate, you're a major talent. I want you to let me take you on."

"You can take me on any time you want, darlin'. Starting right now."

"You know what I mean—" My phone dings. *Damn it.* I reach over the back of the couch to my bag, pulling out my phone. Another message from Travis. "I know for a fact they have better things to do." I turn my phone off.

"I'm sure the hoedown is lighting up with the news that we snuck off together."

Nate's hand is on my back. He gently but firmly bends me over. He lifts the hem of my dress, pulling it up and easing it over my head. His hands are on my thighs, sliding up, and it feels so good I moan, arching my back a little.

He rips my panties and the shred of lace falls to the floor. If I wasn't so damn turned on, I'd laugh. "Did you just—?"

"Quiet," he growls. I bite my lip as he forces my legs wider. My back arches further. I feel his strong, warm hands slide higher, exploring silkily. Opening me. He circles, dipping his fingers into the moisture, until I'm squirming along with his movement. His rough fingertips skate over my clit.

Nate kneels behind me and I feel his *tongue*. I give myself to him completely, letting him do anything he wants to me. He eats into me hungrily, feasting like a starving man as his fingers tease my clit. He pushes his tongue deep, playing, stroking, rubbing, forcing the pleasure to an overpowering swell that breaks into tumbling spasms.

And still, he eats me like he can't get enough, until the waves start to calm.

Then he lifts me, turning me and taking me in his arms as he kisses me again. I slowly push him backward until we're almost on the bed. I fumble with his buttons, needing him, running my fingers over his warm cinnamon skin.

I undo the button of his jeans, easing the zip down, reaching in to grip him, running my fist along the huge, hard length, using my fingers to circle the broad, slippery tip. "I need you," I whisper.

His belt buckle thunks on the plush carpet as he jeans fall to the floor.

Nate leans back on the bed, pulling me along with him until I'm straddling him. "Climb on up, darlin'. Ride my big cock like a good girl."

He raises my arms and guides me to grip the top of his oak headboard.

Nate stares into my eyes until I'm drowning in him.

His breath is warm against my lips. "Hold on," he commands me.

And then he grips his hot, engorged cock and positions me, sliding thickly into my slippery, still-quivering pussy as I sit down onto him, taking all of him by slow degrees. He's so freaking big and hot, I'm already coming again from the thick-skewering pleasure, feeling every ridge as he forces me to take all of it, and again, deeper, harder.

My orgasm milks him as he roots himself to the hilt, over and over, his thumb stroking my clit. I'm raised and lifted, holding on for dear life, wondering if I can survive another shattering release.

And another, washing through me with fresh, shimmering heat.

He belongs to me. He's mine. I know it. I feel it in every throb and every groan.

I'm riding him, dazed by the sheer magnitude of feeling, when he grips me and growls, his cock bucking and surging in violent pulses that set me off *again*, filling my body and soul with heat and love and life.

He pulls me down to kiss him. It's forceful, and I can taste his desperation. *"Roxie. Roxie."*

"It's okay. I'm here, Boone. I love you."

MOMMY. Daddy. Where are you?

From deep within my dream, I wonder if it's me calling out, like I used to do. How could they just disappear like that? How could they just be *gone*? Forever?

"Uncle Nate. Uncle Nate."

My eyes open at the same time as Nate's.

"Shit," he murmurs, climbing out of bed and hastily pulling on jeans and a t-shirt. "She's having a nightmare. I'll be back."

I can hear Daisy's sobs through the monitor, and Nate's, deep, husky, soothing voice. "It's okay, sweetheart. You're okay. I'm here now." He sounds so sad, because she is.

I get out of bed. In the low light I manage to find a clean pair of panties in my bag. I grab a white button-down shirt of Nate's that's slung over the back of a chair, that hangs almost to my knees.

I go down to Daisy's room and lightly tap on the open door. I don't want to intrude, but I sense that he might need me. I wonder if maybe I can help a little. I know what it feels like. I remember the things people said to me that made it almost more bearable.

Daisy's in her tent and Nate's lying next to her, with his long legs mostly out of the tent. A small lamp inside the tent fills it with soft golden light. There are piles of cushiony pillows and blankets. Daisy's tucked in snugly.

"Miss Roxie," Daisy sniffles. "Do you want to come into my tent with us?"

"Is that okay?"

"Yes. Here." She pats some pillows next to her. "You can be next to me."

I climb inside and lay next to her and I can see that the inside of the tent has been decorated with hanging homemade glittery stars. And with photos. Of Daisy's parents. Of the three of them together. And of Nate too, laughing with Jed when they were young. There's the same photo that's framed in the hallway, of Nate holding Daisy when she was a baby, with Jed and Laney in the background. "This is *such* a beautiful tent."

"We always come in here after I have nightmares," Daisy tells me earnestly, fresh tears filling her very-blue eyes. "We put pictures up so I can remember them. I don't want to forget them."

"You won't." I smooth a strand of her hair back from her damp little face. "Did I ever tell you that I lost my parents too? Exactly the same way you did?"

Her breath hitches. "You did?"

"I did. And you know what? I never, ever forgot them. Because I know they're always right here." I put my hand over my heart. "I can feel them. In the beat of my heart."

Daisy puts her hand over her own heart. "Here?"

"Yeah. Right there."

She's quiet for a few seconds, concentrating. "*I can feel them too,*" she whispers.

"They'll always be there. They'll always be a part of you."

Nate's holding Daisy's hand, watching me. *Thank you,* he mouths silently.

More tears wet Daisy's cheeks and she turns to Nate. "But what if I can't *stay* with you, Uncle Nate?" She's crying harder now. "What if I have to go live with Aunt Amanda? We don't even *like* her. My Mommy said she's *mean.*"

"Hey," Nate croons, wiping her tears. "That's not going to happen, sweetheart. Who told you that?"

"I heard Grandma Lou talking to Grandma Betty-Ann. They didn't know I was listening. But I was. I don't *want* to go to Ohio. I like it *here.* What if I have to go there and I have a nightmare and you're not *there.*" She sobs like her little heart is breaking.

Nate looks like his heart is breaking right alongside hers. He gently turns her face toward his and wipes more of her tears. "Daisy. Sweetheart. You don't need to worry about that for a single second. I'm going to make sure you can stay here forever, honey, you know that. We're going to get you a pony for your birthday and some pink cowgirl boots and Aunt Dakota is already planning your birthday party at the pool. Uncle Tobias is going to make you a pink cake with pink candles. You and your friends can take turns riding your pony and it'll be the best party ever. Okay?"

Daisy sniffles, nodding. "Okay."

"So no more worrying about that. You're staying here, end of story. Tomorrow we're going to go down to the school and sign you up for first grade and Harper and all your friends from kindergarten will be in your class. I'll be there every day to pick you up from school and you'll live with me and that's that."

"Harper already signed up for first grade," Daisy sniffs. "Two weeks ago."

"Yeah?"

"Yeah."

Nate's furrow between his eyebrow shows up. The weight-of-the-world one. Like maybe he was supposed to do that but things got busy and it somehow got overlooked. "We'll make sure we do it tomorrow, it'll be fine. Now, how about we read *Where the Wild Things Are* and we'll sleep right here in your tent, all together, you, me and Miss Roxie. We'll make sure you don't have any more nightmares tonight. How does that sound?"

"Good," she says with another hitch of her breath.

Nate tucks her blanket around her more securely and he lays one over me too. Daisy's holding Nate's hand and she reaches for mine. And it's strange, because right then, one of the pieces of me that shattered on a rainy Tuesday night a long time ago feels like the fissure has somehow healed. And I fall more deeply in love with this broken-hearted little girl.

We all have broken hearts, all three of us. And somehow, the jagged, broken pieces have arranged themselves in a way that hinges us together. I think we all feel it. We're stronger together than we are apart.

"I'll stay with you forever," she whispers.

"Forever," Nate whispers back, his eyes holding mine.

Nate starts reading and, soon, Daisy's eyes start to close. I kiss her cheek and lightly play with her hair.

"My Mommy used to do that," she murmurs softly.

Nate gets to the end of the book and Daisy's nearly asleep.

"Miss Roxie?" she coos, her eyes still closed.

"Yeah?"

"I wish you could be my new Mommy."

I'm still stroking her silky hair in feather-light strokes and I hear myself whisper, "Me too."

"Then I would be happy and Uncle Nate wouldn't be so lonely."

Her breathing gets deeper. Nate turns off the lamp. The princess nightlights give off a low glow.

We're still holding Daisy's hands, gazing at each other in our little cocoon in the darkness, listening to Daisy's soft, even breathing.

It's too quiet to hear but I read his lips.

I love you.

22

NATE

My eyes open. The slant of the sun tells me I've slept later than I have in a long time.

We're in Daisy's tent. All three of us fell asleep in here after Daisy's nightmare.

Daisy and Roxie are curled up together like two little peas in a pod.

I spend a few minutes just watching them sleep. Daisy's still wearing her princess outfit. I didn't want to wrestle her out of it last night as I put her to bed and risk waking her up. Her hair's wild from broken sleep and from two back to back parties. She looks like a tiny little mussed-up angel.

Roxie's wearing one of my shirts she must have grabbed on the way down to Daisy's bedroom. Her shiny dark hair is fanned out over the pillows, her lips lightly swollen from my punishing kisses. She's so damn pretty it hurts.

I fucking love her more than I can bear. I love them both so much.

A feral variety of contentment settles into my chest. They're what I want. These two. After years of not really knowing and always working like a maniac to try to distract myself from my own discontent, here they suddenly are. The two people I would kill or die for. That's it. I want to give them everything they want and need for the rest of time. I want to shield them and help them thrive to become the happiest, best versions of themselves. I want to take such good care of them they have no choice but to live their best lives. It's my entire reason now.

Roxie's eyes blink open.

It takes her a second to figure out where she is.

"Hey, beautiful," I say quietly.

Daisy wakes at the sound of my voice. She gasps, smiling her little gap-toothed grin. *"We slept in my tent!"* she whispers. She's lost her two front teeth in the past couple of weeks and I was almost panicking about my new role as the tooth fairy. Turns out twenty bucks is good money for a tooth. All her friends were jealous.

I lick my thumb and gently wipe some chocolate from her cheek. Another detail that flew under the radar when I tucked her into bed last night. "We did. And now I'm going to make you two the biggest breakfast you've ever seen. What do you want? Pancakes?"

"Yay, pancakes! Do you like pancakes, Miss Roxie?"

"I love them."

"Come on, then." I scoop Daisy into my arms and the three of us make our way down to the kitchen. Glancing up at the clock, it's after nine. "I can't believe we slept in that late. I haven't slept past six in years."

"All worn out," Roxie says, under her breath, giving me a sultry grin.

"Just getting started, darlin'," I murmur back, and her cheeks get pink.

I set Daisy on the window seat where some of her books are still sitting from the last time I cooked dinner for her. Must have been Thursday night. The night before my entire world shifted on its axis.

I notice now that I didn't quite get to putting her toys away, from when she was playing with them that night. They're scattered all over the floor.

I'm still adjusting to the amount of mess a six-year-old makes, but it can wait until after breakfast.

I put on a pot of coffee and pour Daisy a glass of orange juice, to make sure she's getting enough Vitamin C, and one for Roxie, while trying not to get distracted by Roxie's bare legs and perfect, puffy lips. I start getting the stuff out of the pantry to make the pancakes. It takes me a while to find the chocolate chips—which are on a lower shelf and there are a lot fewer of them than there were the last time I checked. "Here they are. And it looks like a little monkey might have helped herself."

"It was me!" Daisy giggles. Then she goes back to her book. "'The night Max wore his wolf suit and made m-miss-ch-chiff of one kind…'" *Where the Wild Things Are* is Daisy's favorite book. We read it at least once every night before bed. "What's miss-chiff again, Uncle Nate?"

"It's like when you sneak into the pantry to eat choco-late chips," I tell her.

Roxie's leaning against the counter with her arms folded, sipping her coffee with an entertained smirk. "The hot Dad even cooks."

I grin and shake my head a little, accidentally tipping the flour over because she's so fucking cute in my over-sized shirt. "Mickey Mouse pancakes with chocolate chips are my new specialty. And I can make a mean grilled cheese."

"I *love* grilled cheese," Daisy offers, not looking up from her book.

Roxie smiles at me, her blue eyes glimmering—and if it wasn't for the little princess reading her book out loud to us from the window seat, I'd already be ravaging Roxie Tucker right there on the kitchen counter. "Stop getting me hot," I murmur in her ear. "You're doing it on purpose."

"Maybe."

"Who's *that?*" Daisy says. She's looking out the window, down to the driveway.

I go over to see what she's looking at, wiping my flour-covered hands on a dishtowel. "Oh, shit."

"Uncle *Nate*," Daisy scolds me.

"Oh, shoot," I revise. If it isn't Travis and Vaughn Tucker getting out of Travis's shiny blue Shelby.

"Who is it?" Roxie asks.

"It's your brothers."

23

ROXIE

Who the hell do they think they are?

I go over to Nate's door and open it. To loud music.

Travis and Vaughn are walking up the stairs. Travis is carrying his speaker, which is cranked up and playing—speak of the devil—the Down Home Boys. Vaughn's shirt is open and untucked and he's drinking out of a large flask with the word **WHISKEY** embossed in bold letters across it. Propped behind one of his ears is what looks like a very large joint. *Damn it.* Vaughn's supposed to be strictly *on* the wagon, no exceptions.

But that lecture can wait. "What are you doing here?" I'm blocking the door so they can't come in.

My brothers are both dressed in their usual denim and leather, with plenty of gold chains, tattoos and too-long hair thrown into the mix. They both look…well, like

219

superstar musicians and two-thirds of the hottest country-rock band in the world right now.

"Roxanne Savannah," drawls Vaughn, "you sly little minx. Making a beeline for the biggest dog in town as soon as our backs were turned."

"Why are you here?" I'm not sure if I'm ready for real life to intrude on my newly-discovered slice of paradise, which still feels like a dream.

Having them show up out of the blue is like a splash of cold water—and not in a good way.

Don't get me wrong, I love my brothers, but I don't need them checking up on me. And that's exactly what they're doing.

Travis kisses me on the cheek. "You wouldn't believe the rumors that are flying around the countryside, darlin'. But now that we've been pointed in the direction of Nathan Waylon Boone's private residence by his own mother—and here you happen to be—it appears the rumors might be true."

When we were kids, my brothers always got a kick out of the fact that Nate's middle name is Waylon. In their opinion, the coolest person in the world to be named after would have to be Waylon Jennings. He's one of their idols and biggest inspirations. Which is inconsequential right now, but it reminds me of how far we all go back. And how crazy this might seem to them.

Still, it doesn't mean they can control me. "Where I

happen to be is none of your concern, Travis Tucker. I'm on vacation."

"Sounds like a fun one," Vaughn bumps his shoulder against mine playfully.

"Also none of your business. I can't believe you guys drove all the way out here just to check up on me."

"We were at Travis's country house. It's not all that far. The girls are busy with their sister and her baby visiting and they're having some kind of ladies lunch. So we had nothing better to do."

"I highly doubt that. Write another album, how about that, while meanwhile minding your own business."

"Your business is our business, Rox, you know that. You going to let us in or what?" Vaughn's impish smirk is one I'm very familiar with.

"Depends on what you're going to do once you get in here."

Nate appears at my side. I'm almost shocked when he slings a burly arm over my shoulder, protectively. And possessively. It's an intimate move. And it confirms beyond a shadow of a doubt what my brothers are here to find out. Then again, I'm also wearing Nate's shirt, which is huge on me, and no pants. "Hey, boys. Fancy seeing you here."

"Hey, Nate. Yeah, fancy that." Travis and Vaughn both grin at Nate. I *think* they're friendly smiles, but there's clearly a very protective curiosity behind them.

Kade was always the one I was most worried about,

as far as reacting to this news, but both Travis and Vaughn are a lot more hot-headed than Kade. And Vaughn's especially unpredictable.

"Can we help you boys with something?" The deep husk behind Nate's question gives me light goosebumps as it stirs a memory *of what it sounds like in the dark*—possibly not an ideal time to be thinking about that, but I *love* the sound of his voice. And the low menace behind his words makes no mistake about it: my brothers can accept that this is happening or they can take it outside.

I always think of my brothers as big men, and they are, but Nate is even taller and more built. And it's a new dynamic. He's telling *them* how it is.

Instead of *them* telling *me* how it is.

Not that I've ever really felt controlled by my brothers, but it's true that they dominate my life. And it's freeing: I'm making my own rules now. And Nate's here to make sure I can.

"Just checking in on our little sister to make sure she hasn't fallen innocently under the spell of the Heartbreak King of Sugar Falls." Travis's smile is layered.

"Travis, for God's sake. I'm twenty-*three*." *Not fifteen.*

Nate gives Travis a level glare. "I thought that was your title, Travis."

Vaughn glances at Travis. Then at Nate. "I thought it was *my* title."

Nate shakes his head. "Whoever's title it was, it was

six or seven years ago now. I like to think we've all grown up since then."

"Just making sure your intentions are pure, Boone."

Nate's eyes barely narrow. He doesn't owe them an explanation. But he gives them one anyway. "My intentions are to make all her dreams come true." There's so much sincerity in his answer, it catches both of my brothers off guard. "And there's not a damn thing either one of you can do to stop me from doing it."

Travis notices the way I'm holding Nate's arm—and wearing his shirt. "He's already made good on most of my dreams," I tell them. "And it's only been the weekend."

Vaughn's grin widens.

"Either way, I'm amazed that you two think you have any say in it whatsoever."

"Chill, Rox." Vaughn takes a swig from his flask. "It was a good excuse to come see the Boones again. Hell, colorful past or no colorful past, we all know Nate's done well for himself and everyone else. It's all just a lot to take in."

Nate laughs. "Shit, boys, it might be time to start relying a little less on your sister and maybe look after yourselves for an entire weekend. And there's nothing more colorful about my past than there is about yours, Vaughn. Now, are you two here to fight me or do you want to come in?"

"We wanted to make sure our sister was okay," Travis

says. "We wouldn't be doing our duty as brothers if we didn't."

"Fair enough. But I can assure you, Roxie's just fine."

"More than fine," I confirm, just to rile them—even though I have to admit, meddling busybodies or not, their genuine concern for me is sweet. We've all been looking out for each other for a long time, because no one else was going to, and it's a habit that's dug in.

Travis shakes Nate's hand. "It's good to see you, man. It's been too long."

"It has."

Then Vaughn. "I guess it's welcome to the family then, Nathan Waylon. Again."

A soft little voice enters the conversation. Daisy's tugging on Nate's shirt. "Uncle Nate? Who are *they*?"

Nate removes his arm from around me—slowly—so he can pick up Daisy. "Daisy, meet Vaughn and Travis Tucker. Miss Roxie's brothers."

My brothers aren't shocked to see Daisy here. They heard about what happened from Kade, like I did. "You can call me Uncle Vaughn. Us and Nate are practically cousins."

"We're *not* cousins," Nate and I say in unison.

"You have an earring," Daisy says to Vaughn, in that blunt, observant way children have. He wears a little gold hoop in his left ear. With his wild black hair and blue eyes, it gives him an edge of a pirate-gypsy vibe.

"And you have chocolate on your face," Vaughn says

back. Vaughn has a natural way with kids—possibly because he acts like a child himself a lot of the time.

"That's because I *like* chocolate," she tells him.

"So do I," he says, conspiratorially, like they're sharing a secret.

Daisy eyes him up for a second. "We have some chocolate chips we're putting in our Mickey Mouse pancakes. Do you want some?"

"That sounds fu—" Vaughn catches himself, his grin full of mischief, as always. "Fun. And fantastic."

"You can't bring that in here, Vaughn." Nate's eyeing the joint above Vaughn's ear.

Vaughn takes it and holds it up. "This? It's plain tobacco. Which I don't smoke." He takes a swig from the whiskey flask he's holding, then holds it out to me to taste. "Water. I like to stay hydrated."

"Why don't you just get a water bottle like a normal person?"

"This is more fun. Helps with the FOMO and all that. And it's working, Rox. I'm sober as a fu—"—another glance at Daisy— "as a fun-loving judge. I'm high on life. I'm all in with clean living."

It's a relief. "That's good, Vaughn."

Nate opens the door a little wider. "Well, come on in, then. You two hungry?"

"Starving, man."

Nate takes Daisy into the kitchen and sets her on the counter. There's the distinct smell of burning pancakes.

"Shit," I hear Nate curse.

"Uncle *Nate*," a little voice scolds.

"Shoot," he corrects himself, waving a dishtowel over the smoke and opening the window next to the stove. "I left this burner on."

"Are the Mickey Mouses burned?"

"It's okay. I've got plenty more batter. I'll make some more."

Travis touches his shoulder to mine. "Nate Boone, huh?"

"It's always been him."

My brothers both stare at me, not expecting that answer.

"Turn the music down some," I tell Travis and he does, but barely.

"So," Travis drawls, "It seems love is in the air all over Tennessee. Kade met someone new the other night."

"What? Who?"

"He's got some new girl in his bed and they haven't left his apartment all weekend."

"He does?" That's the best news.

Vaughn confirms. "I called him and he said the two of them ran into each other on Broadway in the rain. Her name is Stella."

I grin at them. "*Yay.*"

"He's thoroughly getting the ex out of his system, by the sounds of it," Vaughn laughs.

Daisy tugs at the leg of Vaughn's jeans. "Uncle

Vaughn?" She's holding a small bag of chocolate chips. "Do you want some?"

"Of course I want some, darlin'."

She pours some chocolate chips from the bag into his cupped hand and it overflows a little. He shoves the whole handful into his mouth.

Daisy giggles. When Vaughn holds out his hand for more, she shakes her head, grinning at him with her little gap-toothed smile. So Vaughn pretends to chase after her. Daisy squeals and runs to hug Nate's leg.

"Careful there, Daze, I'm just serving these up."

I reach to get some plates for Nate to serve the pancakes onto. Clearing a place on the counter to set them down, I notice all three of the men have stopped what they're doing to stare at the open door.

Someone must have knocked, but with the loud music playing, I hadn't heard it.

Daisy has opened the door for a woman, who's standing there with a mildly shocked, displeased look on her face.

She's dressed in a conservative outfit. A knee-length gray skirt and a blue blouse buttoned all the way up. Her hair is pulled back into a neat bun. She's probably in her mid-thirties but it's hard to tell since she's dressed like a much older woman.

Nate looks briefly for a dishtowel but, unable to find one, wipes his hands on his jeans. "Travis, turn that music down, would you?" he says, walking over to the woman.

He holds out his hand for her to shake. "Nate Boone. Can I help you?"

The woman looks at his hand, which is still wet and partly covered in flour. She doesn't take it. "Ainsley Beal."

I'm not sure who Ainsley Beal is but from the look on Nate's face, something about this has caught him off guard.

"Uh," Nate gestures toward the rest of us. "This is Roxie, Travis and Vaughn Tucker."

"Pleased to meet you, ma'am," Vaughn says, almost stepping forward to offer a handshake but then deciding better of it. It's pretty clear from Ainsley Beal's expression she wouldn't shake his hand either.

Ainsley stares at Vaughn, saying nothing. She takes in his open shirt and bare, tattooed chest. The whiskey flask he's still holding. His mussed-up too-long hair. The fat joint behind his ear.

Then she takes a long look at Travis, equally unim-pressed.

I have no doubt that both my brothers look like hell-raisers to someone like Ainsley Beal—whoever she is.

Ainsley's glance falls on Daisy, who still has chocolate on her face—more now than before. Her hair is a tangled mess and probably hasn't been brushed since before the birthday party. She's still dressed in the same princess outfit she's slept in for two days' straight, which looks it. It's crumpled and dirty.

The music is off now but the scene is chaotic. The air

smells like smoke, there's flour and burnt pancakes all over the counter and toys and chocolate chips are strewn all over the floor.

Ainsley turns to me. The shirt I'm wearing is as long as a mini-dress. But it's not a mini-dress. It's very clearly a shirt. And it's fairly obvious it's Nate's shirt. I notice now the few buttons I've done up are unevenly buttoned. My hair looks like I spent a night either tossing or turning—or having very hot sex.

Ainsley seems almost speechless.

But then she clears her throat. "Um, Mr. Boone, I apologize for interrupting your…*party*. I called the school on my way over here and there's no record of Daisy's enrollment."

Nate rubs the back of his neck. "Yeah, we were planning to do that today."

"School starts *tomorrow*, Mr. Boone."

Nate seems flustered and Daisy picks up on it. She goes over to him and he lifts her into his arms. "We're headed over there soon, Ms. Beal. After Daisy finishes breakfast and gets cleaned up."

More scrutiny over the fact that Daisy's obviously overdue for "cleaning up".

"Yes. Well. There's quite a bit involved in first grade enrollment, Mr. Boone. Most parents tend to organize the stationery lists and so on several weeks in advance."

"I'll make sure it happens today."

"You'll need to."

Nate's expression is layered. He's pissed off. Uncomfortable with this visit, clearly. And his worried weight-of-the-world furrow is back. "Do you…want to look at the rest of the house?"

"No," she answers abruptly. "I think I've seen enough."

Ainsley turns to leave.

Nate follows her. "Ms. Beal, please. You caught us at an unexpected time—"

"That's the point of these visits, Mr. Boone. To find out how the household is run on a day to day basis. Without staging."

"*Staging?* If you'd like to have a look at the rest of the house or to come back—"

"That's not necessary, Mr. Boone." She's already unlocking her old gray sedan. "I got what I came for. I'll be in touch."

Vaughn moves as though to go after her, recognizing that something has gone wrong here and he might have contributed to it. "Hey—" But Nate holds him back.

Ainsley slams her car door closed, gets it running after two tries and starts driving away.

Daisy looks at Nate, her small arms tight around his neck. "Who was that lady?"

Nate lets out a frustrated sigh. "That was the lady who tells the judge whether or not she thinks you should be living with me."

"Uh oh," she whispers.

24

NATE

"SHOULD WE GO AFTER HER?" Travis suggests. "I've got the Shelby."

"We're not going to *chase* after her." It's tempting. "She'd think we're lunatics." And she clearly already does.

"Nate," Vaughn takes the rolled cigarette from behind his ear. "If we did anything to—"

"You didn't, Vaughn. None of us did anything wrong here."

Daisy bursts into tears and wraps her arms more tightly around my neck. "I'm *not* going to Ohio! I'm *not*! I'll run away if that lady makes me do that! She can't make me! I'll run all the way back here!"

I carry Daisy into the kitchen. "Sweetheart, I told you, that's not going to happen." I set her down so she's sitting on a little chair at her toy table. I smooth her nest of a hairdo out of her eyes. Her little face is all serious and she reminds me so much of her dad it makes me want to reach up into heaven or wherever he is, grab him by the scruff of his neck and pull him back down here. *I need you guys, man. Help me make this right.*

"Do you *promise?*"

She hears me hesitate, because *what if I can't keep it?* "I promise. I'm going to call the lady and I'll set up another visit and everything will be fine. You're not going to Ohio. Now, we're going to get you cleaned up, then we're going to go down to the school and get you enrolled so you can see all your friends tomorrow. How does that sound?"

Daisy runs up the stairs.

I'm about to chase after her when Roxie places her hand on my arm. "Would you let me, Nate? I could run her a bath and wash her hair and then braid it or whatever she wants. I'll help her pick out an outfit."

It might be exactly what Daisy needs right now. A calming influence and some girl time. "Thanks, Rox. I'm going to call Ainsley Beal."

Travis and Vaughn are cleaning up the kitchen mess, of all things. The gravity of the situation is clear enough and I appreciate them rallying around us. "Two rock stars cleaning up my kitchen. Never thought I'd see the day."

"Don't get used to it, bro."

Taking my phone out of my pocket, I search for Ainsley's number, from when she called me the other day, and punch the call button, pacing in front of the windows as it rings. It rings eight or nine times and then there's a click as the call is transferred.

"Social Services."

"Can I speak to Ainsley Beal, please."

"I'm sorry, she's unavailable. You can leave a message with me if you'd like and I'll pass it on. She'll get back to you in due course." *In due fucking course?* "If you'd like to speak to her directly, you'll have to make an appointment."

"I'll make an appointment then."

"Right. Let's see…" There's a pause. "She only has one free appointment this week. There was a cancellation. Tomorrow at two o'clock."

"I'll take it."

"Fine. What's your name, sir?"

"Nate Boone."

"Do you know where we're located, Mr. Boone?"

"No. Hang on, I'll get a pen." I find one of Daisy's crayons. "Right, go ahead."

"5633 Montgomery Street. We're two blocks off Broadway."

Shit, they're in Nashville. It's a two hour drive and Daisy starts school tomorrow. I also have meetings— which I'll have to cancel. I scribble the address onto a piece of paper. "Thank you. I'll be there at two."

As I'm ending the call, I look up to see Roxie running down the stairs. "Daisy? Is she down here, Nate?"

"No. She went to her room."

"She's not in her room. Or your room. Or any of the other rooms. I looked everywhere. She's gone."

25

______

NATE

I SPRINT up the stairs followed closely by Roxie. I hear Vaughn calling to Daisy outside on the deck.

I check the princess castle, the closet, the bathroom. Frantic, we go room to room, looking everywhere.

I think of all the times Daisy has played hide and seek and made us worry. Once she went off to see Aunt Lou when Ma was babysitting her and forgot to tell anyone where she was going. Or the time she fell asleep in Dakota's room after playing under Dakota's bed and no one knew where she was for an agonizing twenty minutes.

It doesn't happen often, but she's given us a scare enough times for me to feel sure this will be no different. *Please be okay. Where are you?* Daisy happens to be quiet. She also happens to be freakishly *fast*.

The hot tub cover is locked but I check it anyway.

I notice then that the small gate to the side staircase leading off the deck is open.

Daisy.

And I know where she's gone. "The cemetery," I say to Roxie.

"You think she went there?"

"We go there every Sunday afternoon. We missed it this week."

"Where is it?"

"It's up behind the orchard, by the waterfall. It was their favorite place on the farm."

"I'll come with you," Roxie's pulling on her boots.

"Travis, can you keep searching around the house? Vaughn, go up to Ma's and see if maybe she's there."

"Sure, man. She can't have gone far. We'll find her." I'm suddenly incredibly glad they're here.

I roll the quad bike out of its shed and Roxie climbs onto the back, wrapping her arms around me. "Hold on tight, Tuck."

I push the quad bike for all it's worth. We round the hill and I can see the pink of her princess outfit and the strawberry-blond halo of her hair in the distance.

Thank you, God.

We pull up next to the little cemetery of two that we made just for them. The flowers we brought last weekend are wilted in their vases now. Daisy is sitting cross-legged between the two stones. Her little face is streaked with her earlier tears, but dry now. "Hi, Uncle Nate. Hi, Miss Roxie."

I help Roxie off the quad bike. Then I go over to Daisy and pick her up, giving her a big, wildly relieved hug. "You can't do that to me, sweetheart," I murmur.

"I'm sorry. Sometimes I just need them."

"I know. Just tell me next time so I can come with you."

"Okay."

Daisy sees that Roxie has tears in her eyes too and she reaches for her. Roxie takes her and gives her another one of those heartfelt hugs. "You okay?"

Daisy nods as Roxie smooths her hair.

"That's my Mommy and that's my Daddy," Daisy points out.

Roxie puts Daisy's little hand on her heart. "They're still right here. Always. Just like mine are."

"In the beat of my heart," Daisy whispers.

ROXIE

It's late now. We got Daisy home and cleaned up and Nate took her down to the school as Travis, Vaughn and I finished cleaning up the house.

My brothers left to go see Aunt Lou and Uncle Earl for a few hours before heading back to Travis's country house, where they were going to pick up Ruby and Gigi and drive into the city to see Kade. No one's heard from him in a few days and they wanted to check in on him before going to a gig they wanted to see. I joked that their favorite hobby seems to be barging in on everyone's love lives, but they just said it's because they care. Our hugs felt different when they left. Like we're somehow equals now instead of just big brothers and a little sister. And like we love each other more every day.

Daisy's tucked in, asleep. I helped her lay out her

school outfit and we packed her backpack with the school supplies she and Nate picked up on their way home.

Nate tried calling Ainsley Beal a few more times but it went straight to voicemail. I can tell he's on edge, but tomorrow he'll meet with her and explain whatever it was she didn't understand.

We're sitting in the hot tub on his bedroom's deck, the bubbles fizzing around our shoulders. "What a job," I muse. "Going around judging people and making assumptions about their lives. She hardly even stepped inside."

"I'm sure her intentions are good. I think she just got the wrong impression."

"The part she didn't see is that Daisy's living her best life under the circumstances. A sticky face after a birthday party and a hoedown while wearing your favorite outfit is a good thing, not a bad one."

"Yeah. We know that. I just need to make sure Ainsley Beal does too."

I'm laying on his lap in an underwater molded lounger with his arms around me, his body flush against mine, warm and hard underneath me. His finger twirls a long curl absent-mindedly. "Nate?"

"Yeah?"

"I really, really meant it when I said I wanted to take you on. Your music career, I mean."

"I don't have a music career."

"But you so easily could. Will you let me manage you? *Please?* You can't say no. You're too good."

I feel his chuckle more than hear it, if that's what it is. "One day. When there's time."

I turn over so I'm on top of him, facing him. Straddling him. "It's something you should *make* time for, Boone. I can help you. Please let me. I'm going to offer to manage Luke and Leo too. They're good enough, Nate. I really think you could all be hugely successful."

"You should offer it to them."

"But what about you? We can figure it out together. You could hire some help for your contracting business. Find some local guys who can step up and help you run it without being so involved in the day-in, day-out stuff. What about Shane?"

"What do you expect me to do, Rox, take off on tour for months on end? That's not really something that can happen right now."

"You could do local shows. Start with Nashville."

He's quiet, still twirling a lock of my hair.

"I have to go back tomorrow," I tell him gently. "I've got a meeting with a new artist I'm taking on. She's flying up from Austin."

"Why don't I drive you in."

"I have a few other things to take care of too. I've offered to take on another new artist as well. Her name's Ivy Laine. She lives in New York. I'll probably have to go and meet with her at some point soon."

More silence.

"Nate?"

"What do you want me to say, Roxie? Go to Nashville? Go to New York? Take on ten new artists so there's no time for anything else? Leave us behind and don't come back?"

It's not what I was expecting him to say. But he's got a point. "I'll come back. Of course I will."

"When?"

"When…I can."

"Well, that's not really good enough, is it?" He's pissed off now.

I climb off him and sit next to him. "Why are you mad? We knew we'd have to figure this out. I can't just move in, like, right now."

"Why not?"

"Well, because I have a job and a life in Nashville. And because…" I saw the way Ainsley Beal looked at me, dressed in his shirt and very little else. Like I was some kind of hussy who would no doubt be a terrible influence on Daisy. It doesn't matter that she's wrong about all of that. What matters is that her point of view holds so much weight in this situation. The thought of Nate losing Daisy because of me is one I can't tolerate. "I have a job and a life in Nashville," I say again.

"So, that's it?" he fumes. "You're leaving to go back to your *life* in Nashville? What about what happened here this weekend?"

"It was…perfect. Of course it was. But it doesn't mean I can just *not* go back to all the responsibilities I have and the people who are relying on me. You know that better than anyone."

He stands up, getting out of the hot tub with a splash, and wrapping a towel around his waist. "Okay, then. See you later. Have fun in Nashville."

I follow him, grabbing the other towel and wrapping it around me. "Nate. Why are you acting like this? I told you I had a meeting. I can come back in a few days. Or… soon." I actually have meetings all week and into the weekend, but right now doesn't seem the best time to tell him that.

"Fine, Rox. Maybe I'll see you in another eight years. Just make sure you give me a call when you find out I knocked you up this weekend since we spent the entire time having raw dog sex like there's no tomorrow."

His rage catches me off guard. "What do you expect from me, Boone? To just leave everything behind to move in with you and forget that I have a career and a life that I've spent a long time working my ass off to create? I have to figure out how it's going to work. And I will. But it might take some time."

Nate dries himself off and gets into bed, his body big and insanely…hard, even though we're arguing, if that's what we're doing. The sheet barely covers him. "I don't expect anything from you. Just forget that we finally found each other again after eight fucking years. Forget that we told each other we *loved* each other. Forget that we might have created a *baby*. But, hey, no big fucking deal. You go back to your *life*. Goodnight, Rox." He closes his eyes.

I sit on the bed, the towel still wrapped around me. "Nate. We can talk about this. We can make a plan. I said I would try to start delegating. And so did you."

His eyes open. "Except that there are certain things I can't delegate. Daisy's starting school tomorrow. I'm on the verge of losing her. Especially if I don't do everything I can to make sure she has a stable life and a routine. Which is here, Roxie. Unless I have to move to fucking Ohio because I lose custody so I can make sure she's okay. I can cut back on my work hours if that's what you want me to do. And I'm going to have to do that anyway. Shane's a good idea. I'll talk to him. But I can't move to Nashville. Not right now."

I nod, tears pricking behind my eyes at the sorrow in him. I lay down next to him. "I know. I'm sorry. I *want* to be with you, Nate, of course I do. I just…I don't want me being here to have any kind of negative influence on Ainsley Beal's decision."

"What do you mean? Why would it?"

"I feel like there were certain things that were obvious. And that she didn't approve of them. Or of me."

Nate exhales a laugh, but there's no humor in it. "Are you serious? Roxie. You're a superstar, a shining gem of a human being and the kind of success story someone like Ainsley Beal could only aspire to. Plus Daisy adores you. It goes without saying that *I'm* on my fucking *knees* for you. We've spent too long letting other people get in the way of us. The last thing I'm going to let happen now is for Ainsley Fucking *Beal* to get in the way of us. You let *me* handle Ainsley Beal. Okay?"

"Okay," I say softly.

"Roxie, I *love* you. I want to *marry* you. I want you to move in and I want to live with you and give you babies and grow old together. That's what I want. What I *don't* want is to waste any more time. I've done enough of that."

The thing is, he's right. I wasn't expecting it when I drove out here this weekend. To never leave. Or to never want to leave. But sometimes things happen for a reason. Sometimes, the timing feels just right. "You know what I want, Boone?"

"What?"

"I want to figure out how to make this work so much that I know we will. We're both going to start delegating a little more and I'm going to figure out how to spend more and more time here. Because it's where I want to be. And stay. And live. With you." I slowly lower the sheet. "You know what else I want?"

"What," he rasps.

I let my towel fall open. "I want you to agree to let me manage you. Because you're that good and you know you're that good." I ease my fist around his thick length, gently sliding my fingers over the moisture seeping from him as he gets fully hard. "What did you build your own recording studio for if you never wanted to use it, Boone, tell me that."

"We'll see," he groans.

"No. We're not going to 'see'. All you have to do is say yes. Say it." I touch my tongue to him, licking playfully. Flicking my tongue. Teasing him. "Say, 'yes, Roxie, I'll let you manage me.'"

"Okay." The word is low and husky.

"Yes?"

"*Yes.*" It's more of a growl than an answer, but I'll take it.

"Good boy. I'm going to reward you for that." I take more of him into my mouth, sucking and playing, then slowly releasing him. "You know what else I want?"

"What?"

"Your babies."

Nate's eyes are dark. With oceans of emotion.

I lick him again, coyly. "I mean, you *are* the love of my life, I've always known that. And a girl doesn't *not* want to get down and dirty and knocked up by the man of her dreams, especially when he's *this* freaking hot and well-hung, come on. And *especially* when he's the one she's been holding out for all this time."

Nate holds me and rolls me over, his heavy weight above me. His cock slides barely into me. But then he holds himself still. "Marry me, Tuck."

I blink up at him and I can't hold back my smile or my tears. "Yes," I whisper. "I'll marry you, Boone."

He kisses me and drives all the way inside me, the thick-skewering bulk of him forcing me to take everything. To *feel* everything. To drown in the pleasure of him.

There's a desperation to this lovemaking. We feel our losses and our fears. But we also feel the beauty of this life and the gift we've been given. Of finding each other again. Of diving in with everything we've got.

And never letting go.

ROXIE

"It was so nice to finally meet you, Sky. I'll let you know as soon as I hear back from the labels. I expect it to be soon, maybe even by the end of the week."

"Is it okay if I give you a hug?"

"Of course it is."

She's absolutely over the moon. It's such a fun part of this job. I'm literally making Sky Rose's dream come true and it's an amazing feeling.

I've only managed my brothers so far, and now Sky and a crazy-talented new artist, Ivy Laine, who just signed with me—and now Luke and Leo, who I talked to this morning and they're more than ready to run with it. I know I'll be able to convince Nate too, hopefully. We haven't finished that conversation yet, but I can sense the yearning in him. If he could just allow himself to follow his dream instead of only his duty.

"I wish I had more time to show you around Nashville tonight, Sky, but I've got some things I need to do today."

"I'm actually staying with some friends who live here, so they're going to show me all the hot spots. Thanks for everything, Roxie. Really. I still can't believe you're my manager."

"The talent is all yours. You're going to be selling out stadiums before you know it."

I invited Sky to meet with me in my apartment off Broadway, the one Kade keeps for me. I don't know who's at our warehouse right now and I wanted to meet with her uninterrupted. We've talked a few times over Zoom, but it's been fun to meet her in person. She's gorgeous and curvy, like a Texan pin-up girl, with a to-die-for voice.

She was actually referred to me through a very random phone call I got a few weeks ago, out of the blue, from a guy in New York. It was a crazy phone call. The guy introduced himself as Cash Maddox. I later looked him up and he's a billionaire who runs a hugely successful investment company in New York called Invested Enterprises. He was really honest about the situation he was in and it was actually sort of sweet and endearing. He said he'd totally fallen head over heels in love and he was doing everything he could think of to impress the girl, who happens to be Sky's sister, Dusty. Cash was trying to make all Dusty's dreams come true, he said, and one of those dreams was her sister's success. Cash told me he'd pay me for my time and basically begged me to check out Sky's Spotify.

So I did.

I could immediately hear the potential. She's put out two albums' worth of songs and has a decent following in and around Austin.

I have contacts at a label that's looking for young smoky female vocalists who walk the country-indie-pop line and who write their own catchy songs with interesting lyrics. It's a description that fits Sky to a T. And she's very, very hungry. She wants this more than anything, so I know she'll go the extra mile—which is what it takes for unknown solo artists to make it.

So I called Cash back and told him to put us in touch, I offered that day to manage her and she signed within the hour.

Once I see Sky to the elevator and we say our good-byes, I take a minute to call Nate.

"Hey, Tuck." I can tell he's driving.

"How'd the school drop-off go?"

"I stayed for a while to make sure she was settling in okay. She was a little nervous at first, but the teacher is real nice and Harper's in her class, so she was fine. I told Kristie I had a meeting in Nashville and she offered to pick Daisy up from school and take the girls back to their place."

"That's good, Nate. So you don't have to rush. Do you want to meet up after your meeting?"

"I was thinking about taking you out for an early dinner if you have time."

"I'll make time."

"Good girl. We're getting better at this, Tuck. You'll be happy to know I gave Shane a call and we're going to meet and talk about him maybe coming on board. He's job-hunting anyway and he was very interested. It kind of makes sense too. He knew Jed and Laney. He's got those same people skills that Jed had. So it could work. Thanks for thinking of it. I don't know why I never did."

"I'm so, so happy to hear that, Nate. I was actually thinking about calling Kristie after I talk to you. I've just met with Sky and she's fantastic. And I stopped by to see Luke and Leo like I told you I was going to. They had their pens ready before I even walked in the door. They signed with me."

"Sounds like your roster's getting pretty full, then."

"I've got room for one more."

I can hear his smile. "We can talk about that tonight."

"All right." I almost offer to come to the meeting with him, but I'm not sure that would be helpful. I'd be fully clothed this time, at least. But I figure he'll know best how to handle it. "Love you, Boone."

"Love you more, Roxie Tucker. I'm still not sure the entire weekend wasn't something I dreamed up."

"I keep having that same feeling myself. We can pinch each other and see if we're real."

"I had something else in mind."

I'm standing here grinning like a fool because I don't think I've ever been this happy. "That could maybe be arranged," I say coyly.

His laugh is husky. "Maybe?"

"Depends on what you had in mind."

"Well, it involves you being naked and wet and on your knees."

"Oh, well my plan was to be naked and wet with *you* on *your* knees."

"Dirty girl. You're right, that sounds even better." His deep, rasped voice makes my body clench in a *very* intimate place. "I can hardly wait. I miss you, darlin'."

"I miss you too, Boone."

"I'll give you a call as soon I can."

"Okay. I know it'll all go well at the meeting. I'll be thinking of you. Talk soon."

We end the call and I go check myself out in the mirror to make sure I don't look too hot and flushed because I love him and miss him so much.

Then I head down to the warehouse to see how my brothers are getting on with the next album they're supposed to be working on.

ROXIE

Our expansive warehouse complex in central Nashville takes up almost an entire city block. It has six apartments, a recording studio, an open area for hanging out, offices and meeting spaces, a large practice studio set up with most of our gear, and a roof garden. It also has a garage underneath it that's big enough to fit many of my brothers' cars and various motorcycles, cars they've bought for me, my pick-up truck, and even a tour bus.

The warehouse has been the beating heart of the Tucker Brothers Band operations for years now and is our headquarters and sometimes our home.

It's less busy than usual, because we've just come off of a tour and a lot of our crew are taking some time off. And there are fewer hangers-on now that Vaughn and Travis are both in serious relationships. Kade has always been a one-woman-at-a-time man and, since he apparently has a new one, there's not a single groupie in sight.

In fact, the place is empty except for loud music coming from the practice studio.

It's a miracle. They're actually practicing. Like they're supposed to be.

I walk past the main open area, with its walls covered in framed platinum and gold records, along with framed photography of the band and tour posters.

It always feels a little surreal, the juxtaposition of these symbols of success casually scattered amongst worn old furniture we've dragged along since those early, struggling days. It's an eclectic blend of superstar-level expensive furniture and hand-me-down thrift store purchases from long ago, mismatched armchairs and mid-century sofas that have seen so much traffic but tonight are empty.

We've kept it this way deliberately. Our apartments and homes might be glam and luxurious, but the main space in the warehouse has always been a reminder of our roots.

There was definitely nothing glamorous about our upbringing. We like having at least one space that spans from then until now, so we never lose sight of where we came from and how hard we've worked to get here.

It's one of the reasons we're so close. And why I can't be too mad at Travis and Vaughn for their dedicated interest in my well-being.

And now I get to see how Kade is going to react to

the news of his childhood, teen and early-twenties best friend shacking up with his little sister.

Of all my brothers, Kade and I are probably the closest. We talk to each other about stuff I wouldn't talk about with Travis or Vaughn. We have a lot of heart-to-hearts. And it was him—or how he might have felt about it at the time—more than anything else, that kept Nate and I apart.

I open the door.

The cavernous room vibrates with music. Twinkling string lights crisscross the dark-beamed ceilings. A large industrial-looking window runs along the top third of the far wall. It's tinted on the outside so no one can see in from the buildings around us and it lets in a muted light. Lamps are strewn around the space and Persian rugs are all over the floor. Someone once told us they were good for the acoustics so we've been collecting them ever since.

Vaughn is on his drums, banging away like the powerhouse he is, Kade's spinning out a new riff I haven't heard before and Travis sings along to its melody as his guitar harmonizes with new, intricate notes.

I notice Gigi sitting on a couch in the corner, reading a book—although I don't know how she can concentrate. Her long strawberry-blond hair catches light, like it always seems to do.

I'm a little surprised to see her here, but then I remember that the four of them were coming back here last night to see a gig.

They all look up when I walk in.

They play the last chord of the song, holding it. And then they stop.

All eyes are on me.

"Hi," I say, sort of amused that they're all staring at me like that. "Hi, Gigi."

"Hi, Roxie."

It occasionally strikes me when I see them, after not seeing them for a little while, that my brothers are stunning-looking men. They *look* like the rockstars they are. I'm their sister, so I don't think about it often, but when I look at them with fresh eyes every now and then, it's easy to see that my brothers would be considered extremely hot to most of humankind.

Vaughn spins one of his drumsticks. "See?" Maybe to Kade. "She's got a glow."

But they are, in fact, my brothers. And they annoy me as much as they endear themselves to me. Possibly more. "I do not have a *glow*."

"You sure do, honey pie."

I check out Kade's vibe. Exactly the way he's checking out mine.

"Hey, darlin'."

"Hey." I walk over to him. He definitely seems... lighter. The grimness that's been hanging over him for five straight months is completely gone. "I'm in love with him so you're just going to have to get used to it."

He gives me a slow, almost-amused, measured look. "Is that right?"

"Yes, it is right. *I* get to choose who I want to be with and I want *him*."

Kade smiles, almost like he finds the new "glowing" me sort of fascinating. "Well, shit."

"You're not allowed to be mad. It's up to us. Not them," I vaguely gesture to the others, "and not you."

"I called him."

This stuns me for a few seconds. "You did? When?"

"Half an hour or so ago."

God. They're eternally meddling in my life, all three of them. "What did you say?"

"I asked him what he was doing with my sister and he explained that the only reason he hasn't been with you all these years is out of respect for you and out of respect for me. But that if I tried to come between the two of you now he'll beat me to a bloody pulp."

"He said that?"

"Something along those lines. Might have been slightly more colorful."

I consider this for a few seconds. "What did you say?"

"I told him I would have killed him with my bare hands when you were fifteen. Maybe even when you were twenty."

"I think he knows that, Kade."

"He did."

"But I'm not fifteen anymore. *Or* twenty. And as much

as I appreciate y'all's undying concern for me, if you try to get in the way of me and Nate you can find yourselves a new manager."

Vaughn laughs and lets out a low whistle.

"Well, then," Kade says. "That's something we definitely don't want."

"Kade, I *love* him."

"So you keep saying, darlin'." I'm not expecting it but he grins. "I get it, all right? You've both pleaded your case and it's obvious this is something that's been brewing for a long time. I didn't see it, but then again, you didn't want me to. And neither did he."

"I'm okay," I promise him. "He's the best thing. Just give us your blessing and leave us to it already."

Kade laughs. Honestly, it's been a while since I heard him laugh.

"You're in a good mood," I observe sullenly, still riled.

"Stella agrees with him." Travis strums. "A *lot*."

"Where is she?" I ask.

"Asleep. In my apartment."

"All worn out by *the Magic Man*," jokes Vaughn, using one of the nicknames Kade was given by past girlfriends and eventually the media.

"Shut up, Vaughn," Travis and Kade say in unison.

It barely lands. "No one understands my sense of humor around here," Vaughn complains. "Except you, Gi."

She gives him a gentle smile.

Now that we've got the hard part out of the way, I'm bursting to tell them. "There were some interesting developments over the weekend. I signed Luke and Leo."

"To do what?"

"To be their manager."

All three of my brothers are speechless.

"They had this hoedown where they all got up and played. I couldn't *believe* it. They're incredible."

"No shit," Travis drawls. "They were always fucking good."

"And Nate."

"What about him?"

"He can sing. And I mean *sing*. He's so, so good. He's going to be your new opening act for the local shows—if I can talk him into it. He hasn't *actually* agreed to it yet but I know I can convince him."

"I don't doubt that," Travis laughs. "Where is Nate? Didn't he have a meeting in the city today?"

"Yes. He's meeting with Ainsley Beal," I tell them. "Now."

"That uptight chick who stopped by his house yesterday?" Vaughn asks.

"Yep. The social worker. Their office is here in Nashville. I think he said Montgomery Street. I'm going to meet up with him after."

Gigi comes over. "He's at a social services office on Montgomery Street? I used to work there."

"You did?"

"I did one of my placements there." I'd forgotten that detail. Gigi's a social worker. She's also an actual saint. She's absolutely gorgeous and incredibly nice, but she's also got this feisty undertone to her personality that I love about her. She's got Vaughn so thoroughly wrapped around her little finger he can hardly see straight.

"Do you…*know* Ainsley Beal?" I mean, maybe Gigi could put in a good word for us.

"Not well. But I do know Jenny Jenkins, the director. She helped me out a lot during my placement there. She and I have coffee whenever I'm in Nashville."

"So she'd be…Ainsley Beal's boss?"

"Yes. She oversees all the cases and makes the final decisions about what's submitted to the judges and so on."

Vaughn's arm goes gently around Gigi's shoulders. "I was drinking out of that whiskey flask, like you told me to do whenever I had the urge, Gi. And I had the rolled-up cigarette. Probably didn't look too good to a social worker."

Gi looks up at him. Then at me. "No, that wouldn't have looked too good."

"Let's go down there," Vaughn suggests. "Gi can talk to Ainsley Beal's boss and explain everything. It might help."

I'm not sure it's a good idea. "I don't know. I could call Nate and see if that would be okay with him."

I try his number but it goes straight to voicemail. Because he's in the middle of the meeting, obviously.

"We'll all go," Travis says. "We got him partly into this mess. If there's something we can do to get him out of it, we should. If it makes even a small amount of difference, it could mean the difference between him getting custody of Daisy or losing it."

"I don't know if we should interfere."

It's Gigi who convinces me. "Definitely worth a try. Besides, Jenny's been begging me to meet the Tucker brothers for ages. She's a *huge* fan."

Kade slings his bass guitar from around his chest and sets it on its stand. "The limo's parked out front. Let's go."

29

___

NATE

"Mr. Boone." Ainsley Beal rises from her chair as soon as I'm shown into her office. She's wearing the same clothes she was wearing yesterday, or something very similar. Her office matches her look. Drab, outdated and like she went out of her way to make all the colors as muted and dull as possible. I can't help noticing there's a tired basket of faded children's toys next to her desk. Like a thousand kids have passed through here, headed to the fate *she* decides for them.

She does not look pleased to see me.

I offer her my hand and this time she takes it, but her handshake is cold and limp.

"Ms. Beal. Thank you for taking the time to see me."

"I saw you'd been added to my schedule. Mr. Boone, it's really not necessary for you to be h—"

"It *is* necessary." *Tone it down, fucker.* I force my voice to sound less aggressive. "If you'll just give me a few minutes to explain what was going on yesterday when you arrived, I'd really appreciate it."

She nods, like she's tuning in to my desperation. "Fine. Take a seat."

I sit.

It's a few seconds before either of us speaks. The door of the office has been left open and there's normal, everyday conversation going on out there. It feels like a sunny day is happening everywhere but in this room. In here, we're somehow mired in gloom.

"Did you manage to get Daisy enrolled for school on time?" she asks, condescendingly, if I'm not mistaken.

Do not lose your patience. Do not lose your patience. "Yes, with no problems at all. She's very happy in her class with the friends she's known all her life. And she really likes her teacher."

"That's nice." Disinterestedly. "Mr. Boone, I've begun to write up my recommendation to the judge. In light of information gathered during the home visit—"

"Ms. Beal. What you think you saw yesterday was not what you actually saw." That doesn't sound quite right but I keep going. "Our visitors were old friends and—"

"Mr. Boone. Please understand I have only Daisy's best interests at heart. Amanda Sullivan-Smith's lawyers have been very thorough in their investigation into your… *lifestyle*, and I'm afraid, now that I've seen it first-hand, I tend to agree that some of your extra-curricular activities are less than desirable. We want the most stable environment as possible for Daisy."

You've got to be fucking kidding me. "She is in a stable environment. I'm sure you're aware that children are happiest when they're in a familiar setting, surrounded by familiar people they know, love and trust. And I don't have a *lifestyle*, Ms. Beal. I work and I take care of Daisy."

Ainsley Beal takes a long look at me. Obviously sticking to whatever judgments she made about me yesterday. "And you sometimes entertain…guests. Which is the kind of activity that might negatively influence and possibly emotionally scar the six-year-old who happens to be in your care."

Emotionally *scar*? "What *activity*, exactly, are you referring to, Ms. Beal?"

Of course I know what fucking activity she's referring to, and I can't help but blazingly see that this conversation is not helping my case. Ainsley Beal probably hasn't "entertained guests" this millennium. Which could explain her atrocious mood.

There's a loud scream from the main office, which makes Ainsley Beal jump.

I get up from my chair and go to see if maybe there's a break-in or something. Ainsley Beal follows me.

There's a stretch limo parked outside the front windows of the office.

What the fuck.

Getting out of that limo are none other than the Tucker Brothers Band. Dressed like they just stepped off stage.

Please, no.

More excitable squeals, from several of the office girls as they watch Travis, Kade and Vaughn get out of their limo.

A girl with long blond hair is holding Vaughn's hand.

And then Roxie steps out.

For a second I forget everything else. The squeals of all the women in the office. The scowl on Ainsley Beal's face. The small box in my pocket, a purchase I made before this meeting. The fact that I'm probably going to be moving to fucking Ohio.

Nothing will fit in my brain except the flood of awe I'm being swept away by, because she's so damn beautiful it physically hurts.

She's wearing the flower-patterned dress she put on this morning, and her cowgirl boots. Her dark hair cascades in waves over her shoulders, all the way down to her waist, those little ringlets at the ends curling playfully. Her eyes are blue even from a distance, her lips full and pink and so luscious my cock starts to thicken despite the hell I'm currently in the middle of. *Fuck.*

I'm so fucking in love with her I feel like it might kill me, right here and right now, as though my heart is getting ready to burst into flames at the sight of her.

A slew of bodyguards surround the Tuckers as they make their way to the door.

They open it.

There are maybe five or six women in the office and every single one of them is squealing and/or crying. One of them, easily the oldest, who might be in her mid-forties, hugs the blond girl who's still holding Vaughn's hand. "You brought him! You brought *all* of them! *Eeee!*"

One of the girls literally swoons and someone helps her into a chair.

The blond with Vaughn smiles at him, lightly running her hand over his tattooed arm, as though showing him off. "Jenny, this is Vaughn. Vaughn, Jenny was *so* helpful when I was doing my placement here. She's become a good friend."

"Well, any good friend of my angel's is a good friend of mine. The pleasure's mine, Jenny." Vaughn kisses the back of Jenny's hand and she has to hold onto the side of her desk with the other hand as she swoons like a teenager.

"I am *such* a huge fan," she gushes. "Vaughn *Tucker*. And *Travis*. *Kade, oh my god.* Would you mind terribly if I got an autograph?"

Roxie comes over to me. All I really want to do is kiss her. "Nate, I tried to call. They thought it might help if they came and explained things themselves. I'm sorry."

"It's all right, darlin'." My voice sounds graveled and defeated.

I'm going to lose them both.

I'm going to end up living in Ohio because what if she wakes up from her nightmares and she needs me? Roxie won't want to move to suburban Cincinnati. She might fly in occasionally between tours and we can pretend that a long-distance relationship is working for a while, until she gets bored with it and decides it isn't.

My soul feels jaded and battered. I have this weird feeling of not caring about anything anymore, because the only two things I *do* care about are slipping through my fingers no matter how hard I try to hold on.

Even so, I don't have it in me not to fight for them with everything I've got. I *didn't* fight for her when I was nineteen and the regret still sits like a big black hole in the middle of my life, inking everything.

Fuck it. I was going to wait until tonight but she's too fucking beautiful to wait for anything. I never seem to get the timing right anyway so now seems like as good a time as any.

I take the small velvet box out of my pocket and get down on one knee. "This is possibly the least romantic place to do this, but there's something I really need to ask you, Tuck. I've waited so long and I've missed you so much that the place doesn't matter. Wherever you are is the right place. You said yes once but I didn't have a ring, so I stopped off on the way here and got you the biggest one they had."

Roxie puts her hands over her mouth in shock. It's not

all shock though. She's smiling and crying at the same time.

The rest of the office goes quiet. I think. I don't care about them. I only care about her.

"Roxanne Savannah Tucker, I've always loved you and I always will. You're the only one I've ever wanted. You're the one. You've always been the one. Please marry me, Tuck. I love you so much."

Roxie's tears spill over, wetting her cheeks. She leans down to hug me. "*Yes*." I slide the ring onto her finger and pick her up, holding her in my arms, kissing her. *Kissing* her. Like we're the only two people in the world.

Cheers erupt. Gasps. Whistles. More of that gleeful squealing.

When we finally come up for air, I glance over at our audience. I set Roxie down but I keep my arm wrapped around her.

Kade walks over to us. He offers his hand and I take it. He pulls me into a man-hug, murmuring, "You know I'll fucking kill you if there's ever a need."

"Not if I kill you first, brother."

It's an inside joke that goes way, way back.

To the room, Vaughn says, "Excuse me, everyone. Since we obviously have some celebrating to do, we'd like to invite you all back to our warehouse where we can continue this meeting and raise a toast to our darlin' sister Roxie and our now-brother in the true sense of the word —even though he's always been that. And just to clarify,"

—to Ainsley Beal—"*I'll* be drinking water out of my champagne glass since I don't partake in any alcohol or drugs of any variety whatsoever. I'd also like to chip in my two cents that Nate Boone over here is the best father to that little Daisy of any father I've ever seen. Hell, I'd ask him to adopt *me*—if I didn't already have my savior and true love Gi looking after me. And I have no doubt our boy Nate is going to make a damn good husband. I mean, *look* at him, what's not to love? The three of them are going to live happily ever after like they all fu—for sure deserve to. So how about it, Jenny? Ainsley? Girls? How do you feel about a ride in the limo, a toast, and an exclusive first performance of our brand new song? I think we could also throw in some VIP passes and front row tickets to our next show. And maybe even a 5-star hotel for the night. You in?"

More screaming, gasping, clutching and swooning.

Ainsley Beal hasn't said a word this whole time. She almost seems like she's in shock.

"Ms. Beal?" Vaughn says. "What do you say?"

Ainsley Beal is gazing at Kade. "You're the *Tucker Brothers*? You're really...*Kade Tucker*? The bass player? *The...Magic Man?*"

"Yes, ma'am," Kade answers.

Travis and Vaughn try to muffle their laughter but can't.

So she's not immune. Even buttoned-up welfare officers have their types, I guess.

So, since it looks like our meeting will resume when we get to the warehouse because Jenny has decided to close up the office early for the day, I scoop Roxie into my arms and follow the Tuckers, Jenny, the office girls and a starstruck Ainsley Beal into the limo.

30

———

ROXIE

Two weeks later...

I SET the little stick on top of its box on the marble bathroom counter. As I wash my hands, I watch the small plus sign vibrantly ink itself onto the little screen.

I really am.

I'm pregnant with Nate Boone's baby.

Not surprisingly, considering what we've spent the past few weeks doing. A *lot*.

I already knew but I wanted to wait until I was sure. Letting myself adjust to the the newness of my unfolding, surreal, enchanted new reality.

I'm almost a week late.

Our babies will grow up here on the farm and we'll give them the same golden summers we had, running free and living their best lives.

After spending the past few days in Nashville, I drove back last night. I wanted to wait until I got *home* to take the test. And this place already feels like it's that. The farm has always felt like home, and Nate's—*our,* he keeps reminding me—house feels like a luxurious haven, with my dreamscape of a little family so excited to see me after a few days away.

Daisy has become my little shadow. She is the gentlest, sweetest child. We already share a surprisingly profound bond, because we both know what huge, tragic loss feels like and we also adore our Nate. We just *love* him, with our whole hearts. And he loves us.

He brings us presents and cooks for us. The three of us read Daisy's stories together and we laugh at the voices Nate uses for the different characters. He plays his—pink, which makes it even better—guitar for us. If we beg, he sings to us. And I fall in love with him all over again.

With Dakota and Tobias's help, we're beginning to plan our wedding. It'll take place at the lodge, of course, with our families around us. Daisy has an important role as the flower girl. We have plenty of musicians on hand to provide the music. We're even going to stay in the cottage with the pink door on our wedding night.

It's been a whirlwind three weeks, no doubt about that. But then again, we had eight years to prepare for it. To pine for each other and to miss out on what could have been. Once we found each other again, we let ourselves fall as fast and as hard as we'd always wanted to.

I'd never thought much about having babies. *Or getting married.* A month ago, I wasn't sure I wanted either. I can now see that, somewhere behind my subconscious, it's because he left that August day and never came back. I wanted to marry *him* and have *his* babies. *He* was the one I loved.

I still can't believe he's mine and that I get to *keep* him. I sometimes wake up and wonder if finding him again was all just a beautiful dream.

Standing in front of the mirror, I place my hands on my flat belly. "Hey, little one," I whisper. "I love you." *I already do, so much it hurts.* The tiny seed of our wild love, planted inside me.

I put on a sundress and brush my hair.

Then I make my way down the curving wooden staircase designed by Jed, Nate told me, taking in the spectacular view of the river and the dappled sunlight outside the wall of windows.

I've set up the home office Nate built for me, and I've hired Kristie Anderson to take on some of my workload. She's fun, organized, whip-smart and she's not easily intimidated. Which makes her perfect for the job. She also has several contacts in the music industry she used to work with—all women who took time off to have babies but are experienced—who might also be able to join our team.

It could work out well since I've suddenly got a full list

of clients but I've also promised Nate I'd spend more time at home.

And Nate hired Kristie's husband Shane to help manage his business. Because Shane's so eager to prove himself, and he's a quick learner and is extremely good at what he does, Nate's been able to cut way back on his hours.

Shane's vision for property development is also very much in line with Nate's. Nate told me all about the group from Seattle who wanted to build seven hundred houses on the farm next to Sugar Mountain, and that he'd killed the deal. Both Shane and Nate are dedicated to developing land so that it makes sense to the Tennesseans who have farmed it for generations. Which made me love him even more, if that was possible.

My hot rockstar of a fiancé didn't actually "sign" with me because we didn't see the need to bother with the paperwork, but he's agreed to cut an album. He already has a recording studio, after all. And it turns out he's got enough original material for three entire records. We're going through them to decide which ones to put on his first album. Kade's going to do some of the production and I plan to start approaching record labels next week.

Luke and Leo got a record deal with one of the bigger labels—the first one I approached—the week after the hoedown. The deal will easily ensure that they can hire as many farmhands as they want as they record and tour. In fact, they couldn't believe it when I told them how much money they'd just made.

My brothers insisted that Luke, Leo and Nate come to the warehouse and show them what I'd been raving about. And it's been decided: the opening acts for The Tucker Brothers Band's next tour will be, on alternating nights, Ruby on one night and Luke and Leo on the other.

Nate's not making any plans to perform. Not until after we hear back from Social Services. We've also decided to wait to take a honeymoon until things are settled. Nate joked darkly about honeymooning in Cincinnati and I told him we'll take it as it comes. What-ever happens, we'll stay together.

I walk into the kitchen to find Daisy and Nate sitting at the table, heads bent over the picture they're coloring. Her homework assignment was to create a piece of art with the first letter of her name, and to get one of her favorite people to help her color it.

They both look up when I walk in. "Miss Roxie, look! My D has butterflies around it! Just like on my necklace you gave me." She hasn't taken it off since I put it on her.

"And they're pink," I smile, kissing her blond head.

"Hey, beautiful," Nate drawls, smiling that slow smile I fell in love with so many years ago. Each time I see it, the love just compounds itself like a spiraling galaxy of stars. I lean to kiss his head too but he slides his warm palm under my hair and kisses my lips.

Daisy grins. "Uncle Nate, you love Miss Roxie *so much*," she giggles.

"I sure do, darlin'."

I go over to the stove to put the kettle on. "I'm craving hot cocoa with marshmallows. Who else wants some?"

"Me!" Daisy says.

Familiar, beloved country music is playing softly in the background. The house is clean and tidy and the flowers Daisy picked from Aunt Lou's garden are in a vase on the table, infusing the air with their soft fragrance.

Everything looks so inviting and homely, I can't help but wish Ainsley Beal could see us now.

As it turned out, Jenny Jenkins decided to take over Nate and Daisy's case after the day they visited the warehouse, declaring it "a high-profile and high-priority case" and one that needed to be handled by the department's director.

Nate's hopeful, but there haven't been any other home visits. Each time he calls, he's told that they're still waiting for the judge's deliberation.

Nate's phone rings from where it's sitting on the table.

We can both see the name on the screen.

Jenny Jenkins.

We exchange a glance and Nate answers the call. "Hi, Jenny…good, thanks…yes…okay…of course…you did? Can you…yes, we're home all day…all right, we'll see you soon."

He ends the call. That little furrow is back, the one

that always shows up when he's stressed about something —and especially when this particular topic is mentioned.

"Jenny's in the area and she said she'd like to stop in to see us."

"Oh. Well, that's good." I was just thinking it would be the perfect time for a home visit.

"Is Jenny the new lady who's deciding if I can live with you?" Daisy asks, her little face worried now.

"Yes. She said she has some news."

I'm almost afraid to ask it. "What news?"

"She said she'd like to discuss that with us in person. She's only ten minutes away."

Daisy's eyes fill with tears. "I'm scared," she sobs.

Nate wipes her tears. "Don't be scared, sweetheart. Remember, we're a team. We stay together no matter what."

None of us says much as we wait. I busy myself with making four mugs of hot cocoa, and Nate and Daisy continue coloring.

There's the crunch of tires on gravel as a car pulls into the driveway.

Nate gets up to open the door.

Jenny Jenkins is dressed in a bright yellow pantsuit. The jacket is open and underneath she's wearing a Tucker Brothers Band tour t-shirt. The one Travis gave her the day she and the others came to the warehouse, signed by all three of my brothers. I'm almost wondering if she's taken it off since then. "*So* good to see you all," she beams, as Nate shows her in and offers her a seat. "You have a lovely home."

"Thank you."

She's a ray of sunshine compared to Ainsley Beal.

No one so upbeat could possibly be delivering bad news, could they?

Jenny places a large manila envelope on the table and we all stare at it. Daisy climbs onto Nate's lap and wraps her arms securely around his neck.

"Would you like a hot cocoa, Jenny?"

"I'd love one, thank you."

Once we're all seated, Jenny smiles. "I *was* in the area, but I also received this this morning and wanted to deliver it to you myself. As you know, I took over your case from Ainsley, partly because it's the least I could do after you basically made my *life* by bringing the Tucker brothers into the office." She sighs and clasps her hands together at the memory. "The experience had a profound effect on us all. The other reason I took over your case is because, after meeting her idol, Ainsley has decided to leave us to pursue her true passion."

Jenny pauses and I can't help myself. "What's her true passion?"

"She wants to become an accountant."

"Oh. Okay." I guess it makes sense. Either way, we've all been hoping and praying that our chances of keeping Daisy are far better with Jenny than they were with Ainsley.

Jenny pats the envelope. "It's from the judge. I was ninety-nine percent sure we had an airtight case. The recommendation I submitted was very highly in your favor. Since we witnessed the proposal firsthand—that was *so* romantic, by the way." More sighing and hand-clasping.

Nate finally says, "Does that mean…?"

"And since you *will* be providing a more traditional family unit once you're married, which was the main concern of Mrs. Sullivan-Smith's, the contesting party really can't be favored for that reason alone."

I can tell that Nate's about to grab the envelope and rip it open. "What was the judge's decision, then?"

Jenny smiles. Is it a letting-you-down-gently smile or a triumphant smile? It's hard to tell. But then she finally says it. "You've been awarded full custody which clears the path for a legal adoption. I can help you start that ball rolling now if you'd like me to. Congratulations."

Daisy's tear-filled eyes are wide as she looks up at Nate. "Does that mean I can stay?"

"Yes, princess. It means you can stay."

Daisy squeals and hugs Nate. Nate looks so relieved he sort of slumps back in his chair.

"You make a beautiful family," Jenny says.

I was going to wait to tell Nate tonight but now seems like the perfect time. "We're actually going to be a family of four in around eight and a half months. Daisy's getting a little brother or sister."

IT'S BEEN A BUSY DAY. Jenny felt like an unexpected friend by the time she left and we've made plans to meet again at the warehouse for a get-together. Then we took Daisy over to the farmhouse and told everyone the good news. It turned into a huge celebration party. And, when I told them our other good news, Aunt Lou and Betty-Ann both had to sit down because they were so overcome with joy.

I FaceTimed my brothers, who were all together working on their album, and in between comments like, *Fuck, that Nate Boone doesn't mess around*, they were as emotional as my brothers get—which was sort of adorably emotional. Before I hung up I told them all I loved them.

It's late now. As we were reading Daisy her story and tucking her in tonight, she said that now she has a Mommy and Daddy in heaven and a Mommy and Daddy down here. She tried the words out and they slid surprisingly easily into place.

I get into bed, savoring the feel of the Egyptian cotton sheets warmed by Nate's big, always-running-hot body. He's reading his iPad, which he puts to the side as soon as I crawl in beside him.

He takes me in his arms and gazes deeply into my eyes. "Have I told the stunningly beautiful mother of my babies how much I love her yet today?"

"Maybe..." I pretend to mull it over... "twenty times."

"Well, that's not nearly enough. I *love* you, Roxie Tucker. Thank you for making me the happiest man in the world." He kisses me with tender lust, which gets hungrier and more intimate, until my entire body is radiating heat.

Then he kisses his way slowly down my body, taking his time, sucking and licking my nipples until they're budded and rosy.

Nate kisses my stomach, lingering there. "Hey, little baby," he murmurs. "I'm your Daddy. We love you so much. We're going to have such a beautiful life together. You've got the most gorgeous mama in the whole world and the sweetest big sister. We can't wait to meet you."

He moves lower, pinning my legs as he takes everything he wants, feasting languidly, sucking, licking, sliding his fingers inside, until the waves crest and break in starry, luscious bursts.

Then he climbs up my body, laying himself over me. He pushes his big cock into my slippery, still-pulsing pussy, until he's deep, deep inside. I'm so tightly around him, pulling his release from him lovingly with my own wild pleasure.

"I love you, Nate Boone," I whisper, until my whispers turn to moans and we come together, drowning and floating in the beautiful bliss of our own happily ever after.

ROXIE

Eight and a half months later...

NATE and I got married on New Year's Eve, surrounded by our family.

The lodge was decorated with candles and white roses. White roses were also embroidered into my veil and into the train of my wedding dress, which was made by an up-and-coming designer named Lila Bailey, whose designs happen to be all the rage. She also designed Daisy's dress.

My dress was fashioned to accommodate my growing belly. We found out what we're having. Another girl. We've decided to name her Jasmine Savannah Louise Tucker Boone. When I told Aunt Lou the middle names we've chosen she said, *child, that's quite a name,* through her tears.

Dakota was my maid of honor and Gigi, Ruby and Stella were my bridesmaids. The groom's party included Luke, Leo, Tobias and all three of my brothers.

Daisy was, of course, the flower girl. She not only scattered white rose petals she also carried our rings, a job she took very seriously and handled beautifully.

Jenny Jenkins came to the wedding and has become a friend. She was able to expedite the adoption process, which can sometimes take up to a year. Daisy legally became our daughter the day after our wedding. We talked it through with her and she decided to change her name to Daisy Abigail O'Leary-Boone.

She's thriving in school. She's made a lot of new friends, but she and Harper are still besties.

Daisy got a pony for her seventh birthday, named Cashew, who we've all fallen in love with. I never knew a horse could have so much personality. And for Christmas, Daisy got a puppy, a little Jack Russell she named Tink (after Tinker Bell). The two of them are inseparable. And since she's had Tink, who sleeps on her bed with her own little pink pillow and blanket, Daisy hasn't had a single nightmare.

Daisy's Aunt Amanda came to visit us with her family just before Christmas. Dakota and Tobias gave them a complimentary cabin at the lodge for a weekend—which was very generous, since the lodge is fully booked out for an entire year in advance. They do occasionally have cancelations, but they also have a waiting list. The restaurant just won some award for top five in Tennessee and the lodge was recently written up in a national magazine, named "Best New Must-Visit Destination."

One of my favorite things about my life on Sugar Mountain is getting to see both Dakota and Tobias on practically a daily basis.

To her credit, Amanda tried to connect with Daisy, as much as a person can do with a child they barely know. Amanda's husband couldn't have been less interested. Their sons, who must have been around thirteen and fifteen, were the kind of teenagers who don't look you in the eye and grunt a returned greeting because they're being forced to. Nate had told me they were both big gamers, and they had that look, of kids who spend most of their time sitting on the couch in a dimly-lit room eating junk food. When Nate asked them if they wanted to help with a fence he was repairing on the farm, they glared at him like he'd sprouted wings.

Amanda had tears in her eyes when they left and Daisy did too, for a very different reason. Needless to say, we were extra thankful that night that things turned out the way they did.

My job has become much easier now that I have Kristie. We've become close. She's so good at her job, I can work almost entirely from home. Nate insisted I take it easier now that I'm getting further along in my pregnancy. And I do get tired. Turns out growing a human is exhausting some days, especially since I had morning sickness for most of the first trimester. Once I hit the second trimester though, I haven't been able to stop eating. Nate brings me cheesecakes and pickles and anything else I crave.

Kristie and I hired a young assistant manager named Tia Oakley—an absolute live wire—who travels with the bands when they're on tour and handles the on-the-ground logistics. With FaceTime and Zoom, we can keep in close contact and I can help make sure things are running smoothly from my home office. It wouldn't have worked three or four years ago, but my brothers have their own fiancées and wives now to keep them in line. And they're more mellow than they used to be. They've seasoned into their fame and status and are more content to take things at a less frenetic pace than we used to.

Their latest album went platinum in one week. Ruby's also went platinum and so did Kade's solo album. Sky Rose's and Ivy Laine's both went gold.

Nate has brought Shane Anderson on as a co-partner in his business. Which means Shane has taken on more responsibility and will earn sweat equity in the company. It also means Nate can take a big step back from the daily operations and spend more time with us.

Nate has enough money for us to retire if we wanted to. I was actually shocked by how much money he has, especially since he's so choosy about the kind of projects he'll take on. He told me that, just because he refuses to sell out to out-of-state corporations doesn't mean the deals are any less lucrative. He's also been investing his money since he turned eighteen and turns out he's very good at it.

I *also* could retire us. All the acts we manage are doing extremely well, especially my brothers. And they gave me a good deal from the beginning. They also have a money manager who handles our own investments. Sometimes I look at my account balances and have to do a double-take.

Stepping back from his business has also allowed Nate to spend more time on his music, something I'm constantly encouraging him to do. We cut his first album —and I'm literally in awe of it—but he insisted on waiting until after the wedding and the adoption were all settled before I shop it.

Now he says that he wants to wait until after the baby. Late one night, I sort of convinced him to let me run with it and he sort of agreed.

I have some news for him. I got the call this morning.

I'm in the bath. It's hard to believe we've been married now for four months. The baby's kicking and I hold my belly gently as she moves around in there. "Any day now, we get to meet you, little Jazz. I can't wait." I'm five days overdue. And definitely a little nervous about how things will go. We have our plan to call my midwife who's based in Sugar Falls, and our doctor, as soon as I go into labor. The hospital is a twenty minute drive. I've got a bag packed and ready to go in Nate's truck.

My husband walks in, looking big and rough and sun-bronzed. And so gorgeous it takes my breath away.

"Holy fuck, my wife is a goddess."

"Hey, Boone."

"Hey, Tuck."

"Look. She's kicking."

He kneels down and kisses me. "Daisy's going to stay the night at Harper's." The girls have sleepovers all the time now. Harper got a puppy from the same litter as Tink and named her Elsa. The puppies are included in the sleepovers. "And Ma's invited us to dinner, if you're up to going out." He kisses my belly. "Hey, little baby."

"Sure, we can go up to the farmhouse. Dakota's back from her week in Montana and I want to hear all about it. Can you help me get out?" I laugh. "I feel like a beached whale."

"Well, you look like the most beautiful woman in the world to me."

He carefully helps me climb out of the bath. He gets a towel and dries me.

His hands are warm. "And sexy as fuck."

Then he helps me to the bed and lays me down, kissing me like I'm a lavish buffet laid out for him. My husband gets very turned on by my fertile body.

"You're getting me very, very fucking hard, Tuck. And you know what they say."

"What do they say?"

"Orgasms help get things started."

"Is that right?"

"Yes, it is right. Listen to your husband."

It's true that I've been seriously horny throughout my pregnancy. Just the sound of his voice is getting me wet. "Then do something about it, cowboy."

"Get on all fours," he growls, and I smile because his gruffness almost clashes with how gently he positions me.

I feel his hard shaft brush up against me and I arch up to him, *needing* him desperately. *"Please, Boone."*

He places his hand on the small of my back, steadying me. His gigantic cock drives slowly into me. I can feel him hesitating. Being cautious. Fingering my clit as he slides his thickness out, then slowly back in.

He feels so damn good, I'm already coming. I cry out, arching my back, taking more of him as I shatter with pleasure, the spasms milking his thick cock, teasing his release, which throbs and spills.

Nate holds me as the ripples calm, then he rolls me onto my side.

I lay still but I feel sort of wired. I'm still coming a little. The light clenches feel good, but also a little bit achy.

Nate goes into the bathroom and brings back a warm washcloth. He cleans me gently, taking his time, checking me and kissing me.

"How do you feel? Anything happening?"

"I'm not sure."

"Do you feel up to dinner?"

"I'm hungry."

He smiles. I'm always hungry. "Then let's go up to Ma's, have some dinner, then we can come back and have an early night."

"Okay."

Nate helps me get dressed in a white cotton oversized dress with lace frills on the sleeves.

I almost feel like I'm in a trance, like a piece of me is watching myself from somewhere nearby. Something is changing. "I think I'm getting close, Nate."

He looks at me alertly. "Should we get you to the hospital? I'll call the doctor."

"No. Not yet. Nothing's happening yet. But I think it's going to happen soon. Maybe tomorrow."

He picks me up like I'm made of fine china and carries me down to the truck. "You just say the word, Tuck."

On the short drive, I figure it's a good time to tell him. I'm sort of bursting with the news. "You got offered a record deal this morning, Mr. Boone."

He slides me a glance. "Yeah?"

It's the kind of reaction I expected. He's very humble about his outrageous talent.

"It's the best deal I've ever seen, Nate. By far the best offer I've ever been a part of. I told them you aren't willing to tour yet, aside from maybe a few Nashville shows. I said you didn't want to be obligated to travel because of your family, and they were fine with that. In fact, when I hesitated over that detail, they doubled their offer."

"Well, shit."

"Does that mean…you'll take it?"

"It means I love you." He takes my hand. "My little dealmaker with the magic touch. I never thought it was something that would actually happen for me, Tuck."

"Until I showed up and heard you sing, you crazy fool. I was *always* going to make it happen. Let's do this, Boone. Let's show everyone how good you are."

"Shit." Nate laughs and shakes his head, but I can see the awe in him. He's done it. He's created a life where he can finally pursue this long-buried dream because there's no longer anything standing in his way. Our gazes catch and he squeezes my hand because it's not the only one. *Both* his dreams have come true. *And all of mine have.* "All right, then. Let's do it."

I'd kiss him but I'm too big to move that far so I kiss the back of his hand. "Let's do it."

Everyone's at the farmhouse tonight. Like the night I arrived just over nine months ago. Dakota's been in Montana for a week, Tobias just got back from a friend's wedding in Nashville and Luke and Leo just finished up their first tour.

We tell them Nate's news and they couldn't be more excited.

Dakota tells us about her week in Montana. She's been dating her rodeo hero for a while now, and she's glowing. She regales us with stories of stepping onto what felt like the set of Yellowstone, making us laugh. But the long-distance detail is less than ideal. And Dakota was never going to leave Sugar Mountain. Or at least she better not, I tell her.

Tobias tells us all about the wedding he went to.

And Luke and Leo might as well be a comedy duo as they describe the last show of their tour.

Nate is close to me and Aunt Lou fusses over me.

The food is served and I sit back and just take it all in. The beautiful, boisterous Boone clan. My home and my family.

Aunt Lou smooths a curl of my hair. "Roxanne Savannah, you're quiet tonight. And you've barely touched your dinner. You're looking a bit flushed, dear."

I *feel* flushed. "I feel like something might be about to happen."

A slow, deep, rolling pain clenches through me with a violence that takes my breath away. I try to stand, gripping the edge of the table.

A gush of liquid bursts inside me and streams down my legs. "Oh my god."

"Lord above, her water just broke."

Everyone springs into action.

Nate's arms are around me. "Come on, Roxie, let's get you to the truck. I'm taking you to the hospital. Ma, call the doctor and the midwife and tell them we're on our way."

But before I can even take a step, another—much, much stronger—wave of pain rolls through me and I double over, groaning.

It's barely finished when another one follows.

I lose all sense of what's going on around me.

Another contraction rolls through me and it's the most painful thing that's ever happened to me in my life. But also, weirdly, the most powerful. The midwife told me not to fight it but to *allow* it. *Let the pain come, and then let the pain go.*

Another contraction hits me.

I hear loud moaning and then realize it's *me.*

"Nathan Waylon, she doesn't have time to get to the hospital. That baby's coming now."

Another contraction rages through me and I get a very, very strong urge to *push.*

I'm vaguely aware of being placed on the big, wide couch in the living room. Gentle hands are undressing me, wrapping towels and blankets around me.

I'm clutching Nate's hand like a vice grip. *I need him.* I can hear his voice, murmuring in my ear. "I'm here, Tuck. You're just fine. The doctor and midwife are on their way. Everything's okay."

Someone's ordering someone else to get towels and boil water.

Someone else is talking about all the calves they've birthed over the years and how it's no different.

People are around me, helping me. Their hands feel

efficient and sure and this calms me. Their voices are so familiar to me, so full of love and protective concern for us, it makes me cry.

The next contraction just about tears me open—or at least that's how it feels. The moans are loud now.

Another contraction comes and this one's different. Much, much stronger but also…there's a give. I can use that. I can *push*.

I *have* to push.

Time becomes elastic. I can't tell how long I've been here.

Nate's low voice is a croon. I'm gripping his hand and he's talking me through it. I use his voice as an anchor I can hold onto. *I've got you, baby, I'm not letting go. You're doing so well. You're so strong and beautiful. I love you so much. Push this baby out, Tuck.*

It happens again and the push is just so wildly painful but it also feels like it's helping. It's moving. There's a relief at the end of it.

And again. It hurts so much the moaning sounds more like a scream.

"That's it, darlin'." Aunt Lou. "I can see her head. Push again."

I do. I have to. I cry out. And I feel a stretching burn that gives way to an unbelievable relief.

"That's a good girl. Here she is. Her head's out. One more push. A nice big one."

The push happens whether I want it to or not—and I

do, so, so much. I go with it, letting the pain come, and letting the pain go.

And I feel the baby slide from my body.

"Lord above, she's perfect," someone gasps.

The relief is indescribable.

The wrapped baby is given to Nate and he holds the tiny bundle of her so carefully, gazing down at her. Then he places her on my chest.

I start to return to myself and I can see Nate's face, so full of love, and I just have never seen anything so beautiful in my whole life.

And then I look at my baby, safe in my arms. They're right. She is perfect. She has a little thatch of dark hair. I fall instantly in love with her and it's the most intense feeling. "She's so beautiful."

Nate kisses me. "Just like her mama." And he kisses our baby. "Welcome to the world, Jasmine Savannah Louise Tucker Boone."

Thank you so much for reading **Nashville Lights**! If you enjoyed this book, please consider leaving a quick review or rating on Amazon.

Want to see what happens with Nate and Roxie two years down the road? Get the free bonus epilogue here: https://BookHip.com/FZBMAQP

Below I've included the first chapter of **Nashville Days,** the first book in the **Music City Lovers** series, starring Travis and Ruby.

I've also included a sneak peek of Vaughn and Gigi's book, **Nashville Nights**.

xoxo,
Julie

Please come join my Facebook reader group, Julie Capulet's Romantics, where I share cover reveals, insider info and we discuss all things romance!

Sign up for my newsletter to receive my free bonus content and get access to sneak peeks and exclusive giveaways!

Visit my website @ www.juliecapulet.com

Every song he wrote was about a girl he hadn't met yet. Then she walked into his life.

Travis Tucker is a country-rock superstar. With four number one albums, sold-out tours and millions of fans, he's living the dream. But somewhere along the way, the spotlight lost its shine. Travis can never find the one thing he's been writing all his songs about: *real* love. So he decides to buy himself a country getaway to work on his next record and clear his head.

Ruby Hayes is a small town girl with big dreams. Finally free of boarding school, she plans on spending the summer writing songs on the piano in the abandoned farmhouse next door. Then she's on her way to Nashville.

When Travis finds Ruby, singing like an angel at his piano, he falls *hard*. Now that he's finally found the girl he's been searching for, Ruby ignites in him a wild obsession that's hotter than the Tennessee sun. And she has no idea who he is.

For Ruby, things get complicated. With a voice that's somehow familiar, like he's already a part of her, Travis is a temptation she can't resist.

The summer becomes a feverish haze of hot nights, shared lyrics, and the kind of spark that blazes into wildfire.

But summer can't last forever. Can their love survive beyond it, with the demands of Travis's high-profile life, Ruby's ambition and a jealous best friend threatening to come between them?

Or is this a love story written in both the music and the stars?

Nashville Days is a steamy standalone small town rockstar romance starring a hot, hopelessly romantic lead singer and the sweet, sassy songbird who steals his heart. Perfect for fans of Elsie Silver.

Music City Lovers

Chapter One

TRAVIS

"I want to thank ya'll for coming out tonight, Austin. You know we love you." The crowd roars.

We play our last song, our newest number one hit. I can barely hear my own voice as a hundred thousand people sing along with me. It's a crazy feeling, having *this* many souls touched by your words and so fully invested, singing their goddamn hearts out. They know every note. They've lived their lives to these lyrics. They've loved, cried and laughed to these tunes. They're filling up the night with their emotion, swaying to the slow rhythm. The lights of their phones shine like a galaxy of stars.

And when we hit that final chord, the thundering cheer of the crowd is deafening. Vaughn climbs down from his drums and the three of us stand there together on stage for a few seconds, taking it all in. The applause of a hundred thousand people is something you don't ever really get used to. The adrenaline rush is just as pure as it was the very first time.

We take a final bow and exit the stage, where a swarm of security surrounds us and ushers us through a bullet-proof corridor toward our tour bus. I can still hear them chanting my name. But we've done our encores after playing for three and a half hours. We're getting close to the end of our 48-show, 38-city tour and I'm feeling it.

The highs and lows and the creeping exhaustion that sets in after giving it everything you've got for months on end. We have two final shows left, both at home in Nashville. It's been by far our biggest tour yet.

I feel lit by the crowd, the music, the whiskey and the wine, the satisfaction of pouring my heart and soul into something real. Something that touches people and connects them. Every single show has been sold out. Our record is number one. Four of our songs are in the top ten. And the momentum just keeps on building.

We get to the bus and it's crowded, with groupies and people from the band and hangers-on. Our opening act, Jackson Cole, and his entourage are here, like they always seem to be. The fame and the women are new to him. He's overdosing and finding his feet, maybe. Riding our wave, to a certain extent, but whatever.

Vaughn pours three shots. Roxie gives Kade a hug, then me. She's relieved. Turns out our little sister is a genius at managing us. This tour has been bigger than we ever imagined. Now we can play our last two home shows and finally take a much-needed break before we start another 12-show West Coast tour next month.

I collapse onto one of the plush chairs. I tip back the whiskey Vaughn hands me. One of the groupies puts her hand on my arm and leans close to me. "Travis, you were amazing tonight. You're *so* good."

Do I know her? I don't think so. She might be a new one. It all starts to blur at the edges after a while. They all start looking the same. I'm no saint but I also need to *feel* something before I'll act on the constant stream of attention and adoration I happen to get. Right now I'm not feeling much of anything.

Kade hands me a beer.

"Hell," he says, sitting in the chair next to mine and clinking his bottle against mine. "Texas always has insane crowds. I could hardly even hear us." As usual, Kade's new-ish girlfriend Carmen is hovering around him. Roxie's not a fan. Come to think of it, neither am I. I don't usually care much who my brothers hang out with, but this girl seems to have an effect on Kade that's messing with his head. He's more moody when she's around. Jackson joked that she's our Yoko, waiting in the wings, whispering in his ear all the time about running away together so he can work on his solo album. I don't think that's his plan. Not now, anyway. We're on too much of a roll. And I can't worry about it tonight.

Vaughn laughs and cranks up the music, chugging from the bottle of Jack he's holding. He's got a fat joint in his other hand. A groupie with a lot of piercings and a ridiculously short skirt puts a pink pill on his tongue. Another girl is unbuttoning his shirt. His black hair is unkempt and long. His eyes are bloodshot, which makes them look even more blue than usual.

Roxie pulls one of the girls away from him. "What did you give him?" She pries Vaughn's mouth open but he grins at her, sort of guiltily.

"Too late," he says.

"*Vaughn*," Roxie scolds him. "Booze and weed is one thing. You said no drugs."

"Come on, Rox, I'm celebrating. Give me one night."

"*One* night? You've had three whole *months* of nights."

"I'll go cold turkey after the tour," Vaughn tells her. "I'll take a break."

We've all heard that one before. My brother is out of control, is what it boils down to. And he's only getting worse.

Vaughn has always walked a fine line. Like our father did, until it killed him. Kade and I can easily keep up with our younger brother when it comes to the whiskey—and usually do—most of the time. The difference is, we have downtimes. We lay off when we're not touring. We clean up when we feel like it.

Cleaning up isn't something Vaughn's done in a while. I'm not sure he's even capable of it at this point. Kade and Roxie and I have talked about it. We decided to finish the tour, then we'll sit him down and talk it through with him. Get him some help or check him in somewhere if need be.

None of which is happening tonight.

We're driving all night tonight so we can get back to Nashville in the morning. There's no doubt this party will still be going when we get there.

This bus has been the hub of our non-stop bender all

the way through. We all got into a groove of it for the first month or two, but after a while you find yourself getting more and more strung out from the total lack of sleep and peace and quiet. Even before we left, we were hounded like this. We have a loft warehouse we've converted into apartments, a recording studio and an office headquarters in downtown Nashville. We tried to keep the location under wraps but our fans found out about it, like they always do.

"That show was mayhem," says Vaughn. Not that he minds. Mayhem might as well be Vaughn's middle name. As if to confirm this, he blows a couple of smoke rings at me.

Tonight I'm not in the mood to fight my way through crowds of people just so I can go to bed.

What I need is some real sleep. Uninterrupted by banging and knocking and people trying to get in.

I need a quiet place to hang out for a while, I decide. A secret getaway. An old house out in the country somewhere, far from the city and the rabid fans and the never-ending parade of groupies, where there's space and fresh air and days with nothing to do except write. I can't remember the last time I was *alone* for more than a few hours at a time.

I'll find myself someplace off the beaten track, where no one even knows I'm there. I'll sleep and daydream and clear my head. Maybe Vaughn can spend some time there too, and dry out. And Kade, without the girlfriend.

All three of us. We'll work on our next record. We'll write our masterpiece, uninterrupted.

I send a message to a real estate agent I sometimes use when I buy new properties. I have three houses: an apartment in Nashville that's part of our headquarters, my own house in Franklin outside Nashville that I need to get a lot more security for because people have set up fucking camps around the peripheral fences, and a condo in L.A. None of them will be either empty or quiet. I have a lot of friends and an open-door policy for the most part, which I'm now starting to severely regret. All my houses have become magnets for hangers-on and their non-stop parties.

I'm looking for another house, I text him. *A farm, maybe, at least a half hour outside Nashville. Something remote. Very private. Surrounded by a lot of land. Maybe with a barn or something I can soundproof and convert into a studio. ASAP.*

Three girls surround me. One of them touches the top button of my shirt. I'm not in the mood to party tonight, go figure. I'm strung out. *Burned* out. I'm twenty-five years old and I already feel like I'm hanging on to the end of a fraying rope. I've been burning the candle at both ends for as long as I can remember and I suddenly feel a new urge for some goddamn solitude.

One of the girls touches my hair. Another whispers in my ear. "You're *so* hot, Travis. I love you so much."

I don't even know her name.

One of the girls weaves her fingers through mine.

"We want to show you something in one of the bedrooms, Travis. *All* of us."

My phone pings with a message. It's from my real estate agent. Damn, he's fast. "Maybe later." I don't know, maybe I've become jaded. I don't want to fuck just for the hell of it, not that I ever really did. I'm not an out of control player like Vaughn and I'm not a soulful romantic like Kade. I fall somewhere in the middle. I have a good time without getting serious.

But sometimes—like right now—it occurs to me that I never quite *feel* as much as I wish I did. Never in a way that makes you want to hang on to it or get excited about it or make it last. Never in a way you'd write a goddamn song about. Which is too bad. Because I write a lot of songs. Songs about falling in love and chasing after that one and only true love because you think your heart will break if you can't spend every hour of every day with her until you die.

The truth is, I'm just guessing. Because I've never experienced anything close to that kind of intensity. Which, tonight, feels sort of … sad. All these desperate souls, looking for that one magical, elusive person they can fall in love with to the point that nothing and no one else matters.

Most of them will never find it. *I* might never find it.

Which is sort of tragic when you think about it.

Like now. Women are literally hanging off me. And I

feel exactly … nothing. No spark. No interest. Just … boredom. A craving for something *real.*

I stand up and move away, as much as I can in the smoky, noisy, jam-packed space. People are getting loose.

I check the message. *I've got a new listing you might want to see. It's been sitting empty for 4 years and needs some work but it's a premium property. Beaut house. 5 bedrooms. 40 mins east of Nville, remote. Sits on 100 fenced acres with its own pond, a large barn and 3 cabins. Listed at 3.5m. It's bank-owned and available immediately.*

I follow the link and scroll through the photos.

Wow. The place is mint, but he wasn't wrong. It looks dusty and unkempt. In a good way. In a no-one-will-ever-suspect-I'm-there kind of way. I'll leave it like that. I'll become a hermit for the next few weeks and completely tune out. There are pictures of the barn too. It's huge and rustic. And the old cabins, dotted around the property.

The offer is almost too fucking good to be true.

I text him back. *Let me know where to transfer the $. I'll pay cash tonight.*

I'll move in immediately. Hell, I'll drive out there as soon as we get back.

We exchange a few more messages. He confirms that the sale has gone through. He'll have the power turned on. He'll courier the keys so they're there by the time I get to Nashville.

A strange longing settles into me that feels almost like

hope. More than that. An eerie sense that something's about to happen.

He's *crazy* for her ...

Vaughn Tucker is the hot as hell drummer of the Tucker Brothers band, whose four albums have all hit number one. Vaughn is drop-dead gorgeous ... and completely out of control.

Gigi Hayes's life is a million miles from packed stadiums and high-profile tour schedules. She's a small town girl who spends all her time working in the library and studying to become a qualified social worker. For ... reasons.

When Vaughn meets Gigi, for the first time in his life, he's the one who's star-struck. But Gigi is saving herself for true love. And even though she's drawn to the beautiful, trouble-written-all-over-him superstar, she's not deluded enough to believe he's capable of such a thing.

Vaughn has already fallen hard. And Gigi's refusals only make him crazier. She's an angel and he may as well be the devil himself.

But when heaven meets hell, all bets are off …

Nashville Nights is a steamy standalone rockstar romance starring an out-of-control drummer and the one woman who's everything he never knew he needed.

Music City Lovers

Chapter One

VAUGHN

I wake up to the sound of birds chirping.

Where the …?

My head is pounding hellishly.

A vivid image of my mother's face fringes at the edge of my awareness. Her dark hair and her green eyes. *I love you, Vaughn.* It's the very last thing she ever said to me.

My eyes are suddenly wide open.

Her image fades but it's jarring. The heaviness of the loss of her is as raw as it ever was. It never seems to soften or fade out.

I look around.

I'm in a barn, sleeping in a goddamn pile of hay.

Which is surprisingly comfortable.

I crashed out after an all-nighter with my brothers, I remember now. We wrote three complete songs.

And drank a lot of whiskey.

Too much whiskey, if my hangover is any judge.

The place is huge, with dusty beams and an old-timey, rustic vibe. Morning sunlight streams through thin gaps in the wood, painting the whole place in stripes of … beauty, maybe. The kind that makes you feel deeply, fully inspired, I realize as I lie here. Absorbing it.

You're a beautiful soul, Vaughn. Don't be reckless. Don't throw it all away.

Shit.

Having my mother speak to me knowingly from beyond the grave is not something I had on my bingo card this morning.

But I'm feeling it. Too deeply, as always. It's a pain I do my best to numb whenever the need arises. I slide my flask out of my back pocket and check its contents. Hair of the dog and all that. But it's empty.

I look almost eerily like my father did but people used to say my mother and I had the same personality. She was fun and enchanting to be around but there was a pronounced vulnerability to her character that was all about her kindness. She cared too much.

I don't see those similarities in myself at all. Unfortunately, my habits mirror all my father's worst tendencies.

No matter how much I wish I wasn't, I basically *am* my father. And it's this realization that makes me want to self-medicate like nothing else does.

Whatever. I don't feel like analyzing my personality flaws this early in the morning. Or ever, more accurately.

I'm covered in straw and I'm dusty as fuck but the slant of the sunlight feels different today. Soft and color-ful. Almost magical.

I must be really hungover.

I climb out of the hay and try to brush some of it off my clothes but to hell with it.

When I step outside into the daylight, the world is basically on fire with blazing sun, blue sky and green, rolling landscape as far as the eye can see. I have to shield my eyes for a few seconds from the glaring brightness of it all.

There's a pond in the distance.

Now there's an offer I can't refuse.

I take a few seconds to adjust to the sunlight and to make sure my equilibrium is more or less intact, then I walk down toward the pond, half-amazed at how scenic this place is. I've spent too much time in the city lately, on tour buses and in hotel rooms. It's good to get away from all that.

I'm running commando so I strip down and wade into the water, which is clear and clean-looking, and dive under.

Damn, it feels good.

I swim for a while and wash off the dirt and the sweat.

It's been a crazy few months on tour. I've overindulged in every way it's possible to overindulge. I've played my heart out and squeezed every last drop out of each day and—even more—each night.

It's just how I happen to live my life. Fast. Hard. Might as well make the most of the more-money-than-I-could-spend-in-this-lifetime, the whiskey on tap, the God-given gifts I happen to appreciate the hell out of. I have blue eyes and black hair. I'm 6'3" and built as fuck—in every regard. Women give me whatever I want whenever I want it. I thank my lucky stars for all of the above by enjoying the ride every chance I get. Why wouldn't I?

I'm famous, not just because I was recently listed among the top five drummers in the world but also because I tend to make headlines for a variety of reasons.

I prefer to let my fire burn bright.

I'm borderline out of control, maybe, but who isn't?

Anyone who tells me they're *in* control is full of shit, I figure. Even if such a thing was possible, it wouldn't be something I would aspire to. I have zero interest in living my life by a set of arbitrary rules that might be considered "acceptable."

To who?

No one *I* happen to know or care much about the opinion of, is what I've come to realize.

Even so, I can admit I feel sort of wrecked. Not just

physically, from all the insane excesses. Those are easy enough to bounce back from. I'm 24 and brimming with virile energy and blazing lust. It burns hot and borderline feral, all the time, so if I don't *use* it I feel like I might spontaneously fucking combust.

It's the existential exhaustion that hits harder. Sometimes it dawns on me that it would actually be nice to care about what other people think of me.

But all those impulses died on one particular stormy night, years ago now. Its effect still has the ability to exhaust me from time to time. Lately the memories have felt like more of a black cloud than usual. Having my mother revisit me in a surprisingly realistic hallucination out of the blue makes me realize how jaded I am. Maybe I'm closer to the edge than I thought.

The cool water feels nothing less than miraculous, like I'm somehow in the process of being reborn.

After a while, I walk up the sandy beach and grab my clothes but I don't bother putting them on. I'll dry off in the sun. There's no one around. I happen to be a person who's intensely comfortable in my own skin, with good reason. I don't know if I'm arrogant or just secure enough to know from experience that I happen to look like a guy who can show a girl the time of her life on around ten different levels. And then deliver on each and every one of those promises in spades. At least for one night.

That's just the way it is.

I notice, up a slope, there's a cottage situated in a small grove of trees. Travis mentioned that there were two or three of them, along with the main house and the barn. Part of the property he bought only days ago. He wants me to move into one of the cabins for a while.

I know my family worries about me. I take things further than either of my brothers or my sister. Travis and Kade mostly stick to whiskey and Roxie doesn't drink at all.

But, hell, we all have our demons and we all handle them with different medicinal remedies. I tell them there's nothing to worry about.

I walk up the slope to check out the cabin.

It's got a small front porch with two wooden chairs and a nice view over the pond and the hills. I'm mostly dry so I pull on my jeans but leave them half-zipped. I toss my shirt onto one of the chairs and check the door. It's unlocked.

Whoever Travis bought the property from left everything behind, like they were planning to come back to it but never did. The house is furnished and so is this cabin. It's rustic and dusty but fully equipped as a guest house with all the modern conveniences. There's a small kitchen, a table next to the window, leather couches and a fireplace. There's one bedroom with a king-sized bed and a small but luxe bathroom.

Perfect.

There are even paintings on the walls. One is a geometric design, in black and white. It doesn't really go with the rustic furnishings or the wood of the interior, but I like it. It shakes things up.

After our next tour, which is only twelve shows, I might settle down right here and Jack Kerouac my way through a couple of weeks to see if I can create some music that digs so deep it goes down in infamy for the rest of time.

Or something.

All three of us write music and we all have different styles. Travis's is more country, Kade's leans toward blue-grass-meets-edgy-folk and mine is more rock 'n roll.

Yeah, that's what I'll do. Write. Let the angst and the regret and the feverish love of life pour out of me without distractions.

I find it interesting that the urge to write feels remark-ably like lust. It's a spiritual lust but it spills over into a physical lust that's fiery and more voracious than any other kind.

Right now, I'm feeling it. I want to write something down and then fuck my way leisurely through a steamy afternoon with some willing nymph. Of which there are always plenty. Except that I'm out in the middle of the countryside and around fifty miles from civilization.

So I'll start with the writing, which can only be good if I'm feeling as feverish as I do right now.

Here I am, standing in the doorway of my new digs,

leaning my shoulder against the doorjamb, jeans only partly zipped, appreciating the view as I contemplate the state of my own raging lust, when into that view walks … down by the pond …

A girl …

"All I wished for was to experience that spark you read about, just once. What I wasn't expecting was the Fourth of July and heaven on earth all rolled into one." ~ Stella

Bass player Kade Tucker is known as the Magic Man, and not only for his riffs. After breaking off a disastrous relationship, he swears off women. Only problem is, five minutes later, he might have just met the love of his life.

Stella Bell has always done what's expected of her. Until a secret letter and an unwanted proposal on the same day prove to be her breaking point. For once in her life, she's going to do something for herself. As fate would have it, that means taking a spur of the moment trip to Nashville.

A hopeless romantic, Stella has been hiding her true self for far too long. And when a gorgeous, mysterious stranger rescues her from a torrential downpour, she decides to go with it. The hot, dreamy Kade Tucker proceeds to enlighten Stella in every possible way, until she begins to realize that some dreams really can come true.

But will Kade's twisted ex and Stella's family secrets – and a very accidental pregnancy – get in the way of their HEA? Or is this a match made in Music City heaven?

Nashville Dreams is a sexy standalone rock star romance starring a hot musician and a sweet & sassy dreamer who's the one he always knew was out there somewhere. Now that he's found her, he has no intention of letting any one of her dreams go unanswered.

Music City Lovers

Curious about Cash Maddox and Dusty Rose—the sister of Roxie's new client Sky Rose?

You can read their story in **Billionaire Boss**, a fun, sexy billionaire romance.

Our deal was simple. One night. Fake names. No strings attached. Until it turns out he's my new boss...

I couldn't believe my luck when I got sent to a work conference in Hawaii. Living the dream after years of pulling myself up by my bootstraps.

The sand, the palm trees and the blue water were straight out of a romantic fantasy. So was the guy at the beachfront bar, let's be honest. Blue eyes. Broad-shouldered in his business suit but with a rough-around-the-edges swagger and a filthy mouth.

We laughed and had a night of crazy passion that enlightened me in every possible way. I understood what dreams coming true might actually feel like.

And then I left without saying goodbye.

That was two months ago and I've mostly been able to put him out of my mind. I've been busy landing my dream job in New York City.

Imagine my surprise when my new boss turns out to be Mr. Dirty Talking Swagger.

He's been thinking about me too, he says, his blue eyes dancing. He's been searching for me since that night. And he wants to see me in his office…

Billionaire Boss is a steamy billionaire romance and the first book in the New York Billionaires series, starring the four Maddox brothers. Each book in the series is a complete standalone with an HEA.

New York Billionaires

ALSO BY JULIE CAPULET

I Love You Series

The Obsession Begins (free)

XOXO I Love You

XOXX I Love You More

Love You the Most (free)

Sexy Standalones

Max

Cowboy

McCabe Brothers Series

Hopeless Romantic

My Hero

Arrogant Player

Music City Lovers Series

Nashville Days

Nashville Nights

Nashville Dreams

Nashville Lights

Hawthorne U Series

Lovestruck

Paradise Series

Devil's Angel

Wild Hearts

New York Billionaires Series

Billionaire Boss

Billionaire Grump

Billionaire Devil

Billionaire Romantic

Standalone Rom-com

Beautiful Savages

ABOUT THE AUTHOR

Julie Capulet is an Amazon top 20 bestselling author of contemporary romance. She writes steamy he-falls-first romance with heart, heat and fairy tale HEAs. Her stories are inspired by true love and she's married to her own real life hero. When she's not writing, she's reading, traveling, walking on the beach and watching rom-coms.

www.juliecapulet.com